THIS BOO~

WALT ~~~~~

WITH THANKS ——

ALL THE BEST,

MARCH 2013

TAG! YOU'RE HIT!

A Novel By

Howard Jenkins

*With Foreword by Las Vegas
Police Detective Scott Black*

authorHOUSE®

AuthorHouse™
1663 Liberty Drive
Bloomington, IN 47403
www.authorhouse.com
Phone: 1-800-839-8640

First published by AuthorHouse 5/16/2011

ISBN: 978-1-4634-0352-2 (e)
ISBN: 978-1-4634-0353-9 (dj)
ISBN: 978-1-4634-0354-6 (sc)

Library of Congress Control Number: 2011906933

Printed in the United States of America

"Most criminals are stupid or they wouldn't be caught."
Oscar Goodman, Las Vegas Mayor and
former criminal defense attorney.

"Some criminals are smart and it may take a while to catch them. Some are lucky *and* smart and may never get caught."
Anonymous.

www.howardjenkins.com
e-mail: howard@howardjenkins.com

Foreword

Since beginning my work as a graffiti investigations detective in Las Vegas, I have frequently observed one recurrent truth: There's no other type of crime that garners such intense, passionate outrage from the public. In fact, significant portions of the community believe that activities such as illicit narcotics use, vice related offenses and even some street gang activities are not important issues for law enforcement to focus on. Graffiti, however, is only supported and defended by those who are involved in creating it along with the very small segment of liberal society who believes the individual's right to self-gratification trumps society's right to protect property and enforce the law.

The reason that nearly all citizens detest graffiti is not merely that it is the single most costly crime involving property. It is because graffiti represents an infringement on the rights of those who desire to live in communities which have the appearance of being safe, not to mention civilized. Graffiti is offensive. It repulses dignified society, and it personally threatens the individual citizen because it brings with it an invitation for lawlessness and societal decay. The public outcry graffiti causes results in our civic leaders demanding that their police departments and citizens fight it tooth and nail. This is because graffiti is symptomatic of greater evils. It is a warning of what we fear the most: victimization. This is why in movies, television programs, video games, and music videos the backdrop for a high crime area, a place-out-of-control, is always covered in graffiti. It is synonymous with urban decay, rampant crime, and anarchy.

Another interesting fact I've noted is the increasing number of cases of citizens taking the law into their own hands and exacting their own justice upon graffiti vandals by assaulting, beating, torturing, and even shooting them. I've also witnessed the tremendous hatred generated by graffiti vandals in otherwise law-abiding citizens. On more than one occasion while arresting a graffiti vandal I've advised them that they should feel relieved that it was I who caught them, and not angry citizens, who in revenge-mode rarely abide by the strict standards to which police officers are held. They have no rules and regulations, no supervisor eager to take a red felt pen to their use of force report, no citizen's review board. They only have rage against that which threatens them, and the urge to punish.

I've also noted that it is often the productive, otherwise upstanding citizen, who seems to exhibit the greatest passion for punishing graffiti vandals. I've investigated many cases involving various levels of vigilantism: an elderly army veteran who set booby traps for graffiti vandals using techniques he'd learned fighting in Korea in 1950's; the case of the Tar & Feather Crew, a group of seemingly normal citizens who prowled areas frequented by graffiti vandals, covering them in their own spray paint and rolling them in the dirt to create a tarred and feathered effect; and numerous cases of beatings and assaults exacted upon graffiti vandals by citizens who were tired of graffiti and "at the end of their rope." I've seen graffiti turn peaceful, everyday citizens into ruthless vigilantes with a mind for revenge. Graffiti is the most prevalent property crime there is. Statistically, it affects more citizens than any other criminal activity, and increasing numbers of them are fighting back.

I first met Howard Jenkins while I was instructing a training course about investigative methods involving graffiti. We talked about the way that particular criminal activity was proliferating in Las Vegas, and how it contributes to other types of crime, including crimes of violence. As Howard explained the basis and plot for his novel, *Tag! You're Hit!*, I couldn't help but sense that we would become friends. He understands this crime and how it generates strong and often violent emotions from otherwise law-abiding citizens. I share Howard's affinity for novels written with attention paid to truth and accuracy, and was excited and honored when he invited me into the world of *Tag! You're Hit!* I agreed with Howard that this story demanded realistic elements of criminal investigations in Las Vegas. It had to be presented with the real pressures of present day Las Vegas and its police department, one of the most famous police departments in the world.

In *Tag! You're Hit!* the reader is drawn, without compromise in regard to individual viewpoints, political agendas or personal beliefs, into a gripping, reality-based fictional crime novel. Many of the circumstances of the story are based in fact. Howard has captured the true essence of an intense and pressing police investigation involving a proliferating criminal element of society, a savvy and capable killer, and a group of dedicated detectives determined to stop him. *Tag! You're Hit!* reaches deep into the sinister underworld of graffiti, investigative police work, human emotion, and sheer violence.

Detective Scott Black

Detective Scott Black has been a police officer since 1994. He is an expert in the area of graffiti investigations and authored the state of Nevada's graffiti law. He provides training and consultation to local, state, and federal law enforcement agencies nationwide.

Prologue

The covered bridge was in some disrepair in spite of the efforts of county officials, the local Chamber of Commerce and a few volunteers who cared about the history of this area of rural Iowa. The Chamber organized painting and repair parties every couple of years or so. The fading red paint and cracked fascia boards actually looked the part of an edifice that declared "come take pictures of our old and picturesque bridge." The chamber hoped, through colorful brochures, that visitors would take pictures, spend the night in the only motel and eat at one of the two restaurants in the small town that featured either greasy breakfasts or large prime steaks, from genuine Iowa corn fed cattle.

The bridge spanned a creek bed that before all the surrounding agriculture took most of the available water, flowed abundantly around and over the hundreds of small to medium stones lining the creek bottom. Other than when heavy rains fell, continuous year-round water flow was another historical fact, remembered by only the most senior residents. Upstream from the bridge were thickets of low shrub with large oak trees spotted about and as if posing for the next wannabe photographer, enticed to the area by Chamber of Commerce printed material.

Ryan and Robby dressed in Levi's, sneakers and tee shirts, angled along the compacted dirt and small stone road, trying to keep from the center of the seldom-used byway. Typical of twelve year-olds, they weren't as cautions as they should be and Ryan shook the can of black spray paint, so that the ubiquitous marble in the can echoed off the hardpan. The old bridge came into sight as they rounded the gentle bend in the road.

Upstream, perhaps by thirty yards, thirteen-year-old Ben Morgan could sense the Quail moving through the underbrush ten feet below the tree. He had been perched in the crook of the old oak tree for nearly two hours. Waiting. Waiting. He was wearing his military camouflage and his high-powered pellet gun was still light in his hands. He was gifted with patience and stamina well beyond his years. Typical for a late summer's day in the middle of Iowa, the smell of the cornfields and drying grass was heavy in the air, etching this moment deep within Ben's memory. He loved hunting. He loved shooting. His father, a straight laced Iowa farmer, was a decorated US Army sharpshooter and had trained Ben well in the art of hunting and precise target shooting.

Two of the target birds emerged from the brush, pecking the ground and looking around nervously for predators, not seeing Ben line up the rifle's site on the largest of the birds. "Center mass." His dad told him during is tutorial years. "It does the most damage and it's harder to miss."

Come on. One more foot and turn to the right. Ben's trigger finger expertly started its gentle squeeze. The unsuspecting but wary prey nodded and bobbed among the grass and dead twigs. *Come on. Turn!*

The rattle of the marble in the paint can was enough to send the flock to flight. Flapping wings, scuttling brush and twigs and squawks of fear from the bevy of birds scurrying to the safely of distance from the sound. *What the h...?* Ben relaxed his trigger finger and grimaced in disgust as the birds fluttered away.

Ryan and Robby bolded by the apparent absence of prying eyes emerged from one end of the covered bridge, climbed over the faded paint and cracked timber plank supporting one side of the old structure, and crept along the narrow ledge, about fifteen feet above the creek bed. Ryan continued to shake the can of flat black paint and urged by Bobby started to spray a large letter.

Thud! A small hole appeared just above the first small smattering of the fine black spray on the fascia board. Bobby froze. "What the hell was that?"

The boys, coiled to bolt, looked in the direction of the 'pffft' that had preceded the thud just above Ryan's hand. With the rifle pointing directly at them, Bobby and Ryan saw the boy approaching them, stepping over rocks, tree limbs and brush, keeping the gun completely level. Continuing to point directly at them.

"Shit. It's that weirdo Ben Morgan," Ryan hissed. "Come on let's get outta here." The boys stepped over the board and started to move away.

"Hold it!" Morgan yelled, quickening his pace toward them.

The boys stopped. Bobby squinted at the approaching menace that they only knew slightly from school. Morgan's reputation was all too well known around these parts and Bobby and Ryan didn't want to have anything to do with him. Morgan, from a paramilitary father, had a standing within their clique that the young Morgan should be avoided at all costs. He was creepy and fought at the drop of a hat when provoked by someone's immature or nonconforming behavior.

"What the hell are you doing?" Morgan's gun, level and steady continued to point directly at them while moving toward them. "You are defacing property." His voice rose. "I can't stand it when people do that."

"Jeez Ben," Ryan said, his voice quivering. "Lighten up. We were just having some harmless fun. No big deal." Ryan placed his hand over his chest as if trying to protect himself from an impending shot. The tee shirt he was wearing, decked by a large Iowa Hawkeye mascot, didn't feel very formidable to him. "You won't shoot us because of this." He boldly stated, trying desperately to hide his fear.

"Try me. You defacers." Ben Morgan was now on a level with the boys. "I should make you paint the entire bridge."

"No way" the boys almost said in unison. Bobby, continued, "We hardly put any paint on it."

Morgan lowered the rifle. "I know you guys and I have half a mind to tell your parents or the sheriff what you were doing here. Maybe I'll tell them both. Serve you right, trying to deface this old bridge. If I hadn't been here you'd have finished whatever bad thing you were going to do."

Ryan and Bobby could now see why Ben was so different from the other boys.

"Maybe I'll tell the sheriff you shot at us," Ryan said, feeling a little bolder now that the gun was pointing at the ground. "You can't go around shooting at people!"

"Go ahead and tell 'em. I'd love to show the evidence of your spray versus a small hole. I'd deny it." Morgan spat the words.

"You are weird, Morgan." Ryan stepped farther away; convinced

Morgan wouldn't really shoot them now. "Come on Bobby," Ryan said grabbing Bobby's arm. "Let's get away from here."

"Don't be calling me weird." Morgan pointed the gun directly at Ryan. "Put down the can and get outta here." He moved the gun, pointing down the road with it.

"Okay. Okay." Ryan dropped the can and backed away. "You are weird Morgan!"

"Go on. Get." Morgan continued to motion with the rifle. "Don't let me catch you here again and don't call me weird you scumbags!"

Ben watched the would be taggers walk down the dirt road until they broke into a jog and disappeared around the bend and behind a grove of Oak trees. He picked up the offending spray can with a gloved hand and placed it in one of several large pockets in his pant leg. *So they thought I was weird, huh?*

They just didn't understand that cleanliness was next to godliness.

Chapter One

Ben Morgan squinted through the night vision scope of his Dakota T-76 Longbow rifle. It was his third night in a row of kneeling beside a low retaining wall near an open construction site, waiting for graffiti vandals with their hissing spray cans to come along. His all black garb, including a black knit watch cap and black shooting gloves, belied the summer heat of Las Vegas. Even at this late hour - nearly midnight actually - the daytime heat that had soared to nearly one-hundred ten degrees was still hovering around the mid-nineties. The automobile traffic was light and the occasional large truck and trailer passing beneath the bridge, Morgan was watching intensely, seemed to clear the overhead structure by only a few inches.

Morgan was used to staying in uncomfortable clothes and in uncomfortable places for hours at a time. Positioned as he was, across the freeway, he had a clear view of the highway bridge, and could clearly see the beautifully adorned southwest designs of birds, Native Americans in silhouette and jagged Aztec patterns spanning I-15, just north of downtown Las Vegas. The green directional sign, lit by fluorescent lights, indicated traffic to downtown Las Vegas, should be in the right lane. The sign, Morgan thought, detracted from the overall design and appearance of the bridge.

Tonight his patience and military training finally paid off, again. The powerful .330 Dakota Magnum's telescopic site located two young men, one carrying a spray can, the other seemed to be holding a length of rope, creeping around the fencing on the bridge. The crosshairs found the spray can-holding target as he started to work his defacing deed. Tightening his finger, Morgan squeezed off a round and saw his target disappear from view. *We don't need your stinkin' graffiti,* he muttered to himself. *Goodbye scum.* And as the other offender scrambled behind a bridge column, he added, *Don't come back.*

His mild adrenalin rush began to subside, but his gloved hands were steady as he retrieved the lone shell casing from the dirt several yards away before running back to his black Jeep Cherokee. In seconds, he had disassembled the rifle and deftly returned it to its custom made gun case. Driving with his headlights off a few hundred feet to a deserted street near the construction site, he stopped in the dark shadows of an oversized Palo Verde tree, removed the cotton booties from his shoes, as well as the hand made tire covers, and the false license plate from the rear of his Jeep and picked up a Coke can flattened on the roadside. *Fucking litterers.* Then packing everything neatly in the duffle bag on his back seat, he drove off, a good night's work done.

#

"Listen to this Gil," Las Vegas Police Department Homicide

Detective Maria Garcia, said as she sipped on her highly sweetened morning coffee reading the night shift's account of the shooting. The homicide office was sparsely occupied this time of the morning. The only other person within earshot of her comments was her partner, Gil Radcliff. "In all my years with LVPD I don't recall anything quite like this."

"The victim was sixteen to twenty-five years old," she said. "His chest, what was left of it, was splattered on the bridge above where his body was found. Apparently he died instantly. Initial measurements of the single entrance wound would indicate at least a 30-caliber bullet. Bullet fragments were found on the ledge where the youth must have been standing. Traces of spray paint were observed on the bridge structure and matched the can found a few feet from the body. The LVPD Crime lab was called to determine the direction of the shot."

Gil grunted acknowledgement, obviously engrossed in the *Las Vegas Review Journal* report of the same incident. "I'd love to find the officer that gives out this shit. The paper assumed somehow it was a gang related killing"

"Maybe the reporter has it wrong," Maria said, matter-of-factly. "I think our Public Information folks do a good job. Besides, it probably *was* gang related."

"Could be, but I doubt it," Gil replied, running his fingers through his short curly blond hair. "Wasn't it Mark Twain that said something like, 'If you don't read the newspaper you are uninformed, and if you do, you're misinformed!' But the paper still labels it as a gang related incident between rival taggers or rival gangs. I wish they wouldn't use the politically correct term. They're not taggers. They're vandals. No. Worse than vandals. More like scum sucking defacers."

"You make a good point," Maria said. "Graffiti is the one crime almost everybody in the community hates. I've heard old ladies suggest that we cut the balls off a tagger when we catch them. Maybe we should just let gang members shoot each other, until there aren't any left," she added in a jocular tone.

"I don't think it's a gang member shooting rival gang members," Gil said, paying full attention now, "It's not what they typically do."

"Vegas gangs stopped being typical long ago," Maria said, looking up from the report, brushing wisps of her black hair away from her face and looking at him with her dark tantalizing eyes. "That's not why we got this assignment, because of the paper. This is the fourth shooting in two months and you know as well as I that the boss believes it's gang related and wants us to work more closely than ever with the gang unit. Regardless of your theory, which by the way you ought to keep to yourself, we're still responsible for homicides and the gang unit has to take responsibility for graffiti crimes and gang activity even if you have another theory."

"I suppose you're right, Maria," Gil, said with a reluctant grimace. Walking over to the coffee machine, he poured himself a cup of coffee that was as thick as brown sweet crude pumped directly from an oil field.

"Now that I think of it," he continued, "it might be worse if the media thought it was some vigilante at this stage of our investigation. Then they'd really be on our backs. We know these gangs, or at least most of them, and shootings just don't occur like this. The fifty odd shootings last year were mostly hot-blooded reaction killings. I think this is the work of an angry citizen."

"Gil, you've only been in the homicide department for six months," Maria said, lowering her voice, "but you know we track over four hundred gangs every year. You ought to know by now that they're capable of anything. Trust me. These shootings are gang related."

Gil shrugged and rolled his eyes, "I wish the gang unit investigated homicides rather than dump them on us, but when we get the ID of this victim and ballistics data, I'll bet we find that rival gang members have been shot with the same sort of weapon."

"Right, the same sort of weapon, but not the same weapon," Maria argued. "They probably have a lot of high powered weapons like that, including AK47's. They could start a real war if we let 'em. The gang unit guys I know are always a big help to us; but they would love to investigate homicides on their own, but it's *our* job."

"The forensics folks are very competent," Gil said. "They'll come up with enough bullet fragments from all four shootings to make a match. I'll wager an expensive dinner in a restaurant of your choosing that it's the same weapon and the same shooter."

"You got it," Maria replied, grinning. "Make it dinner at The Strip House at Planet Hollywood. You seem to be so sure of yourself on this one. Did you see something like this when you worked in Oklahoma City?"

"No, I didn't," putting his feet on his desk. The thought of her sitting at a cozy booth with him made him smile. "The gangs in Oak City used mostly small revolvers or semi-automatics, nine millimeter being the gun of choice. The biggest gun ever used was a 12 gauge."

"Well then, the gangs here are superior to those in Oklahoma," Maria retorted. "In fact, Las Vegas is superior to Oklahoma in almost any category you can think of."

"Yeah, the heat and traffic accidents." Gil was smiling broadly.

"Better than mosquitoes and boredom. From what you've said. Oklahoma leads the nation there," Maria said, laughing. "Speaking of which, when is your ex going to let you see your daughters this summer?"

Gil glanced at the pictures of two blond girls on his desk. It had been taken last year when they were nine and ten respectively. He hadn't seen them since last Christmas, and sometimes it seemed as though he missed them more each passing month instead of less. Maria's phone rang, pulling Gil out of his reverie. She grabbed the incessant instrument.

"Garcia," she said, "yes, I know where that is. Detective Radcliff and I will be right there."

"Let's go," she said, turning to Gil. "CSI thinks they have the shooter's location."

Twenty minutes later, Maria pulled the unmarked Crown Victoria police car to a stop at the end of the cul-de-sac near a vacant area of land recently carved up by a bulldozer. Yards of crime scene yellow ribbon surrounded the area and several police cars, their blue and red lights blazing away at full tilt. Gil was sure that the lights were adding to the heat of the day. The Crime Lab van, parked askew on the dirt, doors full open revealing drawers, testing equipment and dozens of metal boxes. Several uniformed police and lab technicians were scouring an area near a low wall. Some of the other officers were just standing around in small groups and chatting. Typical, thought Gil.

"It's already hot and it's only ten o'clock," Gil grumbled as they ducked under the tape and tramped across the vacant land. "Must be about two hundred degrees!"

"Don't be such a wuss," Maria told him as they approached a group of crime scene investigators that had placed several pins in the ground. One of the techs was taking pictures. "It's only ninety-five."

"I'm Garcia and this is Radcliff from Homicide." She said, flashing her badge.

"Glad you could make it," one officer said, his eyes hidden behind dark aviator sunglasses, an identification badge hanging from his neck. "I'm Jeffers from CSI. We've met."

From the few cases that she had worked with him, Maria knew Jeffers to be pleasant and professional. Of medium build, he sported cropped gray hair with a widows peak and was not nearly as studious looking as some of the other CSI'ers.

"This is Detective Gil Radcliff," Maria said. "He joined Homicide about six months ago. What do you have?"

"Nice to meet you." After shaking Gil's hand with a vice like grip, Jeffers pointed across a wide expanse of roads and freeways. "We took bullet fragments from the bridge over there," he said. "It's about two-hundred yards. Helluva good shot. The bullet fragmented a lot from entry into the vic, but the fragments and splattered blood gave a good indication of the angle of impact. When we started looking backward we saw this low cinderblock wall, and while searching the area, found two or three things worth noting, including GSR on the other side. As you know, Gun Shot Residue doesn't usually last long enough for us to find. We got lucky because after about six hours it's mostly all but gone."

"I know that," Gil said, feeling like a tenderfoot for being told what GSR was. Gil proceeded to change the course of the conversation. "So you say the perp was at this spot when he fired?"

Jeffers grinned at Gil, "I guess you aren't from here. We use the term suspect in Vegas. Perp for perpetrator, I guess, is used elsewhere in the country."

"I'm sorry and you're right; it is used almost all over the country except here. I moved here from Oklahoma and can't shake the habit of using perp." Gil's face turned even redder. "Go ahead. What did you find?"

"Two other things were interesting," Jeffers said, "the foot prints and tire marks."

"Great." Maria said, encouraged. "What about them?"

"Look here," Jeffers said pointing to the ground. "The suspect kneeled here and rested the butt of the rifle there. However, he covered his shoes with something, maybe surgical scrub booties. He'd been there for some time based on the trampling, but no good footprints. All we can tell is that they were about a size 10 or 11 and that he is of medium build based on the depth of the impressions."

Maria bent down to look closer. "What about the tire tracks?"

"Also very interesting. All four tires had some sort of fabric boot on them so we have no good impressions of the tracks. We did determine that it was a four-wheel drive, and based on the depth and width of the impressions, probably an SUV. This guy was certainly covering his tracks. No pun intended."

"I wouldn't think a gang member would go to all that trouble, would you?" Gil said. He could taste that dinner.

"You guys are the homicide experts," Jeffers replied. "You tell me."

"Okay," Maria said, "I'll admit I don't know of any previous gang members that were so meticulous or sophisticated, but we can't rule out anything. What about fibers from the booties or his clothes where he kneeled?"

"Nothing yet, but this is a big lot and it'll take us another hour or more to completely comb the area," Jeffers said. "However, I'm not holding my breath that we'll find anything. The good news is that this is the first one of four similar shootings in which we've been able to actually pinpoint the shooter's position. We'll also check the surrounding area, but I can't imagine that whoever it was went very far with his tires covered."

"So in the other similar shootings, you didn't find where the shot came from?" Maria asked.

"Not exactly, we had some good guesses, but no GSR, shell casings or anything else for that matter at the probable locations. I think Lemke in your department handled the follow-up."

"That dinner is going to taste soooo good!" Gil said as they climbed in the car after Jeffers agreed to send them everything he had on the previous three incidents.

"Not so fast, buster," Maria warned him. "We don't know anything yet. And there's no indication that we're going to - at least not soon enough for you to make a reservation."

#

Earlier that morning Ben Morgan had been amused to read the newspaper account of another gang shooting, although he had little time to think about it, thanks to the busy day mapping the southwest part of Clark County for his employer – WebMaps, a company that was trying desperately to compete with the likes of MapQuest, Google and other on-line and database map services. Ben's job was to document and survey new streets and enter them into the database as fast as WebMaps could take them. And since Las Vegas and its surrounding area was one of the fastest growing sections of the country, a full time, on-the-ground-surveyor was needed if WebMaps wanted to be able to claim that they were the most accurate and up to date service available. Cruising around the Las Vegas Valley gave Ben all the opportunity he needed to fight taggers.

#

Back in the office, Maria looked at her calendar, "Shit," she exclaimed. "I forgot I scheduled a lunch for us with Rodolfo. You are coming along aren't you, Gil?"

"No way, Maria," Gil replied as he booted up his computer. "My Spanish isn't that good yet, besides, it gives me a headache trying to figure out what you guys are saying. Look, Rodolfo's a great gang unit undercover cop but you don't need me there. I think I'll stay here and do some national inquiries on our sniper, if you don't mind. Chances are he may have done this somewhere else. Maybe I'll even try to do a map of the known shootings and see if I can correlate anything. Have a good time."

"*Ya reserve una mesa por tres, tengo hambre.*"

"If you reserved a table for three, you're really hungry. You can eat two meals, if you like," Gil said, trying to impress her with his little, new knowledge of Spanish.

"You did pretty well translating that for a gringo!" Maria told him. "And it's *not* the same sniper. Catch you later."

As Gil watched her shapely rear end sway down the corridor, it occurred to him that here was a formidable woman who could make his life far easier or a good deal more complicated.

Chapter Two

Ben Morgan parked his black Jeep and walked up to the side of a new bridge on Clark County's beltway, set to open in a few weeks. The bridge, located in Summerlin, ten miles west of the strip, was normally beyond the taggers' range, but graffiti had started springing up here too. Morgan swept the horizon from left to right with his digital camera; he would examine the digital images later that night before deciding on his next stakeout position. The new medical building appeared to be a likely spot to watch for taggers. He was thinking like the enemy, something he learned during his sniper training in the Marines. You had to ask yourself where they would approach, where they would hide, and which way they would run? Most of the time, taggers traveled in pairs or threesomes. Previously, by using his knife and a handgun equipped with a silencer, he had on occasion, been able to get more of the little bastards at the same time. In the more open spaces of Las Vegas, and thanks to the long-range capabilities of his sniper rifle, it proved to be an efficient means of making a kill, even though it often gave the other taggers a chance to hide before he could get off a second shot.

In order to keep the cops guessing, he had decided that he wouldn't attempt another shooting for several weeks and that when he did, it would be in this new area.

After parking in the half-full lot of the medical building, Morgan, carrying his briefcase, cruised around all four floors of the building as if he were a patient or a drug salesman. Dressed as he was in khaki slacks and plain polo shirt, he knew that, as always, he wouldn't draw any attention. There were no video surveillance cameras anywhere that he could see, and just the standard intrusion detection on all the exterior doors. As for the burglar alarm panel near the rear door, it was a standard monitoring and fire alarm set-up. The door, just off an alcove, would be the one he would likely use to enter, and was at the rear of the building, instead of at the end of a long hallway. Morgan stepped into the alcove and waited a few moments. Taking a magnetic strip from his briefcase and with his latex gloves in place, he opened the rear door and placed the strip on the sensor. Only a trained security expert would spot something like this. Now, he thought, the alarm was useless. As usual, first things first.

#

Gil printed the map of the Las Vegas Valley complete with little red spots pinpointing the locations of taggers that had been shot over the last three months in an attempt to see if a pattern emerged. Last night's shooting had taken place just north of downtown on I-15, while the third shooting was in Henderson, at the I-515 and I-215 interchange and the second at the new freeway sound wall on I-95 west of downtown. The first known incident had occurred at a temporary wall around the construction site of a new lofts tower being constructed just south of downtown. After labeling each red spot with a time and date, he saw that the shootings had taken place approximately three to four weeks apart, on different days of the week. Based on time of death estimates, the shootings had happened between ten PM and three AM.

As part of his analysis he tried to establish a geographical pattern, but nothing jumped out at him, although downtown *could* be the center of activity. Certainly the shooting in Henderson appeared to be an anomaly in terms of distance from downtown.

Navigating to the national law enforcement web site he tapped in some crime parameters to see if similar patterns appeared elsewhere in the country. While the little hourglass turned, cranking the query, he walked to the break room for a bottle of water, considering as he did so, the likelihood of accomplishing his three major ambitions which included having dinner with Maria as a first step in what might become a more than budding friendship, proving his sniper theory, and solving these crimes - in that order.

Returning to his computer, he found a site labeled: "List of graffiti suspects killed or seriously injured while committing the act," which when opened, contained a voluminous list. However, the unsolved cases to date in Las Vegas, other than the recent shootings, did not involve bullets from a large caliber rifle, and annotations indicating all the gang related deaths from stabbings, handguns, beatings, or stranglings were so numerous he would not be able to see any kind of pattern. Most important, no pattern involving sniper activity had emerged from his query.

So what did they have here? He supposed that a sniper might have moved to Vegas from some other city and just started taking out taggers. *Hell, everybody moved here from some other place.* He knew other cities had a worse tagging problem. *Why had this sicko all of a sudden started shooting here?*

#

Squinting into the midday sun, Morgan told himself that the Vegas police would never see a pattern in his previous work in San Diego, Atlanta, and Seattle. Because he had been careful. His next assignment for WebMaps would be Denver. If he felt like it, he might just use a bow and arrow, although it was not far from probable that he would use his knife, it gave him much more pleasure to take out his victims up close and personal, so to speak. In each of the other cities in which he had operated, the police had simply assumed it was gang related crimes. And that was good because it had meant that he could simply sit back and savor the fact that, unknown to anyone, he was responsible for cleaning things up in more ways than one.

#

Maria retuned from lunch just as Gil was marking his sniper map with known locations of gang violence and shootings in the last three months. "Hi," he said. "How was lunch with Rodolfo?" Gil was surprised to hear something that sounded a bit more like jealousy than he hoped. What he hoped for was the true meaning. That she had found out something about the shooting.

He reminded himself to concentrate on the fact that UC's, or undercover cops, might be the key to this investigation.

Maria shrugged indifferently, "Pretty good," she said. "Mostly we talked about his UC work with the Eastside Maestros. He also got a line on the Duques gang that was harassing teenagers at the apartment complex over near Sam's Town."

"Did he say anything about the sniper shootings?" Gil asked her. "Did he have any ideas? I mean he is a very good undercover cop."

"I'm not ready to buy you dinner, but he shares your theory," she admitted, picking up several messages scattered on her desk. "The word's around that the gangs are a little scared, but ready to retaliate if they ID the shooter or the shooter's gang. The problem is we now know that one of the victims was not a member of any known group, just an unattached youth plying his artistic skills. We'll need to keep that fact from the media a while longer."

"You're right," Gil tried not to sound like an I-told-you-so. "I'm going out to the sites and look around again. I haven't heard from Jeffers in CSI yet on any findings from last night's shooting, but I have a hunch. Want to come along?"

"No," she disappointed him by saying. "You go. I have messages to catch up on. Who knows maybe one of these calls is a lead. I'll let you know."

Chapter Three

Sitting at the dinky table in the small kitchen of his single bedroom apartment, Ben Morgan booted up his computer and navigated to the Clark County web site, clicking on future streets in the area he had surveyed earlier in the day. Having correlated the map with the WebMaps' latest version, he added his notes and changes and sent it off to WebMaps. They would, he knew, be pleased he was ahead of schedule as he was their best field surveyor of the half-dozen or so scattered around the country, and they had just negotiated a new contract to furnish Map databases to new cars fitted with navigation systems. Now, done for the day, he could turn to planning the next purge. *It's a good thing that I don't have regular hours,* he thought, although he needed daylight to perform his job for WebMaps. When the occasion arose for him to wait on a tagger, he had plenty of late nights. It had taken him ten straight nights to catch that tagger on I-15. However, before he went on to the next thing, it was time for him to start cleaning his apartment again.

#

Radcliff pulled alongside a construction truck next to the I-95 widening project and flashed his badge to a worker who looked as though he could have cared less. Grabbing his binoculars from the glove compartment Gil squeezed through the temporary sound wall opening near where the third victim had been felled and he moved along towards the spot where the tagger had been nailed by a large caliber bullet a little over five weeks ago. It was hot. Stifling. Ten or eleven paces would do it, he thought. And there it was. Some new paint – desert beige - about four and a half feet from the ground. Cars whizzed by about twenty feet from him as he examined the crime scene. Odd lengths of re-bar were scattered about along with fresh bulldozer tracks indicating that the scene had been busy with construction work.

Positive he was at the right spot, Gil stood with his back to the wall and looked across the freeway at the Meadows Mall, dominated by Macy's, the closest store to the highway. Aiming his binoculars, he started scanning the other buildings that would have been likely sites for a sniper. A tagger standing where he was would be easily seen from the mall's roof. No other sites seemed likely, unless the killer had stopped his car on the freeway and shot from the roadway. He decided to rule out a drive-by shooting. The aim had been too good for that. Could've been a freak shot though, Gil admitted to himself. There were no other bullets. However, both scenarios were unlikely. Too many potential witnesses would have been driving by. *And there were no witnesses.* Granted that it would take some nerve for a tagger to walk this far in the open to start spray painting, but then again, graffiti "artists" didn't let height or openness stand in their way. Sometimes they would actually creep along a five-inch wide girder in order to paint a highway sign fifty feet above the roadway. It was, he thought, insane.

Holding a finger in one ear to block the sound of the roaring traffic, he punched in Maria's number on his cell.

"Hi, it's Gil," he said, shouting over the traffic's din when she answered. "I need to get a hold of Jeffers and ask him some questions about the sound wall shooting on I-95. Do you have his number handy?"

"I can do better than that," Maria said. "He's standing right here. I'll put him on."

Jeffers sounded tired. "I was just briefing Maria on the shooting last night," he told Gil. "We did find some fabric threads from his tire covers, but it's ordinary cloth you can find at Wal-Mart, K-Mart and dozens of other places. Where are you?"

"I'm standing at the site of the I-95 sound wall shooting and I have a couple of questions. Did you guys check out the roof tops of the Meadows Mall? It's about the only place that the shooter could have been other than from a moving car."

"We didn't check it out ourselves," Jeffers said. "I think Lemke, in your unit, did though. I seem to remember him saying that according to mall security there was no way to get on the roof."

"I think I'll go over to the mall and check it out myself," Gil said.

"Okay. Please keep me posted. We're here to help."

"Thanks, I will. Please put Maria back on."

"Hi again. That was lucky he was here," Maria said. "When are you coming back to the office?" she asked him.

"I dunno. Is there any fresh coffee?"

"I just made a pot. So come on back."

"No, now that I think of it, I can't stand to see you drink that stuff. It's bad enough without all that sugar you add," he teased her. "I'm going over to the Meadows Mall and check out roof access, but I had another thought or question really. How do you suppose our shooter knew this was the place a tagger would arrive? I mean, wouldn't he have had to have inside knowledge to be right there at exactly the right time?"

"Great question," Maria told him. "I've been giving that some thought as well, but I can't come up with a good answer. Even Rodolfo told me today that taggers don't announce where they'll go next. More often than not they don't even know themselves until they stumble on just the right surface. But I do know that the gang unit does have some intel and I've already looked at some sites where some of the taggers announce what they plan to tag next. Nothing in the recent web history showed any of the sites in question."

"That too, but our suspect could also be extremely patient," Gil reminded her. "And very, very lucky. I'm really looking forward to that dinner out."

Somehow, Gil wasn't sure how she felt about the wager. And he was less certain how she would react if he were to win.

#

Ben could remember, as though it were yesterday, sitting outside Senior Staff Sergeant Johnson's office, stretching his wiry legs, waiting to be called in for his review. Morgan had been in the Marines for three years then and had learned his craft so well that he had been sure Sergeant Johnson would try to talk him into re-enlisting. "Come in, Corporal," Johnson had bellowed behind the closed door.

Instead, after some congratulatory words about what a hell of a good sniper he was, let alone his mapping and surveying skills, he had asked him if he was happy being a Marine.

"You're one hell of a sniper, Corporal. Placing first in the advanced snipers training was no easy feat and you're making great progress on mapping and surveying," Sergeant Johnson said after they shook hands and Morgan sat down. Johnson opened Morgan's file.

"Thank you, Sergeant."

"Well, don't thank me yet. There are some major concerns. Are you happy being a marine?"

"Yes, I am," Ben had told him, "but I don't think I want to re-enlist."

"Oh, I don't think we want you to do that." Johnson had said to Ben's surprise. "You know Morgan, there's more to being a Marine than just being a good soldier. We're concerned you don't seem to fit in with your platoon."

"What do you mean? I do my job, better than everybody." Morgan had said, stunned.

"No argument there, Corporal," Johnson had said, "but you're too much of a loner. You lead your platoon in marksmanship, hand-to-hand combat, and housekeeping, but you have no sense of camaraderie. Marines are a tight knit group."

When Morgan had tried to talk, Johnson had raised his large weathered hand.

"Morgan," he'd said, "the Corps can help you if you let us. We have great counselors. They may be able to help you…"

"Sergeant," Ben had interrupted. "I don't want any counseling and don't want to be more social. I just want to do my job and leave the Corps next year."

"Suit yourself. I'm only trying to help. I think this interview is over. I do have one question though," Johnson had said, standing. "What do you plan to do in civilian life?"

"I guess, I'll use my mapping skills and find a job as a cartographer or something," Ben had told him, never guessing at the time it would be his killing ability that allowed him to find his ultimate satisfaction in life.

Chapter Four

Gil had brought his girls to the Meadows Mall during their first and only visit after he graduated from his mandatory attendance at the academy and finished his field training, and he had not been back until now. He parked the car near some shade in the massive mall parking lot. The hot Vegas sun beat down unmercifully and the large area of dark asphalt exacerbated the heat. Mall shoppers always fought for the small patches of shade under the trees scattered about inside the decorative cement curbing even if it meant walking a greater distance to the shops. Now, reminded of the previous visit to this mall and the reason for it, he found himself becoming angry again. His damn ex hadn't packed enough clothes for his precious daughters. It wasn't as if she couldn't afford it. Between his child support and her own money, she was pretty well off. *Bitch*.

Trying to recall the mall layout, he remembered it was typical of those built in the eighties with several big box anchors and he found a side door near Macy's. The 'Deliveries Only' area was now being used as a smoker's hangout, the door was wedged open with a matchbook cover so the lone smoker, an overweight man in his mid-fifties wearing one of those cheap suits that all retail clerks seem to own, wouldn't be locked out. Even though Gil was wearing a sports jacket to hide his utility belt and to carry his binoculars and flashlight, he knew the smoker must be sweltering. *Damn cigarettes.*

"Sure hot out here." Gil decided not to reveal he was LVPD. "Can I get into the Mall this way?"

"Not supposed to. The public should enter around the front," the man told him, pointing with his fingers, the cigarette firmly between them. "This is for employees and deliveries."

"Okay, I will come in that way next time," Gil said, opening the door and letting it slam behind him dislodging the matchbook in the process. He didn't let it bother him. A man the size of that needed the exercise.

The well-lit hallway, surprisingly cooler than the blast furnace he had just left, was long and cluttered with pieces of crushed cardboard boxes and other assorted retail trash. Fire pipes sprung from the floor every thirty feet or so and disappeared into the ceiling. There were a half dozen rear doors spaced every thirty feet or so, probably leading to the smaller shops. Gil proceeded down the hall looking for roof access or something. He wasn't sure, but he didn't want to go down Lemke's path of asking mall management or security and perhaps being mislead. He wanted to investigate this potential site on his own.

A metal ladder greeted him as he turned a corner with "Maintenance Access Only" painted in red letters on the trap door at the top, and a single key lock at one edge. When Gil climbed up and pushed on the door, to his surprise, it opened.

Pulling his wiry six-foot muscular frame easily onto the catwalk he saw a faint light emanating from small cracks at the roof joints and ceiling tiles below. Gil switched on his little flashlight in order to examine the latch and found it was stuck in the retracted position held by something that looked like adhesive tape residue. At all events, the latch recessed into the lock. If this was an access to the roof, Jeffers should be informed. He proceeded down the catwalk above the shops.

After climbing yet another set of ladders, Gil found himself on a landing with a door reading, 'Roof Access.' Pushing it open, he was confronted with such a combination of roaring traffic, the blast furnace heat, and bright sunshine that Gil almost recoiled back into the safety of the Mall's attic. It took a few seconds for his eyes to adjust to the brightness and his body to the heat. Getting his bearings, he moved to the north side of the roof. Once at the parapet, Gil could clearly see the sound wall on the other side of the highway. Shading the binoculars against the bright sun with his free hand, he found the place on the sound wall where he had been standing just a little while earlier. Crouching down as if he was trying to hide, he saw that at this precise point that if he had been a sniper he would have been completely hidden and would have a good open shot. Even at that, it would have been one great shot from here.

Examining the wall and the roof's gravel mixed into the softening tar, he looked for clues but failed to see anything and decided that he would ask Jeffers with a lot more expertise than he had, to come back. The CSI team is amazing, he thought. Not as good as the TV series would have the public believe, but amazing nonetheless.

Meanwhile Gil needed to find mall security and ask them some serious questions. Either Lemke hadn't actually tried the access door, or he had simply accepted mall security's claim that the public couldn't get to the roof.

But they were not talking about the public here, Gil reminded himself. *They were talking about murder.*

#

After Morgan collected his mail from the apartment's mailbox clusters, he climbed the stairs to the outside entrance of his second story apartment. He shuffled through a WebMaps remittance advice showing that his paycheck had been deposited into his San Diego California Bank, some junk, a Nevada Power bill that he always paid on-line and on time, and an envelope of forwarded mail, to which his boss in San Diego had attached a note.

> Ben, Here's your weekly mail I've collected for you. I see a DMV notice for registration for your Jeep and some other junk. As we agreed, WebMaps will pay for your California registration, so let me know what it is on your usual expense reports and I'll get you reimbursed quickly.
> S.

Thank you Shirley, he thought. It was so good of her to let her field surveyors use her home address while they were traveling about the country.

Tonight, he decided, he would stakeout his new location, and this time, not let so much time pass between his attacks. That would keep the cops off guard. It would take him a couple of nights to make sure he was in the right location and that his Jeep could be parked in a secure spot. So far, he had picked the perfect spots just as he had successfully succeeded in covering his tracks. Things were going even better than he had planned. But the Jeep was dusty and he couldn't have that. He reminded himself, not for the first time, that cleanliness was next to godliness and he wasn't about to let anyone forget it.

#

Even though it was almost quitting time - if there was such a thing for a cop - when Gil returned to the office, Maria was on the phone as usual. Gil was surprised at how glad he was to see her. Sometimes her overbearing ways, her certainty that she was always right, annoyed him, as did her ceaseless calls on the phone. But right now, looking at her as she swung her wisps of black hair back from her face and smiled at him, he realized that all that didn't matter.

"How'd it go?" Maria asked, hanging up the phone. "Find anything?"

Gil explained what he found at the Meadows Mall and told Maria that he had asked Jeffers at CSI to have a look also. Mall security had been shocked when he had pointed out the open door leading to the area above the stores and that the roof access door over Macy's was unlocked as well. However, mall security had not noticed any unusual activity around the mall at the time of the shooting or noticed cars parked for any inordinate amount of time that night, but they had promised to look through their parking lot video surveillance tapes for the period surrounding the date of the shooting. Although they weren't optimistic that the quality of the images would be any good or if the system had even been working on that date. Furthermore, they had pointed out there were always cars parked overnight, by car-poolers, etc.

"I don't think mall cops are very competent," Gil said. "Or should I say, tuned to our wavelength. I'm sure they do a good job patrolling the parking lot and issuing fire lane parking violations, but probably that's the extent of it."

"Well good job, Gil, but I'm not sure what that gets us," Maria said. "Unless Jeffers turns up something, you still only have a theory."

"You have to agree that the theory is starting to sound pretty good though, don't you. And say. Even though you can't buy my dinner yet, how about stopping somewhere for a drink?"

"Stop talking about that damned dinner and let's go for a drink right now," she said. "I know just the place."

Murphy's Pub, a long time fixture in Las Vegas, had become a safe hangout for off duty Las Vegas police officers and DA staff. Friendly locals, police department staff, and prosecutors used their end-of-shift hours to decompress at the conveniently located bar, which was just a few minutes drive from both the advertised homicide headquarters and the unmarked facility that housed the Gang Bureau. Bob Murphy had long since passed away, but the new owners kept the friendly neighborhood feel, hiring and retaining friendly wait staff and competent short order cooks. The traditional jazz emanating from the speakers scattered about the place helped to make it a pleasant refuge.

Mounted on Murphy's tall barstools, Gil was all too aware of Maria's proximity at the small table. Off duty cops and some 'civilians' were nursing tall beers, watching one of the several big screen televisions, the sound muted, or absently playing video poker machines inset into the long bar.

"Hi, what'll you have?" the waitress asked.

"A Patron shooter with ice water back," Maria shot back.

Gil smiled at her and whistled. "I'll have Grey Goose on the rocks with a splash of water and big hunk of lime," he said. "Say Maria. A shot of Tequila. I'm impressed."

"Well as long as you gringos profile us Mexicans, I might as well order the drink of our country."

"Touché," Gil said, and then moving on to business, "You've worked with Bob Lemke a couple of times haven't you? What kind of detective is he? It seems he missed the fact that there was easy roof access at the mall."

"Bob's a good guy, and very dedicated," Maria told him. "I think he hates homicide and would like to do something else. And even if he's not a good homicide field man, he sure does good analysis. He works well with technology, and does an excellent job at sorting through data and sorting out bogus SSN's on violent illegals. He's managed to get a good many of them deported."

"I hope he's better at analysis than I am," Gil said. "That NCIC query didn't cross correlate any previous sniper shootings for me. I probably need to write better queries. It's hard for me to believe this sniper just started here in Vegas."

When the waitress arrived with their drinks, Maria held up her shot glass and said, "Olay," as they clinked glasses.

"Well, well, look who's here." Maria nodded her head to the entrance and waving, "Speak of the devil, Lemke just walked in. Let's get him to join us."

Gil gave Maria a dirty look. *We don't need any company.*

"What do you have, some sort of clairvoyant powers?" Gil said as Lemke came toward them like a broken-field running back. "I call to get Jeffers and he's with you. I bring up Lemke and he appears."

"It's a power you don't need to know anything more about." Maria told him, grinning.

Bob Lemke, an African-American was taller than Gil, heavy set and his shaved head shone like a bowling ball. More like a playing weight Charles Barkley.

"Hi Bob. It's nice to see you again," Gil said as they shook hands.

"How goes the wars?" Lemke asked, ordering a Fat Tire.

"Same old, same old," Maria told him in a way that told Gil that there was nothing between them.

"So, Bob, I went over to the Meadows Mall today," Gil said, wanting desperately to pursue his theory. "I was following up on the I-95 sound wall shooting and guess what?"

"Does this mean we're going to talk shop?" Lemke asked, glancing at Maria and rolling his eyes. He smiled broadly, showing the gap in his front teeth. "Okay, I'll bite. What did you find at Meadows?"

When Gil had described what he found at Meadows Mall and postulated his "sniper" theory, Lemke took a long sip of his beer.

"Well, that's very interesting," he said, "And no, I didn't actually climb up and check the overhead door, because the security guard assured me they check all doors for security when making their rounds at night. I trusted what he said, but I realize now that I shouldn't have taken his word for it. But, you know, you still have no evidence that the shooter, if it's one man, went there to fire his shot."

"Jeffers from CSI is going to send over a tech to see if they can find anything," Gil said, knowing that he sounded a bit defensive. "I'm not counting on them to produce anything however, because it's been several weeks. Although, they could determine if any locks were jimmied or the tape on the hatch was fresh. I'm positive that's where the shot originated. There's really no alternate site that I can figure."

"Gil did a query on NCIC looking for similar patterns in other cities." Maria chimed in. "That is, taggers being shot while doing their dirty business. Nothing surfaced. Perhaps, because you're so great at looking through this kind of data, you could give it a shot.

By the way, I'm not personally convinced this just isn't gang related. One of them could have been trained in the military."

"That could be," Gil said, thinking that Maria was really good at getting others to help. It would still prove my theory to be correct if we found it to be a gang member as a sniper. "However, we now know that one victim wasn't a gang member, so my theory softens a bit," he added.

"True," said Maria, "But, maybe looking through a telescope or night vision scope he couldn't tell if they were members of a rival gang or not. He never waited long enough for the taggers to write much."

"Or for that matter, whether they were part of his own gang or not," Lemke said. "I'll give it a shot tomorrow or the next day. I'd like to do something more cerebral. You guys are lucky to have taken this case from me. All I had to do today was follow-up on some cockamamie leads on that drive-by shooting last weekend. So boring!"

"Great Bob, I appreciate that." Gil said, relieved. The conversation sounded to Gil that Maria and Bob were coming around to his way of thinking. "Do you need anything from me or do you have all the details you need from the previous shootings?"

"No. I can get what I need from the reports and what you've told me," Lemke said. "Did I ever tell you the trouble I got in with my Sergeant regarding taggers when I was in patrol?"

"I don't think so," Maria said, raising her eyebrows. "What was that?"

Gil and Maria moved to the edges of their seats as Lemke looked around to make sure he couldn't be overheard.

"Well. It was some time ago, when Sid Dalton and I were on night shift," Lemke began, "and we came across a kid writing on a power box up in the Lake's section, using a large black Marks-A-Lot pen. Stupid jerk didn't even see our car. Anyway, we catch this kid. He's maybe thirteen or fourteen years old at the most. We didn't feel like writing him up and taking him to his parents, so Dalton and I painted his entire face and head with his own pen and told him to get on home. He was scared shitless." Lemke laughed.

"So, why did your Sergeant get involved?" Maria asked frowning. Gil wondered if Maria was showing sympathy towards the black faced kid or proud of Lemke and his partner for dosing out a non-lethal punishment.

"Well, apparently his parents," Lemke continued, "who were well-to-do and well connected folks, filed a police brutality complaint with internal affairs. Next thing I know the Sergeant is bellowing at us. 'I know it was you guys,' he said. 'The kid described you both perfectly, said it was a big black man and a red haired cop. So fess up.' But we continued to swear it wasn't us. God, the sergeant, and the Captain were pissed but they never wrote us up or anything. All the sergeant said when we left his office was 'don't let me ever hear about you guys doing something like that again.'"

Maria and Gil exchanged knowing looks. The image of that kid painted all black must have been a far better sight than a body torn apart by a large caliber bullet.

"Should I make reservations for dinner, or do you want to wait a few more days?" Gil asked Maria when Bob was gone.

"Let's not wait to prove this either way." She told him. "I'd love to go to dinner with you soon. We can go Dutch until one of us is proven wrong." In the meantime, Maria's finger circled her empty shot glass, eyes dilating. "Can I buy you another drink?"

After that, their conversation turned to much more personal matters.

Chapter Five

Parking his car a few blocks from the new medical center, Morgan, who loved to walk anyway, thought he would park there again if the medical center proved to be a good location. The parking lot was empty. Approaching the rear of the center, he peered through the glass exit door and put on his gloves and cotton booties. It was just after eight at night and not yet that dark.

Making sure he wasn't being observed, he took out his lock pick set and expertly opened the door, knowing the alarm would not sound because of the metal strip he had installed earlier. Stepping into the alcove he waited for any telltale sounds of alarms or people. Nothing.

Stepping silently up the rear stairs, taking two at a time, Morgan arrived at the fourth floor and walked down another hallway to the roof access ladder and the unlocked door. Shoddy security practices often worked in Morgan's favor and the unlocked door was another example. Emerging on the roof between two massive air conditioning housings, he crouched down and walked to the far edge of the roof. He raised his head just above the parapet and took out his small spotting telescope. He could hear the roar of the beltway traffic. Scanning the length of the new bridge and surrounding concrete work, Morgan figured he would have a good shot and imagined a tagger emerging from the shadows on the far side of the beltway. He'd be walking low to the edge and then duck under the fencing. Pow! He pulled his finger on his imaginary gun and saw, in his mind's eye, the bullet traveling across the almost two-hundred-yard expanse and tearing into the tagger's torso. *Perfect.* He would come back tomorrow night and wait right here.

#

Arriving home after plans had been made with Maria for dinner on the weekend, Gil called Planet Hollywood, made reservations for Saturday night, before going for his evening jog. He was making good progress with her, he thought. They worked on these cases very well together. Leaving Oklahoma and his daughters, Liz and Joni, had been difficult but the opportunity with the Vegas Police Department had made it worthwhile, particularly since it meant that he wouldn't have to deal with an ex-wife turned shrew on an in-person basis. Landing the job with homicide shortly after attending the police academy and his mandatory stint as a patrol officer was perfect. Finding Maria so competent and attractive was icing on the cake.

Since his daughters were avid computer users and had their own e-mail accounts, Gil composed a long message to them as soon as he got home and then prepared a dinner using one of his favorite recipes – Thai Chicken Stir-fry. He received a great deal of pleasure preparing dinner, and stirred and seasoned to his heart's content. As usual, before he settled into his couch potato mode for the evening, he organized his clothes and checked his utility belt. As a Homicide Detective, Gil carried a gun, handcuffs, an extra magazine, pager, and cell phone, as well as his badge and picture ID on his belt clip. Removing his compact black Glock, he checked the chamber and magazine before placing it back into the holster, and plugged his cell phone into his bedside charger.

The process he had had to go through to select his weapon here in Vegas had amused Gil. In Oklahoma it had been easy. He'd just used the department issued 9mm Smith & Wesson. He remembered the pleasure it had given him to go through LVPD's list of authorized weapons and talking to some of the seasoned cops. Glock, Beretta, Smith & Wesson, Colt, Kimber, Springfield Armory, Sig Sauer, Heckler & Koch, Para Ordinance, Ruger, and a few others. Barrels 3.5" to 6", black or stainless finish were available to purchase. The very stylish Beretta 92fs 9mm was the most popular with the older seasoned cops, a model also used by the US military.

Gil had settled on the relatively inexpensive Glock because it saved him some money. No "wow" factor for Gil. He just needed an efficient tool to get the job done. Now he put the extra magazine back in the clip holder, placed the belt on his nightstand, went into his living room, settled in front of the TV and fell asleep quickly, after downing a much-needed beer. For the moment at least, life was good.

#

When he arrived early at the office the next morning, Gil scanned his e-mail. Surprisingly, Maria's desk was still unoccupied. It wasn't like her to be late or not let him know where she was. There was an e-mail from Mike Jeffers indicating that, yes, in fact, the hatch above the ladder had apparently been taped open with standard, buy-anywhere duct tape, but there was no other discernable evidence of lock picking, or fingerprints, and no signs of forced entry on the side door. However, a good pick set wouldn't leave any marks, Jeffers explained, and there was probably no other evidence along the wall on the roof because, thanks to the summer Monsoon season, it had rained several times since the crime.

After writing Jeffers, Gil also sent an e-mail to Lemke thanking him again for doing the queries. Maybe it would help him remember to get on with it. The weekend's homicide activity reports and other open homicide cases were neatly stacked in his report box and he sighed at the thought of pawing through them all.

By the time he was pouring his third cup of coffee, Gil was just starting to worry about Maria when she came into the office, her mouth not smiling, but her eyes still full of energy, looking more desirable to Gil than she had before. She dropped her backpack with a thud. "Sorry to have kept you up so late last night," he said.

"Oh we could've been a lot later than that!" Maria said. Now, she was grinning with her entire face. "I went for my usual bike ride this morning, and when I returned to the house I had a voice mail from the captain who wanted me to assist on the shootings over at East Sahara Avenue on my way in. But one of the victims was taken to Sunrise Hospital before I got there, so I had to go there to get his statement."

"I didn't hear anything about that," Gil said grabbing the overnight reports in his in basket. "There's nothing in the overnights."

"It should be there," Maria said matter-of-factly. "The night shift took in a couple of members of the Downtown Vaqueros Gang as probables. Don't worry, it wasn't a sniper shooting, just the slicing, dicing and beating kind of crap."

"You could've let me know where you were," Gil said, frowning. "We are partners you know."

"Sorry 'bout that, but I was sure the captain would call you too, or at least let you know where I was. What have you been doing this morning without me?"

"I sent an e-mail to Lemke, hopefully to remind him about my queries. Jeffers from CSI said there was nothing much at the Meadows Mall. Lemke did call me back and we discussed the sniper's M.O. He said he would get the queries off today. Oh, and I made reservations at The Strip House for Saturday night at eight. I'll pick you up at seven, okay?"

Spending the rest of the day in the field, Maria and Gil followed up on several other open murders and apparent suicides from the previous night. One was at an apartment complex near Nellis and Charleston where a frightened couple had reported hearing a violent argument outside just before two random shots came through their front door almost hitting their six-month old baby. Another Hispanic youth was found dead on the sidewalk."

"God, I hate this," Gil said at one point between locations. "Even young babies almost getting hit by these animals. Maybe I'll go to work in traffic!"

"No way I'll let that happen," Maria told him grimly. "I have no intention of dealing with this scum without someone like you."

It was, Gil knew, as close to a compliment as he was apt to come by. This was a woman who knew what she wanted, and for now at least, he was not about to cross her.

#

Morgan carefully examined his proposed parking spot near a construction staging lot about two blocks from the medical center, and deciding it was safe enough, he pulled his Jeep into a shadow of a lone tree. It was almost dark. He covered his feet with booties but decided not to do the same for his tires because the asphalt debris made it unlikely that he would leave tracks. Removing the counterfeit Nevada plate from his duffle bag, he snapped it into place with magnets, which were sealed into the cardboard edges.

Entering the building and getting to the roof was a piece of cake. *God is with me.* Raising his head just high enough to look over the low wall, he scanned the new Beltway Bridge with his rifle's state-of-the-art night scope.

A tagger would come along.

He was sure of it. And his Marine training had taught him to be patient. It was three-thirty before he quit for the night.

Chapter Six

Only two months before graduation, high school senior Ben Morgan had walked down the empty school hall to meet with his counselor. Ben, a straight B minus student taking minimum credits, always dreaded these sessions. He knew he would enlist in the Marines in a few months and be gone from Iowa. Having been excused from the tiresome shit about presidential elections in his social studies class for his appointment with the counselor, he absently turned the corner and spotted a boy, probably a ninth grader, bent over and cutting something into the surface of a locker. Morgan went light on his feet as he came closer. The boy was using a straight edged razor blade and had already cut "C O" into the green paint. Silently taking a heavy textbook from his backpack, Morgan bashed the unsuspecting boy in the back of the head so hard and with such force that the boy's head crashed into the locker and he slumped to the hall floor without, as Ben was to learn later, seeing him walk away.

Feeling all gussied up, dressed in a blue blazer, open collared blue linen shirt, and khaki Chinos', Gil took a deep breath and rang Maria's doorbell. She lived in an older but well maintained neighborhood on the east side, about five miles west of Sam's Town Gambling Hall and Casino. She greeted him wearing a simple black dress with petite diamond stud earrings and a single strand of pearls. Her normal tightly pulled back ponytail was long gone and her face was framed with gentle curls with wisps of bangs and streams of hair that touched her shoulders. Gil hadn't seen Maria's hair cascade about her shoulders before. *Gorgeous.*

"*Buenas noches Maria,* "he said. *Usted parece magnífico.*"

"*Usted mira hansome también, No un saludo malo para un gringo.*" Maria said as she ushered him in.

"I tried to look a little less police-womanish tonight." Maria said, whirling around, her dress fanning out to reveal her legs, ordinarily covered with tight fitting denim and jeans, to mid-thigh. "Gil, you don't need to try any more Spanish tonight. Your accent is terrible. Do we have time for a drink?"

"Probably not," he said, glancing at his watch, "but maybe we could have a night cap after dinner? Ready to go?"

"I'm almost ready," Maria assured him. "I'll be right back. Make yourself comfortable."

What was it about all women? They can't just go; there was always the last minute do's such as putting on mascara, freshening lipstick, or loading their purse with a few more feminine necessities. Nevertheless, this time, Gil did not mind. Because, if he had anything to say about it, this would be an evening neither of them would forget.

#

Wealthy Forrester Smead tapped his salad fork nervously on the end of the eighteen-foot European crafted dining table while he stared grimly at his Rolex. His wife of twenty years and fifteen-year-old son were over fifteen seconds late joining him for dinner. Hilda, the cook, knew he'd go into a rage if she were late putting his wine and salad on the table precisely at six-thirty. Gloria and Tim knew that also as they rushed to join their husband and father.

As usual, Smead bellowed, ranted, and raved about punctuality, and announcing that his home building empire would be nothing without discipline. Dinner was unpleasant.

After dinner, lying on his bed staring at the ceiling, Tim swore to himself he would get out of this crazy house soon. He didn't care that his father's wealth had provided everything that he ever needed and more. Carefully, Tim removed a piece of carpet in his closet and lifted out his guide to white supremacist gangs. He'd show the Hispanic and black communities some fear. Placing a marking pen in his pocket for later use on his usual reflective walk through the neighborhood, he would continue to plan his emancipation and join the gang full time.

Settling into their seats at The Strip House Restaurant, Gil concluded his winning argument that he would pay for dinner. "True," he said. "Not all the evidence is in on my sniper theory, but I want to buy dinner anyway."

The Strip House Steak Restaurant, inside the completely remodeled Planet Hollywood Hotel and Casino, had been getting rave reviews. Gil looked at the prices and could see why. But, what the hell. This was going to be a nice evening.

"Now you see why I wanted to come here," Maria said. "It's a fabulous menu. I read that Chef John Schenk's menu is scrumptious. I'll have a Bloody Maria with salt. Please." Maria continued to scan the menu.

"You mean Bloody Mary don't you?" Gil said.

"Nope," she said. "A Bloody Maria is made with tequila instead of vodka; I have to keep up my tradition."

"Mmmm. Maybe I'll have one of those too." Gil raised two fingers. "So Maria, I don't know much about your life before LVPD. Where'd you get your Criminal Justice degree, again?"

"Since I'm a native Las Vegan, I decided to get my degree right here at UNLV," she told him. "My mother and father had relocated to Los Angeles, before I graduated, but they came back for the commencement. They're proud of me. I'm the only one of my brothers and sisters that went to college."

It was, Gil found, surprisingly easy to talk to Maria. Within minutes she was telling him about the brother that was killed in a gang shooting, something she claimed she rarely talked about even though it was the reason that she had gone into law enforcement.

"I'm so sorry to hear about your brother." Now Gil understood what drove her to homicide cases. "What about your other two brothers?"

"They finished high school in Southern California and are working for our uncle, learning the air conditioning business in the Simi Valley," she said. "Simi's near the San Fernando Valley."

"I'd think Las Vegas would have more use for AC than there," Gil said, searching about, while he asked the question, for something more stimulating to say. He wanted to impress her. He had to admit that. But perhaps because she was his senior he found casual conversation a bit forced. "The heat is unmerciful."

"Yes, well, their long term plan is to come back here and start a company," she told him. "Vegas has a lot of AC companies, so it will be hard to get a foothold, but they're young and ambitious."

They were, he realized suddenly, both treading water. Filling in their past. Which was, he supposed, only natural if they were going to be friends. He talked about his own youth and trouble keeping up with his older brother. His older brother, Rob, did better in school and sports than Gil, perhaps because he didn't have the passion at that time in his life. Rob was now a successful criminal defense lawyer working in Tulsa.

As for Gil, as he told her, he had decided on criminal justice and had taken night college courses after a stint in the Army, while he worked at various jobs around Oklahoma City. "I wanted to lock 'em up and my brother wanted to release 'em," he said. "Guess we're pretty competitive that way."

He went on to explain that he had been working in real estate when he'd met his wife to be, Joanna, whose dad owned the business. Soon after they married, Gil told her, he had gone to college full-time and earned his CJ degree shortly before his first daughter was born.

"Tell me what happened between you and your ex," she said, making it sound almost like a command.

If it had been anyone else, Gil might have clammed up. But there was no use pretending to himself that this woman absolutely intrigued him, sexually and every other way.

Gil selected the most inexpensive bottle of wine he could find on the list. Inexpensive at $50, was relative!

"Well, there's not much to say really," he told her as the waiter brought her peppered rare Ahi Tuna and him a bone-in NY steak. "We were the classic not-really-made-for-each-other couple. Joanna was the moneyed, country clubbish type. Eventually, she stopped trying to make me quit the police force and withdrew from the marriage. Being a cop is tough enough, but when you have a wife that hates the hours, and the calls I received at all times of the day and night, well… you get the picture. I was in a lot of pain, but I liked being a cop so much that I just couldn't quit. Her father even tried to set me up in his business, but I was stubborn and wouldn't even consider it. Joanna was already out of love with me and I figured that even if I quit being a cop and became a corporate weenie for her and my girls, we wouldn't last. So I took this opportunity in Vegas. You know the rest."

"She doesn't sound like a shrew though," Maria remarked. "She was just trying to get you to be home more. Not sure, I blame her. Cops' spouses have it tough."

"Trust me on this; she became a nagging, always complaining bitch," Gil insisted, "She is a good mother though. I'll give her that. I'm now a distant dad, but I remain in contact and I see my girls as often as I can. I'm still a cop."

Gil held up the glass of Australian Shiraz and swirled it around. He saw his ex-father-in-law do it hundreds of times and never had the nerve to ask what he was looking for. He thought it looked cool and so he did it without knowing why.

"So, I've told you about my love life, so to speak," Gil added, sipping the wine he had splurged on. "Some of the phone calls I've overheard you take leads me to think you have a boy friend."

"*Had* a boyfriend," she told him. "Hell, I've been through several boyfriends since I was engaged to Grant about four years ago."

"Grant?"

"Yes, my dear Grant," Maria said thoughtfully. "He was the program director for Channel 4 News. He got a promotion to General Manger of a TV station in Albuquerque. We were about to call the whole thing off anyway but when he moved away, it ended officially.

By then, we were grasping at straws to keep it going, because our lifestyles were so different. As you know, I like being active and keeping myself in shape. Grant was always just ready to collapse in front of the TV, go out to eat, or hit a casino. He worked hard at his job, but hated any form of exercise. I was madly in love with him though."

Gil found himself wondering if the kind of exercise Grant disliked included sex, although he couldn't imagine any man not being turned on by this woman. She must have read what he was thinking in his eyes, because she rapped his fingers with a spoon.

"Stop it," She admonished him. "But you're right, he didn't mind that kind of exercise, although, over time, that slowed down quite a bit too. I guess that's normal in longer-term relationships, right?"

"I'm not sure it has to," Gil told her. "Joanna and I nearly stopped making love completely after Joni was born."

"So did you have any girlfriends after you broke up with Joanna?" Maria asked. "I mean, you've been here for a couple of years now."

These were, Gil realized, no idle questions. Maria was not just trying to be polite. She really wanted to know, and she had no qualms about letting him see that she did. Suddenly there was a tension between them that had not existed before. They were both interested in one another, and he found that enormously exciting.

"Well, yes and no," he said. "During our separation, I really didn't date. And once the divorce was final, well I just threw myself into my job and spending time with Liz and Joni, so I didn't have much time to date or socialize that much. And then, when I came here, I realized that work provides opportunities, too. For example, there's that single blond over in public affairs who…"

"Hey buster, you're with *me* now," Maria interrupted him, pretending to be offended. "No talking about blonds, you prejudiced, blond, blue eyed piece of crap. Actually, I was about to mention that I have some cheesecake at home that's better than anything we can get here. In fact…" Her phone rang.

"Shit," she said looking at her cell. "It's the night shift sergeant. This can only be bad news."

Gil tried to remain expressionless, but found himself wanting to bang one fist on the table. Her reference to cheesecake had been a double entendre if ever he had ever heard one.

"Okay," he heard her say. "Radcliff is actually with me. No need to call him. Has CSI been called?" Then covering the mouthpiece she asked Gil, "How long to get to the Beltway and Town Center? There's been another shooting of a tagger."

"By the time we get the car from valet, I would think thirty to forty minutes."

"We'll be there in twenty minutes," Maria told the sergeant. "Probably beat CSI there."

"Does this mean the nightcap and cheesecake are off, or really late?" Gil said frowning.

The look in Maria's eyes had told him it was the latter, which was going to be more than all right with him.

Chapter Seven

With a screech of brakes, Gil stopped the car on the middle of the Town Center Bridge. Several police cars and a paramedic truck, lights blinking, were askew on the roadway, and a LVPD volunteer was directing the light traffic around the emergency vehicles. Several officers were standing on the rock-covered embankment below the bridge where a latex gloved paramedic was squatting over a body. The flashing lights highlighted a large bloodstain on the concrete just below the top of the bridge.

"God, I hate going to crime scenes dressed like this," Maria said as she opened the car door.

Maria and Gil were hurrying across the remaining stretch of bridge when an officer shouted, "You can't go there."

"LV Police," Maria said, as they fished out their badges.

Maria had a tough time negotiating the rock embankment in her low-heeled sandals. "Slow down," somebody said, "he's dead."

Leaving Maria beside the body, Gil, his back to the blood stained concrete wall, began to assess where the bullet might have come from.

"God damn, Gil," she said, bending over the body. This kid's barely fifteen years old, if that. Caucasian, light brown hair, nice shirt and shorts. Nike shoes."

"Dollars to doughnuts that kid is not a gang member," Gil said, turning to scan the floodlit side of the bridge, noting that a chunk of concrete was missing in the area stained with blood.

He heard one of the officers tell Maria that there had been no ID on the body, and that the only evidence he had bagged was an uncapped marker, it's cap missing. "No, Ma'am," the office continued. "The kid has nothing at all in any of his pockets. The way he's dressed, I say he was a resident of Summerlin. Probably lives close by."

"Shit," Gil said, joining the group surrounding the body. "What a shame. Probably a good kid just trying to make his mark. Although I'd have to say there's nothing good about a tagger. Look what it got this one."

"Gil, if this is that same shooter, we've just got to get him," Maria said. "This is such a waste of a life."

"He's the kind of tagger that, at worst, should have been warned and fined," he agreed. "Defacing property is a crime, but he didn't deserve this."

Maria nodded in agreement. "See any potential origination locations up there?"

"Other than the roadway from the other side, the only building I was able to see is that medical center over there," he told her. "You'll see what I mean when we climb back up."

"So who discovered the body and did anybody see anything?" Maria asked one of the officers.

"A motorist traveling north on the other side saw the boy fall and called 911 just over an hour ago," he said, reading from his small note pad. "He thought the boy had fallen or jumped from the bridge. After the dispatcher took the information he left and didn't return to the scene. The only other thing he could tell us when we contacted him was that he didn't hear the shot or see anyone else."

"Gil. What were the previous estimates on TOD?" Maria asked Gil.

"The estimated times of deaths were all between ten at night and two in the morning. So this doesn't quite fit our sniper from that standpoint."

"Maybe the tagger doesn't fit the time frame," Maria said. "Could be that older taggers are out and about later than this kid."

"Let's go over and check out that medical center building," Gil suggested. "We can come back after CSI gets here. Perhaps they can find a bullet fragment up there somewhere. It's my guess, based on how the chunk of concrete was blown away, that it will be in the rocks near the top."

The rear of the four-story structure, illuminated by the emergency lights that glowed from several of the offices and medical suites, as well as a number of street lamps. A single fluorescent bulb, that haloed the recessed door in the small overhang, lit the opening. After dowsing his headlights, they scanned the area. No cars.

After they circled the building on foot, separately, they met by the portico, each of them reporting they had seen nothing out of the ordinary.

"Let's drive around the general area and see what we can find," Gil suggested.

As they drove around the area adjacent to the medical building, passing vacant lots, construction sites, and a residential area, Gil began to wonder precisely what they were looking for.

"I doubt that the killer parked in the parking lot." He mused aloud, "and even if he did…"

"Stop," Maria interrupted him. "See that man walking a dog. Let's ask him if he's seen anything. Roll down the window."

Gil thought it was still way too hot to be walking a dog. Getting out of the car and holding up her badge, Maria introduced herself, "Excuse me, we wondered if we could ask you a couple of questions. Nice dog. Is he dangerous?"

"No, she's friendly," the man said frowning. He looked to Gil like he was in his mid-fifties, and wearing shorts and a golf shirt. "What did I do?"

"Nothing at all," Maria assured him. "There was a shooting about an hour ago over at the Town Center Bridge and we were wondering if you might have seen anything or heard anything unusual?"

The big dog licked the back of Maria's outstretched hand. Gil stayed in the car. "A shooting!" the man exclaimed as Maria let the Great Pyrenees continue to lick. "Was somebody killed? I sure haven't seen a thing."

"Yes, a kid was murdered," Maria said. "Are you sure you didn't see anything out of the ordinary?"

"Well, come to think of it," he told her. "I did see a car parked up the street. There was a car, or rather an SUV tucked up against the side, near a construction lot."

Gil and Maria got out of the car and followed the man to an area covered with broken pieces of asphalt and hardpan. "I'm pretty sure this is the spot," he told them.

"What kind of SUV?" Maria asked. "Did you notice the plates or anything else about it? How long ago would you say it was there?"

"Oh, I dunno," the man said. "Maybe an hour and a half ago. It was black, maybe a Toyota, Jeep or something like that. They all look the same to me. I think it had Nevada plates, but it was kinda dark and I'm not sure."

"Any detail you can give us would be a great help," Maria assured him, "even if it was just a number on the plate or a letter."

"Nope," he replied, reining in the dog who was becoming impatient, "but I now remember noticing the car was very clean. Odd for a black car parked near a construction lot. It shone in the darkness."

"Interesting that you noticed that the SUV was clean, but don't know the make?" Gil said.

"Sorry," he said, "but I'm not really into cars, and gas guzzling SUV's are all the same to me."

After Maria asked the man to make a statement into her digital audio recorder to be transcribed later into the field witness database, she gave the man her card, recorded the man's name, address, phone number, and thanked him very much. Maria joined Gil in patting the panting dog goodbye, before returning to the bridge. The CSI van had arrived and a tech was taking pictures of the body as they gingerly made their way back down the rocky slope. After reporting on the fact that a strange SUV had been seen at the building site nearby Maria asked that the CSI tech pass the information on to Jeffers since it could be significant.

"Hey Detective Garcia," a police officer standing at the top of the grade bellowed. "There are television and *Review Journal* reporters here who'd like to ask you some questions."

"Be right there," she called back and then muttered to Gil, "Shit, that's all we need."

"I wouldn't say anything about a sniper right now," Gil warned her.

"I'm not stupid," she assured him, and with that, she scrambled up the embankment, leaving Gil to observe most of her shapely legs and a flash of white panties. She was mighty fine, he thought.

It was a half hour later before they were ready to leave. "So Maria, about that nightcap?" Gil said as they settled into the car. "I don't live too far from here, you know."

"Great, let's do that," Maria replied. "Do you have any cheesecake?"

"No cheesecake, but I have some vodka and beer, not to mention three week old Krispy Crème doughnuts."

"You have doughnuts?" Maria asked jokingly.

"Sure," Gil said just as jokingly. "I have doughnuts, just in case nobody believes I'm a cop."

"I'm game for anything after this shooting crap," Maria told him, still laughing at his little doughnut joke. "Since, presumably, you weren't expecting company, I can check out what kind of housekeeper you are."

"Fair enough." Gil, genuflecting on the inside, thanked the gods above that he had cleaned and tidied his house today, not to mention having changed the sheets. If he were going to be lucky tonight, Maria would notice that too.

While Gil busied himself with getting ice and generally making a clatter in the kitchen, Maria wandered into his small office and took note of more pictures of his daughters, along with several Commendations from the Oklahoma City Police, for "bravery" and "service above and beyond." There was also a framed newspaper clipping.

"Homicide Victim's Mother Honors OCPD Officer"
Oklahoma City, OK. OCPD Homicide detective Gil Radcliff was honored today at a ceremony for his

tireless work at bringing to justice the murderer of
Socialite Nancy Dexter's eighteen year old son...."

She broke off as Gil arrived with the drinks.

"Well, here's to whatever," she said, raising her glass.

Whatever it takes to get you into my bedroom, Gil thought, while asking her if she wanted to catch the late news.

"Actually," Maria told him, "I had something else in mind."

She certainly believed in getting straight to the point, Gil thought, finding his reaction was mixed between absolute delight that he should be getting so lucky so soon, to a mild discomfort based on the question of whether or not she would have been this direct about what she wanted had their professional positions been reversed. Perhaps, he thought, this was what women meant when they said they felt as though they were being used, and then told himself not to be ridiculous.

They became ravenous, hurried, and moved so quickly to the bedroom that Gil's head was spinning. He had not, after all, had sex for months and months and although he wasn't sure about Maria's previous activity, she seemed as ready as he was. In fact, she helped him shuck his shirt over his head. "I've had this in mind for a while," she told him as he pulled her dress down to her waist, and undid her bra.

"So have I," he assured her, kissing her breasts and firm nipples.

When he pulled off her dress and panties she pushed him down until he was kneeling before her. She ran her fingers through his hair. "Oooh yes!" she cried. "That's the right spot."

Pulling him onto the bed, Maria opened her legs to his eager mouth. And determined to please her, Gil concentrated hard. Maria's groans of pleasure provided all the feedback he needed to confirm he was accomplishing his goal. She came with a whimpering and a set of powerful convulsions.

"I want you inside me now," she gasped, pulling Gil on top of her.

Gil penetrated her easily. His strokes were slow and patient. As their lower bodies performed that familiar dance, he kissed her ears and neck. Every few minutes, they changed positions, stopping occasionally to explore each other with tongues, fingers and lips. Maria had several orgasms and Gil's was one of those satisfying, curl-your-toes types after which they finally collapsed in each other's arms.

"Oh my, I needed that," Maria told him, and Gil found himself intrigued by her eagerness. She had all but initiated the encounter and she certainly had been an active participant in it. It was a refreshing change from the usual attitude of the women he'd known, most of whom had approached sex as if they were doing him a favor.

When their breathing had returned to normal, they talked for several minutes: the shooting, snipers, the gang unit, politics in the Homicide Unit, Las Vegas, ex boyfriends and an ex-wife. When Maria suggested they make love again, all Gil could respond with was, "I'm really tired; can I go to sleep for a bit right now?"

Maria would not be denied, and declaring she was not sleepy, proceeded to fondle his limpness and testicles. In spite of Gil's protestations, Maria continued her insistent ways, as she continued to massage and pull on him. "I think it's getting ready," she breathed into his ear as she stroked and kneaded him.

"Oh yes, Gil. It's ready!"

Chapter Eight

Ben Morgan's routine on Sunday mornings was always the same. Read the paper, do the crosswords along with the Jumble puzzle, and clean his bathroom and kitchen. This Sunday was no exception, but he was anxious to read about his accomplishment of the night before in the newspaper.

Police seek link with five recent shootings of Graffiti artists

(Las Vegas Review Journal) Las Vegas Police are trying to determine whether some kind of gang warfare is ongoing around the Las Vegas Valley.

Another youth was killed last night at the New Town Center Bridge over the Southwest portion of the Beltway, apparently shot while starting to paint graffiti on the new bridge. The victim's gang affiliation, if any, and identity is being withheld because of his apparent age. According to police spokeswoman,

Maria Garcia of the LVPD Homicide Unit, a suspect is unknown
at this time. They are working on several leads, she said.

Police said the five shootings likely are gang-related, and are
probably linked.

Morgan grinned as he read the account. It had been the same in
all of the previous cities in which he had initiated clean-up operations.
He re-read the line *'gang-related and probably linked'* several times as
he sipped on his coffee. *'Working on several leads!'* Ha! Suddenly he
remembered his first such incident in San Diego nearly a year ago
when he had strangled his first victim with his bare hands. What
an adrenalin rush that had been. And it happened quite by accident
when he had come upon a Hispanic kid painting some obscene
words on a seawall. The remaining murders had been planned with
meticulous care, however, in order to make sure he would never be
caught. There had been five stranglings in San Diego, six knifings
in Atlanta, six more in Seattle using his 9mm Browning, which had
been equipped with a silencer, and two knifings on the road between
Seattle and Las Vegas. Las Vegas now had five dead scum, thanks to
him. He might have time for one, maybe two, before he had to move
on to Denver for WebMaps.

Morgan stared into space remembering that life changing
moonless night in San Diego. It had been well after midnight, and
Morgan had been walking on a remote stretch of beach north of
The Silver Strand. He was in such turmoil about his life, he had
walked almost eight miles from his house, thinking, re-thinking,
and praying. The gentle sounds of the small waves lapping at the
shore had no effect on the incessant negative and unclear thoughts
he was experiencing. Continued to experience. Over and over. He
had no real friends, his plan to become some sort of hired assassin

had not come to fruition, and he was in a dead end job playing a geek to novice PC users. Furthermore, while he could converse with people, he hated being sociable and didn't know how to mix with the right, or in this case, the wrong people. Something was definitely missing in his life. He often prayed for guidance from God, but as he contemplated his life, he had heard footsteps on sand covered concrete above him and to his right. However, when he stopped to listen, he only heard the ocean waves lapping.

Morgan crouched down, his back to the ocean. Listening and looking. There was a small dinghy, barely visible, lying on its side beneath a long ten-foot tall wall that he supposed kept the houses perched above safe and dry at high tide and during winter storms. An opening illuminated by a low post mounted lamp cast a small light on the wooden steps that rose to the neighborhood above, where yellow-orange light leaked out of a few windows of the expensive seaside homes .

Suddenly, a youth wearing shorts, a ball cap, and tee shirt appeared above the wall. Looking in both directions, he cautiously ventured down the wooden steps to the beach to the left of Morgan. Marine Corps training took over as Morgan crouched lower and pulled in all is energy to become invisible. If the youth looked in his direction he would be nothing but a mass of inorganic compound, like a rock.

The youth stepped onto the beach and looked around, even more cautiously this time, before taking up a position near the dinghy, facing the wall. The sound of the marble rattling around in the spray can was unmistakable, and Morgan tensed as the youth started to paint initials, gang name, or whatever expletive he had in mind. On his feet, moving now, Morgan stole toward the boy, grabbing him just as he had one letter, predictably, an F, sprayed onto the wall. In an instant, Morgan had him by the throat squeezing the life out of him. Morgan's well trained fingers and thumb pressed deep into the taggers neck and air passage; his powerful hands continued to squeeze as the boy's legs kicked and squirmed.

"Defacing public property is a crime, you worthless piece of shit!" Morgan whispered in his ear just before the Hispanic kid took his final gasp. The dead tagger slumped to the sand, eyes still bulging with fear.

During his eight-mile walk back home, Morgan repeatedly thanked the Good Lord for finally giving his life direction and meaning. His new calling meant he would meticulously plan and carryout foolproof execution of these defacers in a manner that would defy detection.

#

Gil got up early and made sure that the first thing Maria would smell on awakening would be sausage frying. Minutes after he had put them in the pan, she emerged, from the bathroom, wearing one of Gil's terrycloth robes. Maria walked into the kitchen where he was cooking wearing only his boxers and a LVPD tee shirt. His glimpse of her naked body before the robe closed made him smile too.

"My, that smells mighty good," she said putting her arms around him as he stood by the stove, flipping the sausages around in the pan. "Good morning."

"Well, good morning to you. Did you sleep well?"

"Like a brick." Maria told him, snuggled against his back. "Have you been up long?"

"Oh, about twenty minutes or so. Want some coffee? Oh, you should see the paper on our shooting last night."

"They spelled my name right at least," Maria said, sitting herself in Gil's small dinette. "I wonder if they identified that poor young boy yet."

Gil was glad that she had said that. It had, he realized now, bothered him more than he had thought that she appeared to be so callous about the boy's death the night before. Perhaps, he thought, it was because of the loss of her brother. Perhaps, she couldn't allow herself to feel too much too directly.

"I suppose we could call in to find out, but let's eat breakfast first. How do you like your eggs?"

Maria was very complimentary to Gil's cooking. "This is pretty good, Gil," she said washing down a bite of English Muffin with a sip of coffee. "Too bad you didn't cook for your wife. She would never have let you go."

"Too bad she didn't cook for me," he retorted, grinning. "I wouldn't have *left her.*"

Breakfast banter continued as they explored each other's lives in more detail.

"I know the Sergeant originally gave you some time off at the end of next month when your girls visit," Maria said. "But what are you going to do with them the other days when you have to work?"

"I dunno exactly," Gil told her, "but when I last talked to my brother, my sister-in-law, Loretta, indicated that she'd be willing to come to Vegas and watch them when I have to work. I need to firm up the plans. I suppose when push comes to shove, I can find a baby sitter or something." He gave Maria a sideways glance, "You interested?"

"Oh good God, Gil, you don't want me watching your kids," Maria said, laughing heartedly. "I'd poison their minds, with lots of feminists stuff. Come on, let me do the dishes, although I don't want you to ever think I'd do it on a regular basis."

"You mean I can't count on you coming over for breakfast on a regular basis." Gil said patting her rear-end. "And don't bother with the dishes, because I can think of something else…"

The chirping of her cell phone buried deep in her purse, which she had thrown on the couch the night before, interrupted him. "Shit, let's hope that's a personal call," she said.

"No shit, captain," Gil heard her say. "Oh, man, it's going to hit the fan… Yes, I can call Radcliff…" She winked at Gil. "Okay, we can be there, but I think you ought to invite Bob Lemke too. He was running some queries for us… We'll give you a single sniper theory then too… Okay, see you then."

"What was that about?" he asked.

"That was the Captain Rodgers." She said, a faraway look in her eyes.

"No shit. I gathered that. What happened?"

"They ID'ed that kid from the shooting last night and guess what?"

"What?"

"Do you know who the biggest home builder in the valley is?"

"I dunno, Pulte, KB, who and why?"

"It's Ace Homes. You know the guys with the tag line, "There's no Place Like Ace"? Well, the kid that was shot last night is the fifteen-year-old son of Forrester Smead, owner and CEO of Ace Homes, the guy that owns that twenty room house in that gated community on the golf course. Seems his kid sneaked out of his bedroom window last night."

Oh, oh, Gil thought. Now the pressure really would be on. It was one thing for gang members from the wrong side of town to be killed, and quite another when it was the son of an important member of the community.

"Anyway, the kid was obviously bent on putting some graffiti onto the bridge when he met our sniper friend. Smead is already all over the Mayor and the Sheriff. Going to be a lot of news this evening and the *Review Journal* will have all kinds of coverage tomorrow morning. The Captain has called for a special meeting at noon today. You may have heard me suggest he invite Lemke. Maybe he has a line or something."

"Shit, that's all we need," Gil sighed. "All that pressure from the top, with no real help, either clue wise or resources."

"Here in Vegas we call those "Tower Capers," Maria told him. "Perhaps now the press coverage will scare our sniper off or at the least get some other citizens to come forward with something they saw or heard. Right now," she added, "we have nothing. It might be the right time to give the press our sniper theory, and let them help out."

"What do you mean our theory? I guess that means our next dinner is on you now. I'm thinking Alizé at the top of the Palms."

"Damn, Gil," Maria said, teasing him with her eyes. "I'll have to take out a loan if we go there."

It had been a long time since Gil had laughed that long, and he found himself wondering just how long this feeling of being on top of the world would last, particularly since he knew that, in many ways, that was completely up to Maria.

Chapter Nine

As Morgan finished rubbing a nearly invisible spot from his kitchen countertop, he looked about his kitchen and thought, *now that's what I call clean!* Plopping himself down on his easy chair in his tidy living room, he picked up his latest *had to read book* from the perfectly aligned stack. Morgan was surprised that he had not read *The Art of War* by Sun Tzu before. It was full of important information about resourcefulness, momentum, cunning, flexibility, integrity, secrecy, speed, positioning, surprise, deception, manipulation, responsibility, and practicality.

Several passages reminded him he had made just two mistakes in his effort to stomp out graffiti vandals. One mistake was the happenstance encounter on the beach in San Diego, and that had been *the* mission-defining event for him. The other mistake had been another accidental encounter at a roadside rest stop in Oregon. That had been so unplanned that he had taken the ultimate risk and let his emotions get away from him. The one lucky thing about it had been that there had been no witness, and apparently no video surveillance.

Morgan had looked forward to being reassigned to Las Vegas from Seattle. WebMaps was a good employer, and they loved the fact that he was single and able to move about the country to whatever location he could be best use to them. He had been particularly anxious to use his sniper rifle that Uncle Sam had spent so handsomely on training him to use, one that he had successfully stolen from a big house in a rich Seattle neighborhood. Being a night person, Morgan had decided to drive as far as he could toward Vegas, starting out after sundown. Late his first night on the road, or actually very early the next morning, he had pulled into one of Oregon's nicely decorated and well-maintained rest stops just north of Grants Pass in order to empty his bladder and catch a few minutes nap.

Morgan pulled his Jeep into the parking spot away from the lights and the truck parking area, where a few trucks, their diesel engines idling, were parked at the far end. Except for a dirty old suburban van parked close to the restrooms there were no other vehicles in sight. The diminishing sounds of the few passing cars and trucks were like waves in a distant ocean.

Just in case he encountered trouble, whether in the form of 'highway robbery,' or a 'gay' mugging, Morgan took his briefcase from his backseat, lifted up the false bottom, and retrieved his ten-inch custom-made hunting knife, which hadn't made many appearances since he left Atlanta. Once outside his car, he strapped the knife, contained in its quick draw scabbard, to the small of his back, and slipped into his windbreaker. Except for his shoes, whose soles Morgan had painstakingly made smooth with a very fine file to avoid leaving any footprints, and except for the fact that he was not wearing black pants, black sweater and ski hat, he was in his Atlanta hunt for taggers uniform. His Seattle 9mm Silenced Browning was safely secure at the bottom of one of his cardboard boxes bound for Las Vegas in a Graebel moving van.

Morgan walked toward the restroom keeping to the edge of the parking lot, past the "pet area" which announced itself by the smell. Emerging from the shadows so he could walk parallel past the van, he half expected to find a driver sleeping in the cab, but it appeared empty.

Approaching the restroom, he heard muffled male voices. "Shit," someone said, "don't write fuck. Everybody does that. Write sumpin' about the fuckin' goddamn government or sumpin."

The hair raised on Morgan's back and arms and sweat formed in his armpits. He moved closer to the closed door, and pressed his ear to the vent. "I'll write what the fuck I want. You always tellin' me what to do. I got the goddamn marker."

Clearing his throat, Morgan waited a beat before pushing open the door and found two scrawny, poorly dressed young men, one standing at the urinal, the other leaning over the sink and about to continue writing on the large stainless steel mirror. If Morgan had closed his eyes to imagine what images he would come across, he wouldn't have been far wrong. The man standing at the urinal was wearing a tank top that revealed more tattoos than Morgan thought would fit on an arm. The other, wearing a filthy tee shirt, swiveled around, and was holding a marker pen.

"Now, you don't want to be going around defacing public property do ya?" Morgan said, repeating the line he had often used in the three cities he had previously lived in.

The man at the urinal buttoned his fly and turned toward Morgan, while the other made an attempt to hide the marker behind his back and said, "You a cop?"

Funny how many of his graffiti vandal victims asked that just before he ended their lives. "Nope," Morgan said, "I just don't like scum like you defacing property."

"Well, fuck you," the man with the marker said. "You'd better get the hell out of here, or we're likely to kick yo' ass."

Morgan was aware of only one thing and that was that he was enraged. Morgan spread his arms away from his waist and stepped closer to the men.

"Hey shithead, like I said," the man by the urinal said, starting toward Morgan, "get the fuck out of here." Morgan, in a fleeting second or less, choreographed his next moves. Extracting the knife from the small of his back he flashed it across the jugular vein of the neck and buried it to the hilt in the second man's chest.

The man whose head had been nearly severed from his body grunted as he dropped to the floor, and the other called out "Christ!" as he fell beside him. Avoiding the sprayed and rapidly spreading blood he opened the restroom door a crack and checked for new cars that may have parked in the area. Seeing none, took his leave of the two corpses.

Stopping in the pet area, Morgan relieved his full bladder on the rocks, rinsed his knife in the drinking fountain, and stepping carefully across the pet area silently swore at pet owners for not using the available plastic doggy bags. Five minutes later he was headed south on his way to Vegas. The rush that had accompanied the murders had made it unnecessary for him to nap. His only regret was that he had been forced to act out of rage with no previous planning. That was, he promised, something he would not do again. Unless, of course, he was unfortunate enough to come accidently upon scum like this again.

Chapter Ten

Maria insisted on driving separately to the Captain's meeting and Gil assumed that she would be only a few minutes behind him. "You go ahead," she told him. "Let's not let anybody see us arrive together on a Sunday."

Now Gil stood at the back of the familiar room trying to decide where to sit, realizing that he might have to stand and espouse his sniper theory in more depth. A few other officers from homicide, the public affairs women, Mick Jeffers from CSI, and Bob Lemke were lounging about on the classroom type chairs in the large briefing room. The Captain had not yet arrived and Gil could only hope that Maria would make it before he walked in. The Captain in his usual form would instantly perch at the lectern and just start addressing the assembly.

Gil was well known now, he realized, as he acknowledged the greetings from practically every officer there. Lemke's thick folder of papers was a good sign, Gil thought, as he nodded at Jeffers who chose a chair next to Lemke and parked himself. "Hi Bob, looks like you got some query responses there."

"I sure did, although I'm not certain they all fit what we're looking for," Lemke said, "but there are some interesting things in this folder, particularly from Seattle, Oregon, Atlanta, and San Diego."

"I can't wait to see it. Does the Captain know what you have?"

"Not yet. He called me this morning and I guess Maria told him I was running this stuff. This meeting has already ruined my Sunday. I promised the wife and kids we would go to the park for a picnic lunch."

"Sorry about that, but in this heat, is that something you really wanted to do?" Gil said, at the same time recognizing that it was ironic that he, a man who had practically abandoned his girls, was feeling guilty about Bob missing a family outing.

Before Lemke could respond, Gil heard someone taking the seat just behind them and swiveled around to see that it was Maria. She was wearing no make-up and obviously, to Gil's inside track, had simply donned jeans and an LVPD tee shirt during her quick trip home. She still looked great. Just as Gil was about to greet her, the Captain walked in from a side door.

Captain Tom Rodgers, a twenty-year veteran, looked just like a man a media guide might have drawn. He was tall and rarely smiled, with job pressure wrinkles around his mouth. A picture of gravitas. Rodgers had worked his way up the ranks, having been a traffic officer, fatality accident investigator, gang unit detective, homicide detective, homicide sergeant and finally in charge of the Homicide Unit. He unfolded a couple of pieces of paper, smoothed them on the lectern, looked at his watch, and cleared his throat.

"Okay," he said. "We have all heard that the fifteen-year-old son of a Mr. and Mrs. Forester Smead was shot last night out in

Summerlin. As the president and owner of Ace Homes, Smead is quite the prominent citizen. The objective of the meeting is to get our story straight for the media and determine what we have in identifying the suspect. Ginny, what does the press have so far?" he asked, looking over at Virginia Rodriguez.

"Up until this morning, the press only knew it as another shooting of a graffiti vandal – possibly gang related," Virginia said, standing. "Now that the identity is that of the fifteen year old son of the Smead's, the evening TV and the *Review Journal* tomorrow will try to identify the death as non-gang related. There's no way we can avoid that. I've already talked to Mr. Smead and assured him we're working on his son's murder as diligently as possible. I gave a statement to the press about an hour ago to the effect that we have nothing new to report, but that I may have something for them later this afternoon. I was waiting for this meeting to give me some direction."

"Okay, that fits with what I told the sheriff," the captain said. "He has already received two calls from Mayor Goodman. Damn politicians. Let's go around the room and see what we've got. Garcia and Radcliff were on the scene last night and she and Radcliff may have a theory. Maria?"

"Jump in here, if I leave something out, Gil," Maria said before going on to brief the group on the progress or lack thereof on the previous shootings. She revealed that one of the previously reported victims was not a gang member, but added that although it was possible that looking, as the sniper must have been, through a night scope he might have not known that his victim did not actually belong to a gang or tagging crew.

This was information, she added, that they hadn't shared with the media, just as they had not revealed the location of the shooting of the I-15 bridge victim. Nor had they revealed Gil's discovery of a potential site from the top of Macy's. They had not shared the information given to them by the man walking his dog near the construction site who had told them that a van had been parked there at about the same time of the shooting. But now it was time to air their theories, particularly in regard to where the murderer had been located somewhere near the Town Center Bridge. "I've already asked CSI to go to the medical building and check it out."

Jeffers was, Gil noted, writing furiously in his booklet. The location fit in with the other shootings, and she smoothly segued into their sniper theory, which to Gil's surprise, she attributed to him.

"So you guys think we have a crazy on our hands, shooting taggers?" the captain said as she returned to her seat.

"Perhaps you should hear what I've found," Bob Lemke said, taking the overhead projector from the side of the lectern and turned it on. "May I use this, Captain?"

"Sure, Lemke, let's hear, or should I say, see what you've got."

"I've been doing some research in the national database, the FBI's NCIC," Lemke said, looking directly at Detectives Hewitt and Hughes, the others from homicide, and opening his folder. "There have been several cities with multiple cases of taggers being killed during their acts of vandalism: in Atlanta, San Diego, Seattle, and St. Louis. All of them unsolved. At first, I threw out the results because they weren't shootings. But," he added, placing a transparency on the projector, "look at this."

The unfocused, hand-drawn, black and white image, was that of a crudely constructed box with lots of black dots. The bottom line had a time line, spanning a year. The bottom right hand date, coming into focus as Lemke twisted the focus knob, revealed the words, 'last night.'

"I've crunched this data pretty well, and I've talked to the police in San Diego, Atlanta, St. Louis, and Seattle," Lemke said, pointing to each of the black dots as he mentioned each city. These dots represent graffiti vandals who were killed while tagging. Notice that, except for St. Louis, these killings are evenly spaced, within three or four weeks of each other. There were six stranglings in San Diego spaced over about three months, the first manual and the others by means of a garrote. After that they stopped and then there were eight knifings in Atlanta, spaced over about a three-month period. All the same type of knife with a ten inch blade. After that, eight people were killed by a 9 millimeter handgun in Seattle over a similar three month span, and according to ballistics, the same gun. Then we have our five rifle shootings here."

"What about St. Louis?" the captain asked.

Lemke smiled, "I just got a call from the St. Louis PD and I didn't have time to take the dots off this chart, but it looks like they caught a couple of gang members who have confessed to several shootings. So right now, St. Louis is out. It didn't look like those fit this timeline anyway. Based on my data and expanding on Gil's theory, I'd say we have someone that hates taggers, that has moved from city to city and changes his MO so these data would confuse us. Further more I have some..."

"You've got to be shitin' us." Hewitt rose to his feet. His partner, Hughes, lounged back in his chair, uninterested. "Come on Bob, that's really a stretch."

Gil turned in his seat, and whispered to Maria, "That dinner is going to taste so good!"

"Bullshit Radcliff, you're just thinking of dessert," Maria whispered. "Give me a piece of paper; I may have to write something down."

"Calm down," Captain Rodgers said. "Let's see if we can put

this together and sort it out. We don't have much else to go on so please wait until Bob has finished. Go ahead Bob, what else do you have?"

"As I was about to say," Lemke said, looking straight at Radcliff and Garcia, "I felt bad about not confirming roof-top access at Macy's, so I asked mall security to look through their surveillance tapes of the dates in question for the sound wall shooting that Gil had already asked them for. And although they had told me they didn't see anything themselves, I did find this."

Placing a grainy picture on the overhead projector, he pointed to a murky spot at the far end of the mall parking lot.

"Over the course of about four nights, including the night of the shooting, this vehicle was parked in approximately the same spot, tucked away in this corner of the parking lot. I asked the photo folks to enhance the image, and they think it's a black Jeep."

Gil swiveled around, looked at Maria, and raised his eyebrows.

"Now look at this," Lemke continued, switching slides. "This photo is from the Oregon State Police taken within minutes of the estimated time of death of two men knifed at a rest stop near Grant's Pass. One of the victims had been holding a marking pen. The surveillance camera takes pictures of Interstate 5 every five seconds. Their photo-interpreting folks think this is a black Jeep also. They couldn't make out the license plate details, but they believe it was either a Washington or California plate. Three weeks later, here in Vegas, our current spree of shootings started."

"Good job, Bob," Captain Rodgers said as Lemke took his seat. "At least it's something more than we had. Okay, let's assume this theory is correct. Hewitt, I'd like you to go out to the witness Maria spoke about and question him again."

"Captain for Christ's sake," Hewitt protested. "This is awfully thin."

Captain Rodgers' eyes narrowed. "Look, we don't have anything better and we need to run down all these leads and circumstances. Do you have anything better to propose?" Rodgers ended the question with a pointing finger.

"No I don't," Hewitt said, almost sheepishly, and then brightened. "I think it's gang related. I really don't think it's some vigilante parading around the country committing serial murders for the sake of cleaning up the planet."

"We'll continue to work that angle, too," Rodgers said impatiently. "but Lemke's data and Gil and Maria's theory needs work right now. So you guys are good about getting a witness to remember more than they think they can. If we can confirm it was a black Jeep parked there last night you can get on with a DMV search. I'm going to ask a profiler to come in on this case. If what Gil and Maria think is true and Lemke's data supports a single suspect, moving from city to city, I'd like to get a line on what this loony is like."

"Captain, that's all good," Maria said standing up. "But if Lemke's timeline is correct, shouldn't we be thinking that this killer may be moving on in a few weeks. Three months or so was all the time this guy apparently spent in the previous cities. What kind of job would allow him to move from city to city?"

"Maybe he's independently wealthy," Hewitt mocked her. "Let me ask another question. I'm assuming that these tagger killings in these other cities made it to the media. It is possible we have several copycats. There are crazies out there and we know that everybody hates graffiti. Nobody hates it worse than me, by the way. These guys are maybe doing us a favor."

"I think it's unlikely." Lemke said, defending himself, holding up the folder. "Why would they start and stop along this timeline? I think we should pursue this as the same suspect. And detective Hewitt, I think it's fair to say that this guy hates graffiti more than you."

Hewitt just stared into space and muttered under his breath, "Coincidence."

Gil couldn't put his finger on it, but it seemed to him that Hewitt was being obstinate and counterproductive.

Gil watched the Captain pace around the lectern, thinking about the latest dialog. "I tend to agree," the Captain said, finally, "that it's more likely to be one killer and not four copycats. Add the possible job changes to your list, Hewitt. Start looking through bank and utility records. We might be able to correlate DMV license plate changes, with new bank accounts or new utility accounts. This guy has to live somewhere. But I want to keep the possibility open that it's someone working alone or with gang members. Or for that matter some other unknown anti-graffiti network."

"Garcia and Radcliff are now on special assignment to Captain Vasquez who will run the day to day operations," the captain startled everyone by saying. "I talked to the sheriff and he agrees. I'm going to undergo some much needed back surgery and will be out of action for about six weeks. I told the sheriff and Captain Vasquez that if we came up with something at this meeting they should support having Maria and Gil coordinate the entire effort. I think we've come up with something very good at this meeting. Captain Vasquez is going to be stretched very thin while I'm out, so Hughes and Hewitt, effectively you'll be taking directions from them on this case."

Gil tried very hard not to smile on the outside, but was beaming on the inside. Maria and I are good team, he thought. *We can handle this.* The only doubt that crept into his head was figuring out how to manage Hewitt and Hughes. The rest would be just plain old police work. He'd have to stay on his toes, and double his effort for the long term. *Long term,* he thought. He hoped beyond hope that this effort didn't screw up the planned visit from his daughters.

"Lemke, you continue to help the team with analysis," Rodgers said. "If Hughes and Hewitt come up with some DMV, bank, or utility records, I'd like you to run the data back through San Diego, Atlanta, and Seattle to see if we can correlate anything."

"Will do, sir." Lemke replied. Although neither Hughes nor Hewitt said anything it was clear that they were not pleased to hear that Gil and Maria were, as of now, running the operation. In fact, Hewitt sank further back in his chair with an 'I-don't-give-a-shit' slouch.

"Jeffers, you and the rest of the CSI folks will continue to provide your excellent support," the captain continued. "That medical center rooftop and surrounding area should be a top priority."

Jeffers nodded, "It already is, Captain."

"Maria, you can get the gang bureau field contacts out there and start asking about what they may have seen," the captain continued. "Someone decided that there's some sort of gang retaliation going on. Let's get a line on that. Our gang bureau said they'd help."

"I've already been talking to Rodolfo and he said he'd try and get some other undercover guys on it." Maria told him.

"Virginia, let's schedule a press conference for four today," the captain continued. "That should get us on the evening news and get Mayor Goodman off the sheriff's back for a while. You can tell them we have a line on a black SUV. Let's not mention the word Jeep right now. Maybe it will jog someone's memory about the previous shootings. Let's recap for the dates and locations of the previous shootings for the media. Stay quiet about our sniper theory and tying into the other cities, but you should say that we believe these shootings are linked. The press has already done that anyhow. We should mention that we no longer think they're strictly gang related. Hewitt, get all of the forensics and police reports on these other killings in those cities."

Virginia raised her hand, "Captain, I can handle the press conference, but I promised Mr. Smead I'd call him and brief him before I told the press anything. Any problem with me doing that?"

"No, but give me an hour to brief the sheriff, so he can brief the Mayor first," Rodgers said. "Now, are there any other questions? No?" He exited the room.

"Great job, Bob," Gil said, shaking Lemke's hand as the rest of the room sat in almost stunned silence. "I'd never have got that information. What made you look at other causes of death?"

"Yes, great job Bob and thanks for doing that." Maria chimed in.

"Thanks," Lemke said beaming. "I dunno exactly, I just saw this huge list of graffiti vandals who had been killed in the act, probably like you did at first Gil. So I took the list and put it into a database and just stated sorting by dates and such, until I saw this pattern emerge."

"Okay," Hughes said, joining them with Hewitt firmly by his side. "I still think the theory stinks but we will get on with what the captain has asked. Is there anything else we can do for you?"

Maria, Bob, and Gil traded glances. "I don't think so right now," Maria said. "If you find some DMV or utility service info I'm confident the captain with his new found powers bestowed on him by the mayor and sheriff would be able to get a search warrant for any bank data you may need. Let's just keep in touch. If you have any luck with last nights' witness, please call me on my cell. If that guy remembers the make of car and it was really a Jeep, we can start to narrow it down, although it could be a huge list of Jeep owners who have moved here from Washington State."

"Hey, Maria," Hewitt said as he and Hughes started to leave, "we heard that you and Gil arrived at the scene last night in the same car and that you were all dolled up. Why was that?"

"None of your goddamn business," Maria said, grinning.

"Okay, Okay." Hewitt said, holding up his arms in a pretend self-defense manner.

Maria held up her middle finger to the now empty doorway and turned to Gil and Bob. "If you guys are hungry. I'll buy lunch."

Chapter Eleven

Asian massage parlors were the same in all cities in which Morgan had resided, and he left this one, shading his eyes from the Las Vegas glare and girding himself for the blast of hot air. Now that he was sexually relieved, he would head home, start manufacturing his fake Colorado license plates, and catch the local evening news. Curiosity over last night's victim intrigued him more than most. Perhaps it was because the image of the youth darting under the chain link fence before Morgan blew him away with his powerful rifle remained ingrained in his mind. The boy had seemed to be well dressed and younger than most of his tagging victims which probably meant that he was not a gang member. He wondered what the police and press would make of that. At least it would confuse them. And the kid shouldn't have tried to deface a brand new bridge. *Hey! I need to get the police back on to thinking these are gang related killings. I need to find out more about gangs!*

Morgan climbed into his hot Jeep, removed the windshield heat reflector, *good goddamn invention*, and headed home. His hand-job this afternoon was as good as any he had received in the past from the young and eager Chinese girl. *You want me massage you there? Onry twenty dolla more.* Ben Morgan's sexual appetite was always under control and had been since a couple of years after he had left the Marines. His routine was to masturbate a couple of times a week while showering, and find an Asian massage parlor on some weekends and pay the extra twenty bucks or so for a hand job. This behavioral formula kept him from being distracted by women, or the urge to find female companionship. He still found his unfortunate encounter with a coworker, before he got himself under control, distasteful.

His honorable discharge from the Marine Corp had been a distant two years earlier then and he had already been on his third job, as a help desk technician at a telecommunications company - working swing shift – 4 PM to 1. The cubicle farm, as it was titled by its inhabitants, had provided no privacy and the din of conversation from the two dozen or so help-desk techs droned on and on unrelentingly.

Morgan was good on the phone and was very helpful to callers having a difficult time getting connected to the internet. His neighboring cube mate, Selene, was a young, unattractive, full-breasted young woman, attending college at San Diego State during the day and working these evenings. Morgan liked to lean over her low cubical wall when she was struggling with a call and stare down her cleavage revealing, low cut blouse. God, he wanted to dive into those soft mounds.

During one of their lunch breaks, Selene told Morgan about an incredible call she had received earlier in the evening. "This stupid man asked me what hours the call center was open and I told him the number was open twenty-four hours a day, seven days a week. And do you know what he said? 'Is that Eastern or Pacific time?' Can you believe it, Ben?"

Morgan had laughed and stared at her breasts, "I can believe it, Selene," he'd said. "People are stupid. You know, I'd love to take you out some night. Actually, I'd love to fondle those two big ones. You know, working in the cubicle next to you drives me nuts."

"Shit, Ben. What a terrible thing to say to me!" Selene had exclaimed.

"Terrible! I thought I was being complimentary. I'm sorry if that offended you. But you do have a beautiful body. How else should I say it?"

She leaned forward and looked around the sparsely populated lunchroom. "Well, you could have stopped after you said you'd like to see me outside of work," she said in a low voice.

"Hey, I was just being honest," he'd told her. "Do you want me to start over and not mention your boobs?"

"Damn, there you go again. Mentioning my breasts. And don't call them 'boobs.' You're embarrassing me."

"Okay, here I go from where I started," he'd said. "I just love being in the cubicle next to you. May I take you to dinner or something on the weekend?"

"Well, to be absolutely frank," she told him, "I'm not sure I should take a chance. You're a good guy, Ben, but sometimes you're just plain weird."

Weird! That rang a bell. Someone had called him that before. And it hurt just as much now as it had then. On the other hand, unless he ingratiated himself with her, he'd never get what he wanted.

"Look, Selene, I'm sorry, it's just that I'm really no good at this, never have been, so please have dinner with me."

"Okay, I guess I'd be willing to go to dinner with you," Selene said. "Maybe I can help your social skills. When, where and what time?"

Anthony's Seafood Restaurant was located on a pier and trapped a good many San Diego tourists into its noisy dining room. The fish was always fresh and the wait staff counted on high table turns to maximize the tight-fisted tourist tips. Morgan and Selene's table was set back from windows which was fine because the sun had already set, and the only thing to see were the few lights from passing tourists' boats anyway. Much to Ben's disappointment Selene was wearing a pullover sweater, which although it accentuated her large breasts, kept him from admiring her skin.

"God, I haven't been here in years," she said picking up the menu. "I think the last time was with my parents when they had my cousin in town. Are we going to have a drink?"

His eyes transfixed on the epoxy covered wood table, Morgan traced the initials and words a previous customer had carved deep into the wood.

"Look at this," he said in an outraged voice. "People are so crazy, defacing property like this. The restaurant ought to throw them into the ocean."

"Oh, Ben, if they did that they wouldn't have any customers," Selene had said, "Besides what harm is it? Everybody does it."

Before the waitress arrived with the wine, Ben explained in rather lengthy fashion, his cleanliness-is-next-to-godliness speech, and how he hated defacers, dirty and untidy people. Selene listened with amazement as Ben quoted scriptures and his feelings about such matters.

The dinner conversation went down hill from there. Selene ate very little. What she did eat, she ate as fast as she could before telling

Ben that the wine had given her a headache and she had a ton of homework. Both of them were silent during the ride back to her apartment. *She thinks I'm weird too.*

In spite of her protestations, Ben insisted on walking her to the door of her second story apartment. And when she put the key in the lock, he asked her if he could come in.

"Not this time," she began and then gave a little scream as he embraced her from behind, one hand on her breast.

"I said no!" she exclaimed, twisting away from him. "Now, Ben, please go home. I don't want to do this. I've had enough of your weird ways tonight."

Weird! Now that enraged him. Pushing her inside, he closed the door behind him, and reached out for her breast again.

"No, Ben," she said firmly, slapping his hand away. "I mean it!"

But he hadn't been able to stop himself. When backing up she stumbled over a small occasional table. He caught her before she fell.

"I promise it will be fun," he said massaging her breast and trying to kiss her.

"Shit, Ben, no!" she cried out as he pulled her close. "I'll call the cops. Get out of here now, and I'll pretend this never happened."

In an instant, Ben circled her throat with one arm and grabbed a breast. But it was hard to hang on because she was stronger than he had thought and actually succeeded in wrestling him around the room until he pushed her down on the couch and held her there, under him.

Selene looked up at him with terror and tears in her eyes. "I'll scream at the top of my lungs," she gasped as he tightened his grip. "I knew I shouldn't have let you anywhere near me outside of work because you're weird! Weird!"

That was when Morgan had let her go. He'd left her apartment without a word, determined to call his boss on Monday and quit. He'd never give a woman a chance to call him that again. Never. From now on, when he wanted sex, he'd pay for it.

Heading to his Las Vegas apartment, Morgan left the massage parlor and his distasteful memories behind. He had also left his sexual desire on a wet warm towel.

#

Maria patted the floral design on the vacant spot next to her on the couch. "Come sit down," She said. "The news comes on in a few minutes and we can see what kind of job Virginia does with the press."

Gil admired the way Maria had decorated her little house with pictures of her commencement, her proud parents, her brothers, including Louis who had been cut down in a gang shooting. She was the kind of woman who was full of surprises, aggressive in her job and in bed, but surprisingly feminine in other ways.

"Man, are we going to have our hands full with this investigation," Gil said, turning on the TV. "I'm so glad that Lemke did such a good job on those queries. I certainly enjoyed our lunch with him. He's such a good guy. Do you think research will turn up something with the DMV?"

"I suspect they won't take the Jeep theory serious until they see if last night's witness can positively identify that SUV as a Jeep," Maria said as he leaned down to kiss her cheek. "I should be getting a call on that soon enough."

As soon as she said it, Maria's cell phone rang. "If that's homicide talking about that witness, I'm going home and never see you again," Gil said before she could answer it. He laughed.

"You can't leave until I let you," She said, grinning back at him.

"Garcia here… Yes… Well, that's something…. He's sure…? Yes, she should be on in a few minutes… Did you hear anything from CSI?... Tomorrow… You going to call Lemke or should I?... Okay great, I'll call Radcliff…We'll be in the station by seven-thirty."

"That was Hughes," Maria told him. "He said our witness can't positively state it was a Jeep and he wasn't quite positive it had Nevada plates. He couldn't recall any numbers or letters either."

"What was that about CSI?"

"Oh, Jeffers told him they were having a tough time running down Medical Center management to get access on a Sunday, but they intend to keep trying, although probably won't get anywhere until tomorrow."

"I hope it doesn't rain tonight," Gil told her. "What about seven-thirty tomorrow morning?"

"We're just going to have a short get together with the other officers and make sure our battle plan is cohesive. The Captain is bringing in a graffiti crimes specialist and we're also going to meet the profiler."

"I don't know about you, Maria. Sometimes I think you're clairvoyant. Maybe we should go gambling. I'm sure we could win a ton of money."

"I have no luck gambling," she told him. "Now shush, here comes the news."

"Good afternoon," the attractive blond anchor began. "We have some breaking news on the shooting last night at the Town Center Bridge and the 215 Beltway. At approximately ten o'clock last night, a passing motorist saw a youth fall from the bridge and called 911. Police arrived on the scene shortly afterward and discovered that the boy had been shot. He was pronounced dead at the scene. We now know that the fifteen-year-old victim has been positively identified as the son of Mr. and Mrs. Forrest Smead. Forest Smead is the CEO and owner of Ace Homes, one of the largest builders in the Las Vegas Valley. Now let's go to Greg Powers live at police headquarters."

The picture of the reporter appeared, his finger pressed on his earpiece. "Thanks, Mona," he said. "I just attended a news conference about an hour ago when Las Vegas Police spokesperson, Virginia Rodriguez, issued the following statement: The Las Vegas Police Department is working hard on identifying last night's shooter," he quoted as the familiar image of Virginia came on the screen. "We have a reliable witness that spotted a black SUV parked in the area at the time of the shooting. We now believe that the four previous shootings may have been committed by the same individual and we are asking the public's help to come forward with any information from the previous locations of similar crimes."

"Ginny's a good spokesperson for us and damned attractive too," Gil said, "but that blond over in her department, now there's… Ow, that hurt!" he concluded as Maria jabbed him in the ribs with a very sharp elbow.

"I told you before, Radcliff," she muttered, "no talking about blonds. Now shut up and listen."

"Thanks for that live report, Greg," the anchorwoman was saying. "We also just received a statement from a Smead family spokesperson, that they are offering a hundred thousand dollar reward for information leading to the arrest and conviction of their son's killer. We'll keep you posted on events in this tragic case. Now on to other news…"

"Shit, that's all we need," Maria said, picking up the remote. "The Captain was hoping for a little help from the public, now we'll be getting a million leads an hour to chase around. Damn!"

"It's alright, Maria," Gil told her. "We'll just let other detectives chase them down, and we can get on with the investigation."

"No, this is going to take more than we can handle, all across the department," she told him. "Let's see if Jay Leno is funny tonight. Meanwhile I'd like a deep passionate kiss."

Just as Gil was delivering in spades, he heard Leno say, "Did you hear about this? In Las Vegas the police think they have a person going around shooting Graffiti vandals. Remember when Las Vegas Mayor Oscar Goodman said they should cut off the thumbs of Graffiti vandals? Well, in his latest statement about these shootings, he says they should cut off the trigger finger of the shooter before they hang him. So I guess what will stay in Vegas is a bunch of thumbs and fingers."

Maria snapped off the TV and grinned at Gil, "You want that dessert now?" She asked him and didn't wait for an answer.

#

Slouched in an easy chair in front of the TV, Morgan snapped off the same newscast. *Damn.* At least they don't know it was his Jeep. That was something to be thankful for, but he'd have to be more careful next time. He needed to make sure he made no mistakes the next time he plugged one of those sonsobitches. After he finished making his Colorado license plate, he'd set himself to reading every one of those books on gangs that he had bought from Borders several days ago because he had to know all about gangs and how they worked for his own protection.

Chapter Twelve

Dr. Jayne Samuels, a psychic detective, worked for an independent consulting firm that specialized in profiling the criminal mind. Having moved to Vegas several years earlier for the simple reason that the LVPD could provide her with so much work, she had no plans on returning to the east soon. She liked this town, even without the criminal profiling work it offered.

Opening her laptop computer, Jayne readied herself for the meeting that had been called to discuss the criminal who was shooting graffiti vandals. Tucking her long blond hair behind her ears and adjusting her black rimmed glasses, she waited for her computer to boot up. LVPD was, she knew, getting used to her incredibly sharp mind and analytical skills to piece together clues to violent crimes. What they didn't know yet was the extent of her personal motivation. Several years earlier her father had been murdered by an unknown killer, and it had been because of her diligent work that the killer had finally been caught and was presently on death row.

In order to facilitate identifying suspects, the profiler's job was to create a composite that might include gender, age, race, occupation, socioeconomic status, marital status, area of residence, educational and family background, social habits, and probable arrest history. She was particularly good at providing the motivation that drove killers because she had a good many years of practice looking into some of the darkest minds imaginable.

"Do you want a cup of coffee, Jayne?" Homicide Captain Joe Vasquez asked. Captain Vasquez's office, which was like him, large and dark, was set-up for a big meeting. His messy desk was a sure sign that he was on serious overload having been given this special assignment out of the blue.

"No thanks, Joe, I'm all coffeed out. I've been up since five. I understand you've been on special assignment working the prosecution of those young men that were out killing homeless men. How did that go?"

"I think we've got it ticked and tied," he told her wearily. "The DA has done a masterful job. We should get a conviction, but I'm kind of glad to be doing regular police work and not just rubbing elbows with attorneys and judges."

"While we're waiting for everybody else, what can you tell me about this graffiti business?" she asked him.

"Actually, not much," he told her, rising to draw the dark shades to keep the heat of the early morning sun out. "The homicide detectives Garcia and Radcliff are taking the lead on this and all other support departments are going to help as much as they can. My other homicide detectives, Hewitt and Hughes, are assigned to help and they'll be here. Did you read what the newspaper had to say about this?"

"Yes, but there's not much there," Jayne said. "Besides, I've also learned that more often than not, newspapers either get it wrong or it's woefully incomplete."

"That's for sure," Vasquez agreed, flipping his badge around and smoothing non-existent wrinkles from his crisp uniform shirt. He pressed his fingers against his salt and pepper moustache. "They misquote us all the time."

After a few minutes the entire team, except Jeffers from CSI, including Detective Sam Brown, a graffiti crimes specialist, had taken their places. Introductions done, sipping on coffees and eating doughnuts, Vasquez, called the meeting to order. Maria went over the single suspect theory at high level; Lemke filled Jayne in with the other cities' time lines.

"Thanks to the research department, we now have all the police reports and forensics from all those killings," he added. "There was a very interesting crime scene report from the rest stop in Oregon."

It was clear that Lemke was enjoying being the center of attention again.

"Seems the killer, based on the report, used a very quick and military like maneuver on the two victims. The other thing worth noting is that the knife used in the eight knifings in Atlanta, match the ten inch knife type used in Oregon."

Jayne took the folder he handed her and she typed furiously into her laptop.

Hewitt reported on questioning the witness and getting a so-so ID on the Jeep and the witness again, declaring how bright and shiny the vehicle was, which was, as the witness had noted, been very strange for an SUV parked near a construction site.

"What about the license plate?" Gil asked. "He told us that he thought it was a Nevada plate."

Hewitt rolled his eyes at being questioned on what he thought was his superior witness questioning skills. "He didn't confirm it to my satisfaction," he said. "He still thinks it *may have* been a Nevada plate. But he would be a terrible witness if cross examined by a shrewd defense attorney."

Gil couldn't put his finger on the reasons, but he hadn't liked Hewitt when he first met him, now he was sure he didn't like him.

Maria, ready to lead, said, "We're going to use the war room next to Captain Vasquez's office. It will better there than in the large Homicide Conference Room. We can leave our notes on the white board as we will be the only ones using the room. Gil and I will keep track of all the evidence and make sure any leads we receive are properly followed up on. Can we agree that we will meet there daily at ten in the morning? That way..."

"Sorry I'm late," Jeffers said, hurrying into the room, "but I just got word, we did in fact find GSR near the parapet on the medical center building roof. We were lucky. Normally GSR fades away in six to eight hours. Good job at spotting that location, Gil."

"Did you find anything else up there?" Maria asked.

"Yes, as a matter of fact we did, but not on the roof," Jeffers said, taking the last empty seat. "We found a metal cover on the rear door that disabled the alarm. So the suspect knows something about security systems as well. He probably placed it there when the building was open so he could come back later. Somebody should question the staff and see if they remember a stranger walking around there. Perhaps they saw someone wearing gloves. We checked out the roof, but I'm not counting on finding any suspicious fingerprints or footprints because this suspect knows what he's doing. We have the metal in the lab, but I'm not counting on finding anything, it didn't have any fingerprints. I wish the building had video surveillance, but it doesn't. I'll keep you all posted."

"I'll get on with questioning the building occupants," Hewitt volunteered, surprising Gil. Gil was still sure he didn't quite trust Hewitt and his nearly silent partner, Hughes.

Jayne was still typing, but managed to make eye contact with the police officers as she entered words at a fast clip into what Gil hoped was a profile that would help them nail the type of sick mind out there.

"I think most of you know Sam from the Gang Bureau," Vasquez said, opening his large hand in Detective Brown's direction. "I'd like you all to hear Sam's experience in dealing with graffiti and the potential and actual vigilantes. Sam, go ahead."

Sam cleared his throat, looked over the top of his glasses at the assembled group. "I'm not sure my expertise as a graffiti crimes expert warrants my involvement here," he said. "What I've heard makes me think it's the other side of the equation that's important. Having said that, from what I've heard today and read previously our suspect hates graffiti as much as most citizens. I will tell you this, though. Based on the crime reports and my caseload during the past few months, crimes involving graffiti have gone down, particularly in high profile places like Summerlin and on traffic bridges and sound walls. It's something people feel strongly about. Remember that graffiti constitutes the most expensive property crime in Nevada, to the tune of thirty-million dollars a year!"

This was, Gil realized, a PR concern of the police along with everything else.

"I can tell you from what people say that a lot of them don't think we do enough about graffiti," Sam continued. "And as a result, I've known a few citizens that take matters into their own hands. Some of them have been caught too, as a good many of you know. And arrested. Fined. But before I go on to tell you about some of my personal experiences, and before this concept of a single vigilante being responsible for these murders takes on legs, let me tell you a little about gangs and graffiti."

He then went on to explain that in the greater Las Vegas area alone more than five-hundred tag crews have been documented. At any given time there are more than a hundred active tag crews placing graffiti throughout the Las Vegas valley. These tag crews operate in an organized manner with a leadership structure and requirements for membership. They often mandate that prospective members place graffiti as an assignment, or "mission," as ordered by a senior member or leader of the crew. The prospective member must perform to the crews' satisfaction in order to gain acceptance and full membership into the crew. Most graffiti vandals are required to remain active in placing graffiti, or "put in work" for the crew in order to remain in good standing and maintain membership. Brown cleared his throat again. If a Graffiti vandal wants to leave the crew for any reason, or discontinues their Graffiti activities, they often face harassment and physical assault. There have been many documented incidents involving graffiti vandals who have been victimized by other vandals for leaving the crew or quitting graffiti altogether. Tag crews have modeled themselves after traditional violent criminal street gangs and have adopted many of their customs and practices.

"Based on previous investigations," Sam concluded his dissertation, "it's clear that most graffiti vandals fit a specific profile just like Dr. Samuels here is trying to establish with the shooter. So, in my opinion, this shooter *could* be a graffiti vandal that was either beaten up or ostracized by a crew and he's trying to get even."

"Are you telling us that you think it's an ex-tagger doing these shootings?" Gil demanded.

"Since we don't know anything yet, my theory is as good as anyone else's at this point," Sam said defensively.

It did not surprise Gil when Hewitt said, "I think you're right on."

"If we're right about this being a single suspect, moving from city to city," Maria said, "someone who's damn clever about covering his tracks, is it, do you think, possible that an ex-tagger is responsible?"

"Yes," Sam fired back. "Many graffiti vandals come from prominent families, or are seemingly productive members of the community. Since 2002, I've investigated the son of a respected local high school principal, a local veteran police officer's twelve year old boy, and a number of other kids who came from prominent families. That Smead boy isn't the first son of a construction company's CEOs to get caught up in tagging. I arrested the son of another manager of a multimillion-dollar construction corporation. Oh! And girls are involved in this sort of thing too, including, if you can believe it, the daughters of an editor of *the* local newspaper and the executive assistant of a highly regarded local judge. They were out joy riding on roller skates and carrying spray cans."

The others laughed, but Gil was turning over all these new theories in his mind. He couldn't come to grips that these shootings were the result of ex-taggers or formerly upright citizens playing vigilante. No. Gil was certain that this crazy was just that, a crazy clean-up-the-planet-type, who was very clever, a good shot, and did, in fact, move about the country.

As taking the laughter as a request to continue, Sam added, "I also investigated and arrested a department manager at a major Las Vegas hotel-casino, a delivery driver for UPS, and a local government employee who worked in the city's parks and recreation department. So it could be anyone. That's my point, even a well-educated, upstanding citizen."

Now you're back on track Sam, Gil thought.

"Wow, Sam." Captain Vasquez exclaimed. "What do you think, Dr. Samuels?"

"I haven't concluded anything yet," Jayne replied. "But I'll certainly note Detective Brown's observations as a possibility. Right now I'd like to hear him on the subject of vigilantes."

Vigilantes, yes, thought Gil, but not some upstanding citizen. But, maybe? He had to admit that this theory may have some merit. He'd like to discuss all this in private with Maria and Bob Lemke.

"Well," Sam said, "I had a case of a discharged Navy Chief that had called us several times about kids in his neighborhood tagging his house. We didn't have the resources to stake out the area, so this fellow spent a night outside, hiding in the bushes, and popped a kid with a high-powered air pellet rifle that was writing on his wall. Long story short, the Chief was arrested for assault after the kid's parents filed a complaint. Although, as it turned out a detective somehow screwed up the prosecution's case by fouling up the Miranda's and no charges could be filed."

After Vasquez suggested that they look up the ex-Navy Chief and see if he was still in the area Maria spoke up.

"I have been coordinating these shootings with your UC Rodolfo," Maria told Brown. "Do you use any other UC's on tagging crimes?"

"I have on occasion," he told her. "But frankly, I've found them to be pretty much ineffective when it comes to this sort of thing. Why do you ask?"

"I was just thinking." she told him. "I'll have to organize my thoughts a bit more before I add anything to this discussion."

"Okay, folks," Vasquez said in the pause that followed, taking charge again. "Let's get back to why we're here. So this is the deal. We'll check on the Chief, and others that have tried to take out their anger on taggers in the past, and continue to work the Jeep and DMV angles. As for you Sam, I don't think you need to attend the daily meetings, but you've been a big help today and we'll certainly call on you again if we need to. Apparently Dr. Samuels needs some time to work up a profile."

"I'm beginning to see a pattern emerge that should be useful," Jayne told him. "I'm going to take these forensic reports, study what you all said, and examine whatever other information is available." Adjusting her glasses, she closed her laptop. "Of course I'll attend the daily meetings as well."

"Okay," Vasquez said. "Let's get on with it. The last thing we want is the sheriff breathing down our necks more than he already is. Maria may I have a word with you? This won't take long."

"What's up?" Maria said as the others filed out of the room.

"I just want you to know that I'll help you in any way I can." Vasquez leaned back in his chair. "But you should know that Hughes and Hewitt came to me to voice their concerns that you and Radcliff will be running this investigation..."

"Hey," Maria interrupted. "We didn't volunteer for this. As far as..."

"Hold on Maria, I know you didn't," Vasquez told her. "I was going to say that in spite of their concerns and petty grievances, I told them they would support the entire force in this investigation and give you and Radcliff a hundred and ten percent support. I reminded them what a terrific detective you are and that Radcliff has homicide experience from Oklahoma, and that if they had a problem with this, I'd kick their asses. I know that Sergeant Hardey would normally be taking his normal supervisory lead on you guys, but his recovery is taking longer than we thought. Now with Rodgers out too, we are really shorthanded, and knowing your leadership skills as I do, I just know you'll excel."

Gil, sat alone in the break room, waiting for Maria. Gil was certainly concerned about what was going on behind the captain's closed door, and was feeling very uncomfortable and anxious. Why was he excluded? He thought, they must be talking about me, but Gil recalled Captain Rodgers saying,' Garcia *and* Radcliff are now on special assignment to Captain Vasquez and will run the day to day operations?' If we're to be co-leaders I should be in there with her, Gil thought.

"Are you sure Captain?" Maria said. "Because if you think someone else should be running this one, I'd be glad to get on the sheriff's calendar and tell him that."

"Actually this was my idea, "he told her. "And I'll tell you why. One, as I said, you're a terrific cop, next in line for sergeant, and two, I know Radcliff wants to show his stuff. I'm a little concerned that he has scheduled a vacation in a few weeks. I may have to ask him to delay that, but this will be a good time for him to show his stuff. Hughes and Hewitt are very good detectives, but they have a piss poor attitude sometimes. You can handle that."

"I'm flattered, Victor," Maria said. "I'll certainly do my best. But I know Gil has scheduled his daughters from Oklahoma to visit. It would be a shame to screw that up, but I understand how critical this is."

"Yes, it is, and I hope I don't have to interfere with his personal life. I'll let you make the final call. I know you'll do your best, Maria. You always do," Vasquez said, rising to his feet as sign of dismissal.

"By the way, how did you know that Radcliff wants to show his stuff as you put it?" Maria asked him. "I would have thought that he would have come out and told me he wanted to advance as quickly as possible. After all, we are close….Er, I mean we work together. I had no idea that he'd formally requested rapid advancement."

"He hasn't requested anything formally," Vasquez assured her. "Don't worry. It was always an option for him when he was brought into homicide. We just didn't have any openings at the time. You sound disappointed. You did know he would eventually have the opportunity to be promoted didn't you?"

"Of course," Maria said. "But it's not that simple. Just taking the test doesn't guarantee that he'll make sergeant. Not in Homicide, at least. But he's a good officer. First rate. We work well together."

"That's what I've heard, Maria," Vasquez said, giving Maria a crooked smile and a wink.

Damn, Maria thought as she joined Gil in the break room. "It's worse than Peyton Place around here," Maria said aloud.

#

Morgan swore under his breath as he re-read the e-mail from his boss at WebMaps telling him that she wanted him to stay in Vegas for another four weeks and survey the northwest side because of all the new construction. This meant he'd have to change his MO again, and get out his knife.

He still had a vivid memory of how he had used it the first time. He had been settled into his little apartment for about two weeks and was getting the lay of the land in an area with the new shops, roads, and bridges. Just knowing the knife was there had given him a sense of security. Skilled in its use, thanks to his Marine training, Morgan used the knife as efficiently as a garrote. But if these crimes were to turn national, he had to be certain that any patterns that emerged would lead the police on a wild goose chase after gang members. Morgan practiced quick drawing and stabbing at the air and imaginary figures. Shadow boxing as it were. Rehearsing his deadly moves.

In Atlanta, after parking elsewhere, he had roamed the streets of areas under construction since they were often lures when it came to graffiti. No one around. Lots of bare walls. That sort of thing.

That particular cold night, he had melted into the shadows of a fieldstone wall until after an hour or so when his back began to stiffen. He had been about to stand and stretch when he had seen a young man come into sight and look around nervously. As soon as Morgan saw him pull a can of spray paint from his pocket he pulled down his black ski mask and circled in order to come up on his victim from behind.

He still remembered how he had savored the feeling of invisibility as the victim continued to spray in patterns on the wall, unaware of the impending doom. Stealthily, knife drawn, Morgan closed the distance between him and the vandal in less than two seconds. Silent. Deadly. To reduce the likelihood of a struggle and avoid a foot chase, Morgan circled the man's neck with his left arm and with a quick upward motion skewered the tagger in the middle of the back behind his heart.

"Don't you know it's illegal to deface property you worthless piece of shit?" he said as the tagger sank to the ground.

Blood had poured over Morgan's' gloved hand as he removed the ten inch blade from the torso of his victim. Knifing was sure a lot more messy than using a garrote. Now he had evidence to destroy. But the excitement, the exhilaration, the knowledge that he had done a good thing had made it worthwhile.

An hour later all he could think about was where he might find his next victim.

Chapter Thirteen

Dean Schmidt removed his glasses, closed his eyes, rubbed the bridge of his nose, and thought about what he had just read in the *Las Vegas Review Journal* about the shooting of graffiti vandals. Poor Smead. It must be rough to lose a fifteen-year-old son that way. Mayor Goodman had chastised taggers, saying they ought to have their thumbs cut-off, but *not* shoot them. His late wife, Gladys, who would have been seventy-five next month, had hated taggers too. It had always surprised him to hear her say 'they ought to cut off the balls of those vandals' when they drove past some desecrated wall or bridge. It was the only violent thing she ever said about anyone. Well, she was gone now, and soon he would be as well.

Schmidt's Oncologist had pronounced, at his last appointment, that he might have about six months to live. At seventy-seven, Schmidt thought he'd lived long enough and couldn't wait to join his dear Gladys in the hereafter. Would she, he wondered now, be proud of the life he led during the three years he had gone on without her? Probably not. Playing video poker all day, every day, at the local casino was not a particularly grand way to approach life's end. What would she say to him if she knew that he was going to feed his addiction by spending the better part their daughter Margaret's inheritance? His life insurance policy wouldn't help Margaret much, particularly with his two grandkids just starting college. If only she and the kids would visit from Maryland more often.

The newspaper's description of the fallen taggers around Las Vegas gave him pause. Would Gladys have wanted him to have been the shooter? Perhaps he could have redeemed himself with her, if he had been the vigilante. How hard could it be to prowl the streets and pluck off these no good taggers?

Dean's eyes snapped open, lifting his aged lids wider than when he would hit a royal flush. He still had his hunting rifle and he was in fairly good shape, even now, that he was suffering from cancer. He had been a good hunter and an excellent shot during his hunting days a few decades ago. Why not make Gladys proud of me now? He still had some time left to make a difference.

Gil waited impatiently for Dr. Samuels so that they could begin the next Tag Team meeting. Maria was efficient. She covered all the bases. But it seemed to him that they were moving at a snail's pace and not getting anywhere. Perhaps the profiler would give them the heads up they needed. At the first of the daily meetings, Sam Brown revealed that the Navy Chief had relocated to Florida after his case had been dismissed and was, in fact, still living there at the time of the shootings. Nobody had any other information, but everybody was hopeful that much of the ongoing analysis would soon expose some data that would be useful. Jayne, in her role of the profiler, had announced that she would provide some preliminary analysis.

"Please forgive me if you've heard some of this before," Dr. Jayne Samuels began, "but it helps me organize my thoughts and segue into this suspect's potential profile if I take a step by step approach. First you should know that I characterize the crime scenes and by extension the criminals themselves as either organized or disorganized. Organized offenders' crimes are premeditated while disorganized offenders act with little or no planning. Our suspect in this case seems to be both organized and disorganized. For the most part, his crimes appear to be well planned and executed. Although presumably the taggers he attacks are strangers to him, when he leaves the scene he's careful to retrieve any spent shells or cartridges, bloody knives, etc. In other words, he goes about the planning of the crime, the crime itself, and its aftermath in an organized way."

"However, this guy, if it's the same guy, has shown disorganized behavior in several of his murders. A very unusual behavior, but not unique. Note that, for now, I based my analysis on the supposition that we're dealing with a single killer. I realize not everyone's on board with this theory."

Was it possible Gil thought, that this woman was discounting his theory that the murderer was one man and only one man? He kept his mouth shut, but only with effort. Why, he wondered, didn't Maria speak up. She was in charge of this operation and she had signed on to his theory.

"So," Jayne continued pressing a button on her laptop to scroll down, "In my opinion, the pattern here is a deliberate avoidance of a pattern in order to outsmart the cops. Serial killers read up on police procedures, collect crime magazines, find out how we operate and investigate crimes. They learn the rules in order to break them, by varying the MO and other variables."

"Okay, so we have a smart killer," Maria said. "But do you have anything else that might help us ID him? There are a lot of smart people in Las Vegas."

Maria's question made Gil feel a bit better, but Maria, in his opinion, didn't come on strong enough to Dr. Samuels about the single killer theory.

"I'm getting to that," Dr. Samuels said, unruffled. "Give me a sec." Pulling a folder out of her briefcase, she proceeded to present an analysis so complete and comprehensive that everyone in the room was mesmerized.

According to her analysis, they were probably dealing with a white male, thirty-five to fifty-five years old, probably military or police trained with emphasis on sharp shooting and hand-to-hand combat. He could have been a Navy Seal, an Army Ranger, or a Marine. He would have done well and most likely have received an honorable discharge, however he may have had problems that would have been documented, like fitting in, non-team player, etc. His use of knife, garrote, small arms, and sniper rifle would prove the point of well-trained military. He was probably a loner and didn't have any close buddies. I'd look for him to show several disorder traits, such as obsessive behavior towards cleanliness and is probably a neatness freak. Most likely he hasn't been married and has a hard time nurturing and maintaining female companionship. If he had been married, and I don't think he still is, his divorce would have been messy. Any children would be under control of his ex-wife and he probably doesn't have visitation rights, or has abdicated them to her. He would be a terrible father.

"He's not actively or latently gay," she concluded, "but he may possess a penchant toward rape, stalking and using prostitutes as his sexual relief. The killing of taggers is his ultimate sexual relief."

Wow, thought Gil, that was a comprehensive profile all right. As Dr. Samuels had been speaking he had conjured up several images of the killer knifing, strangling, and shooting his victims. He also saw in his mind's eye a man struggling to be sociable, no friends and sitting alone in a small room or apartment.

"So what are we looking for?" Jayne continued, flipping over a page. "He's law abiding and feels everybody else should be too. He's become judge and jury. He feels so self righteous that he thinks he's justified to eliminate evil doers, in this case, defacers of property. He doesn't care whether they are black, Hispanic or white. He may even think that he's answering a divine call to save the planet from people who don't take care of the environment. But he's not religious in the sense that he belongs to a church. He doesn't belong to anything."

She went on with her dissertation providing more details for the Tag Team to consider. This was probably a man that up until now had a hard time holding a steady job. He now has either a job that allows him freedom to move about the country, or he possesses a skill that is transferable from region to region, like a construction worker. The latter is harder to imagine as it would require him to get along with co-workers, and that would be hard for him. But not too hard for a few months while he hunts down and kills taggers and then moves on. More than likely, he works for a company that allows him to be independent in the field. Definitely not a sales position. More likely some sort of technical consulting. For example, he could do routine maintenance on machinery or equipment. Medical devices, construction equipment, elevators, security systems, what have you. A skill or trade he would have had to have been trained for."

"Any questions so far, before I go on?" Jayne said, looking around the room.

"I have one," Hewitt said. "Is it possible that the reason this guy strikes so many different places is because he's independently wealthy?"

"I don't think so," Jayne said. "But that doesn't mean it isn't possible. Although most of this is a science, it is still an art and subject to errors and false assumptions. But nothing I've come across yet indicates wealth. Anyway, I don't have much more at this point, but I'd like to focus on his vehicle for a moment. You think it's a late model black Jeep. One witness said it was unusually clean, given the fact that it was parked near a construction site. He hates graffiti. He is a neatness freak. An obsessive compulsive type . So, recapping my suppositions, I believe that we have a single Caucasian male, thirty-five to fifty-five with a background of and military service, and a job that allows him to move about the country. He's most likely a night person, so look for someone that can work irregular hours and has a tremendous amount of patience."

Gil thought that he had conjured up images of a suspect before Dr. Samuels had finished her profile. Now his mind was racing with possibilities of what behaviors the suspect demonstrated. What did he look like? Where might he live? What areas of town did he frequent? On and on his mind filtered, discarded, added, and imagined all the possibilities. Talk about plain old grind it out police work that will be required. He couldn't wait to talk to Maria in private about all this. Gil looked around the room and noted that Hewitt and Hughes had returned to their slouching positions, however Hewitt had asked an intelligent question, or was he just trying to justify his earlier flippant remark about the suspect being independently wealthy? Sam

Brown looked introspective and, Gil was sure, had discounted all Dr. Samuels had said.

"Dr. Samuels," Gil said. "You mentioned that this man probably releases his sexual energy making use of prostitutes and perhaps committing rape. Do you think that he would be committing rape and killing taggers within the same time frame?"

"Good question, detective," Jayne said. "He could, but I doubt it. As I said before, the killing of taggers is his ultimate sexual relief and to that end he's probably sexually relieved for some time after he commits his murders. That's not to say that after a given amount of time his sexual urges take over his need to kill taggers urges. A cunning killer would have figured this out about himself and as I postulated previously, he could be using prostitutes as his sexual relief. Does that answer your question?"

"Any other questions," Dr. Samuels said again, looking around the room. It did not surprise Gil when Sam rose. He was, Gil noted, still wearing a skeptical expression.

"Well, I think that's all very interesting," he said. "I don't doubt that Dr. Samuels probably has this guy nailed pretty well including the logical conclusion she based on serial killer history that this guy is Caucasian and thirty-five to fifty-five. But we need to keep in mind a couple of other possibilities. For instance, yesterday I spent about thirty minutes on the phone with a smoke-shop owner who advised me that he was sick of having to have his walls cleaned because the city has threatened to fine him if he doesn't keep his business graffiti free."

Sam went on to tell about someone who had actually gone out and bought a rifle and threatened to kill taggers if he caught them defacing his wall.

"I gave him the old talk about his having everything to lose,"

Sam said, "and hopefully he's calmed down. But there's no guarantee. The guy was definitely middle-eastern with a heavy accent. I got the impression he'd served in the military, in his home country, and would have no qualms about doing what he said and maybe has 'back home.'"

"Good detective," Maria said. "That gives us a name to run down. But he doesn't sound like the kind of guy that would be wandering around the country killing vandals."

"I'm sure not saying that," Brown said defensively. "Here, Radcliff. This is his name and address." He handed Gil a small slip of paper. "I'm just stating that there may be more than one killer out there. I'd just be careful about getting locked into the single suspect theory and spinning your wheels on Dr. Samuels' profile. Graffiti crimes, as I've said before, bring out the worst in people, and I just happened to have another example occur yesterday."

"Shit!" Gil said, looking at the note. "This guy's name is Qasim Hormoz. Perhaps we need to bring in Homeland Security!"

The minute he said it however, Gil realized that he had been set up. He was not surprised when Captain Vasquez was not among those amused, nor when he reminded them all, with special emphasis when he looked at Gil, that there was nothing funny about this. It was interesting, Gil thought, to see Brown cover his ass.

"Just so you know," Brown said. "I get these kinds of calls from Smiths and Jones just as often too. Don't think this is some fringe group. I'm just trying to be helpful."

"Well, yes, I think we realize that, Sam," Maria said. Apparently realizing that it was time for her to show some leadership. "I think your input has been invaluable. I'm just not sure what we do with…"

"I did talk to Captain Saldeña about using Rodolfo, our UC, in a more aggressive way," Brown interrupted her. "Rodolfo knows how to tap into some of the gangs' e-mail and internet sites. I'll have him coordinate what he learns with you, as usual. I still think this could be the work of an ex-tagger crew and not a single vigilante. It would certainly explain some of the shootings at known graffiti hot spots."

"Thank you, Detective Brown." Jayne said, scribbling some notes. "I'll add this data, but I feel fairly confident that we're on the right track with a single suspect that has the characteristics I've described. If that becomes a dead-end, I'll rethink it. Any other questions or comments?"

Good for Dr. Samuels, thought Gil. She certainly didn't back off the single sniper theory like he thought she might.

"You might want to surf through these MySpace and other web sites," Brown persisted, handing her a folder. "It includes many of the Tagging Krews I keep an eye on. You'll note that crews is spelled k.r.e.w.s. and you'll see graffiti with a lot of K's. I think you may be surprised at my detailed information about the individual taggers. Not names, mind you, but real characteristics of taggers. Our killer or killers could be in there."

"Let's pick up the pace, folks," Maria said. "Do you have a list of Jeep owners that moved here from Washington, Hewitt?"

"We have just three," Hewitt told her. Good Maria, Gil thought. Keep the pressure on him. Gil couldn't imagine that data to be correct and hopefully Maria will take on Sam Brown too. "And we ran two of them down and they have iron-clad stories and we haven't located the third owner yet. According to records, the owner, a Jennifer Thomas, has moved to Pahrump. We'll contact her this afternoon."

"Just three?" Gil exclaimed." that's hard to believe with all the people moving here."

"Let's expand the data to include California and Georgia," Maria said. "Any luck with the utilities?"

Hewitt looked at his notes. "Nevada Power gave us a huge list of accounts with previous service in Washington that were opened sixty to a hundred and eight days ago," he replied. "But we can't do anything with it until we get a cross hit from the DMV or other source."

"I agree," Lemke chimed in. "The data would be too voluminous for even me to churn through. But what about this? How about the oft chance that he already lived here and didn't have to register his vehicle from another state? Perhaps he lived in Vegas before going to San Diego. Do you have a list of all Jeeps registered here?"

"Yes, we do," Hewitt said, "But I don't have it with me. It's a lot bigger list than just the three from Washington. I'll have analysis e-mail it to you. But you won't have any utility records to correlate it to. I'll also run down some of the information Sam Brown gave us."

"Well, I'd like to play with data anyway," Lemke said. "I'm really enjoying this part of it. Besides, once I get the database set-up it will be easy for me to run queries. I can run the list against known felons at least."

Good for Lemke, Gil thought. *His data research is the reason we're all here, listening to the brilliant Dr. Samuels and focusing on solving these single suspect murders.*

"I'd love to run the prostitute angle Dr. Samuels came up with too," Maria told them, "but I'm not sure how to start without a potential name or description."

"Well, you may have more than you think," Jayne told her, looking at her file. "We know his shoe size and probable height and weight. He's likely to be a Caucasian male, five foot nine to five foot eleven, probably thirty-five to fifty-five years old with some sort of cleanliness and neatness fetish. He may even be vocal about taggers. That might give enough to start with, don't you think?"

"Hewitt, ask vice to circulate amongst the massage parlors and known brothels," Maria said. "Looking for a white guy that has these sorts of fetishes."

"Shit, Garcia," Hewitt replied, scribbling on his note pad. "That could be every 'John' or tourist that visits Vegas."

"Not every one of whom drives a black Jeep with Nevada plates," Maria reminded him. "That felony list that shows up on the utilities list, Lemke. That could be checked against anything vice finds. Right?"

"We need an early break," Gil chimed in. "That could create a hit or two and we'll see how long the list of Jeeps that are already registered here is. Bob could bang it against that list too. We should also contact Atlanta, San Diego and Seattle PD's and run the black Jeep and profile by them."

Gil was pleased that the only response was Lemke's, 'I'll take care of it.' He knew that Maria would have thought of doing this a long time ago. And he saw, by the way she looked at him that she knew it. But she recovered herself without missing a step.

'Penchant toward rape.' 'Judge and jury.' 'Possible revenge toward previous tagging Krew.' She wrote on the white board. She underlined tagging Krew and added several question marks. Dr. Samuels nodded in agreement with what Maria wrote and declared she would continue to fine-tune the profile.

Gil knew what had to be done, and he had spoken up. Whether Maria liked it or not, that was the way it was going to be.

Chapter Fourteen

Maria pulled the big Crown Victoria into the parking lot of the fifth Asian Massage Parlor she and Gil had visited today. Parlors which she noted, all started looking the same, most of them being small store fronts in the middle of a mall, all within a mile of the Strip so that cab drivers didn't have to haul their fares too far. Cab drivers that dropped off fares at these locations practiced the long tradition of receiving kickbacks for deposing tourists on their front doors.

These parlor calls followed several daily meetings that revealed no new news or leads. Maria decided that it was time to do some routine legwork. The other detectives, Hewitt and Hughes, had been assigned temporarily to another shooting at an apartment complex on the southwest side. As a consequence, they would not be available to Maria's task force for a couple of days. Furthermore, vice was being slow to respond for her request to check prostitutes and illegal brothels here in Clark County. A request had gone out from the sheriff's office to the other Nevada's sheriffs to ask that the suspect's description and behaviors, as provided by Dr. Samuels, be circulated in the legal brothels.

This fifth parlor of the day blatantly called itself Chinatown Massage with a not so discreet phone number in larger print above the seedy sign, which read simply, 555-6969. It always amazed them, she and Gil had agreed, at how frightened the employees and massage attendants became when police badges were flashed before their eyes.

"You'd think these were whore houses the way they react," Gil had muttered after the first two visits.

"I guess if you give these girls enough money you could probably get laid in any of these," Maria told him offhandedly. "It's standard operating procedure to get jerked off at the end of a massage though. The term around the industry is a 'happy ending.' Most of these girls are almost slaves to the owners. In fact, my friend Terry over in Vice has been assigned to a new group called Human Trafficking. Hard to bust these places as there is always a scumbag attorney stepping in to defend the owners, and the girls are afraid to testify. It's a tough situation. I'd like to work on this problem someday."

"You know," Gil said, unbuckling his seatbelt, "I think Doctor Samuels has a great theory, but I'm beginning to think that Sam Brown has some very good ideas as well. You know, an ex-tagger gone wild so to speak."

"Maybe so Gil, but let's run this Samuels' theory into the ground first," she said. Gil knew she was right. Tenacity was not the attribute that he most admired in women usually. But nothing about Maria was "usual."

Gil and Maria flashed their credentials to the wide-eyed Asian girl sitting behind the reception desk. Drab blackout curtains pulled across the old storefront windows gave the shabby lobby a sleazy feel.

"I wonder if we could ask you a few questions about a man that may be a client of yours?" Gil began.

The little woman rose to her full height which must have been all of four foot eleven. "What kinda questions?" she demanded. "Don't have names of men that come here."

When Maria explained in as much detail as she could the kind of man they were looking for, and what he was driving, the girl looked at her defiantly.

"Not usually look out for what kind car they drive," she said. "Only check to see if get in taxi to pay driver. But we see man get in black Jeep couple days ago."

"Can you describe him?" Maria said, notepad at the ready.

"Maybe a license number or a state?" Gil added.

The girl held up a finger and said, "Be right back. Me ask girl who do massage. She look out door with me."

Gil and Maria traded glances as the girl disappeared behind the shabby curtain draped across an opening to the rear. The sing-songy conversation with intermittent laughter and tittering that followed lasted long enough to give Maria and Gil some hope that they were going to get some useful information on what Gil had earlier described as a profiler's weak shot in the dark!

The receptionist emerged through the curtains followed by an equally tiny young girl whose shorts could not have been any shorter. "This Mei Lei who massage man with black Jeep" the receptionist declared. "I tell her you want know what black Jeep man look like."

"Strong muscles, this tall," Mei Lei said, indicating a height of about five foot ten. "Been here before."

After more questions, Gil and Maria came away with a description of a man carrying no real distinguishing features. Not bad looking.

Military haircut. Pretty muscular. No tattoos. And after lots of tittering and Chinese speak, 'A small cock who 'cum out fast.'

Because the girls thought that the Jeep might have had a California plate, Maria and Gil were feeling good about the prospects about this man fitting the profile and Maria arranged for a police artist to call on the girls. Before they left for the next massage parlor on their list, they determined there was no video camera that may have been pointing at the parking lot.

"Maybe the profiler has this guy right," Maria said as Gil took a turn at driving the Crown Vic to the next address.

"Could have just been a coincidence too, because the California plate isn't the right answer," Gil replied in an almost I-told-you-so manner.

Sometimes he thought that Maria didn't completely buy in to his single sniper theory and Bob Lemke's linkage to the other cities. But their time working together on this case and that they were now lovers, Gil hoped he wasn't being blind to something in Maria's personality.

"Dr. Jayne is more often right than wrong," Maria said in defense of the profiler. "The military haircut fits along with the medium build for his foot prints."

That's my smart detective, thought Gil. She was showing a complete grasp of the complex situation. All he had to do was let her have time to think. She'll figure it out.

"Say, wasn't that photo taken on the Oregon highway either a California or Washington plate?" Gil asked.

Maria swiveled in her seat to face him, "That's right," she said, "and the witness by the Town Center bridge wasn't exactly clear that it was a Nevada plate. We should have analysis look at California in addition to Washington state registrations now registered here."

"We should ask Atlanta, San Diego, and Seattle to place a newspaper article seeking information about a man that may have committed rape, someone who hates graffiti. You never know what could turn up. Remember the ad that was run by that insurance agent in the original *Thomas Crown Affair*?"

"I do remember. Great film."

It was, he knew, not the same thing as a movie, but he was not a patient man. This killer wasn't waiting, and Gil was determined to plunge ahead as fast as they could, no matter what.

#

Returning from the local Borders Bookstore, Morgan placed his most recently purchased books about gangs on his side table and settled into his chair. He scanned the three books quickly trying to decide which one to read first: *Gang Intelligence Manual: Identifying And Understanding Modern-Day Violent Gangs In The United States* by Bill Valentine, *Inside the Crips: Life Inside L.A.'s Most Notorious* by Colton Simpson, and *Gangs And Their Tattoos: Identifying Gangbangers On The Street And In Prison* by Bill Valentine and Robert Schober. He had been lucky enough to find a copy of *Crimes Of Style: Urban Graffiti and the Politics of Criminality* by Jeff Ferrell, as well. He decided on *Gang Intelligence* and settled into reading. *This was going to screw up those cops!*

When Morgan finished another of the books on gangs he threw it across the room in disgust. *Fucking scum. These guys are bad dudes.* One thing he knew for sure now was that there were a lot of gangs in Las Vegas. Hispanic gangs, north, south, black gangs, Crips and Bloods, white supremacy, and skin heads. The most surprising thing about them all was that they were operated from within prisons. How could that be?

Gang activity in Vegas paled in comparison to California where there were over 100,000 members. Still, the Vegas statistics were scary enough. The number of gangs in Vegas was over 300 with a total membership of almost 8,000.

MS13, Lightening Bolts, Daggers, Crips' graffiti in blue, Bloods' graffiti in red, Crowns with five points, crowns with six points. SUR and NOR with specific numbers, 13, 14, 11, 3, 6, 50, 60, 702, 18, 28, 40. Folk nation gangs versus People nation gangs. Morgan's head was filled with numbers, signs, special handshakes and how to answer the question from a gang member, "Where you from?"

In one case, a teacher failed an eleven year Bloods' gang member because he wouldn't write the letter "C" in anything he wrote, because C stood for his gang's archenemy the Crips. Blue was out too, because that was their color scheme. Therefore, he would write a sentence 'The slouds were white and puffy.' The young boy refused to correct the spelling to clouds.

It had been simply an accident, Morgan knew now, that the taggers he had previously killed had been members of gangs. Now all this attention was being focused on the fact that the latest kid he'd popped off was from an affluent household, it was clear from the news coverage that the police were giving more credence to the single killer idea. Well that was going to change now. He was only going to take out verified gang members in order to convince both the police and the press that the killings were gang related. He was going to have to be very careful. Dealing with, or at least being in close proximity to members that did not give a shit about anything but the elimination of rival gangs and the protection of their own was going to be dangerous. Danger never bothered him before, but somehow this was different.

The police web site also provided him with useful information. He learned that the Gang Division Unit was now known as the Gang Crimes Bureau and had been made part of the LVPD's Special Operations Division. Its purpose being to investigate or assist in investigating all crimes that were in any way related to gang criminal activity including the application of graffiti, along with crimes involving religion or ethnicity hate crimes.

The Gang Crimes Bureau participated in the Southern Nevada Community Gang Task Force and supported four additional Federal Task Forces that were individually sponsored by the Bureau of Alcohol Tobacco and Firearms, the Drug Enforcement Agency, the Federal Bureau of Investigation and the United States Marshals Service. This essentially divided the unit into sections which dealt with investigative procedures, task forces, problems involving graffiti, as well as investigative and enforcement in all areas. These squads covered seven days of the week, primarily working swing shift.

The Gang Crimes Bureau also operated the Area Gang Intelligence Center known as "Our Gang Center," a central focal point for all gang related crime information, gang criminal intelligence and gang suspect identification.

It was, Morgan realized, a virtual empire of protective agencies. Which gave rise to the question of why, with all these specialists on hand, was there still so much graffiti? Morgan mulled all this newfound information repeatedly and came up with a plan.

#

To the untrained eye, police sketches looked, Gil thought,

amazingly alike. Perhaps it was the charcoal format, which meant that everything appeared in black and white. The image that stared back at him from the page was a man in his late thirties or early forties with a military haircut, light hair, his piercing eyes set wide apart.

"I checked with the Captain and he has agreed to release it to the press and the TV folks as a person of interest just as you had suggested earlier," Maria said. "We're also going to run this picture in Atlanta, Seattle, and San Diego."

Gil turned his attention to Lemke's database report on black Jeeps.

"According to the DMV database," he said, "we have no good matches on registrations from Washington or California. Damn, that's frustrating. Either our Town Center bridge witness was wrong about the Jeep having Nevada plates or the massage parlor girl was wrong about the California plate. Are we talking about two different Jeeps here?"

"Could be two different suspects too," Maria said. "Did you see Lemke's note on that bundle? I've got it right here." Maria read Bob's note – 'The one witness at a shooting scene in Seattle observed a black SUV parked several blocks away, but he was sure it had Washington plates. Based on what I've been able to find, there's another possibility and that's that our suspect covers his out-of-state plates with forged Nevada plates. We need to pursue this. We know he is clever. Bob.'

As Gil watched Maria read the note, he realized now, more than ever, he was beginning to fall in love with this woman with each passing minute they spent together.

"How the devil do we pursue the making of fake plates? We're not even sure if we have the same Jeep and if it is, it's his!"

Gil returned to the artist's sketch, "I wish we'd had this before

Smead's son's funeral," he mused. "I wonder if our suspect attended. There was a lot of attendees and media coverage. It's not too late to review videos of the funeral and do a face scan."

"I asked Jayne if our suspect was likely to attend the funeral or return to crime scenes," Maria told him, standing up to stretch her cute body. "She said it wasn't likely and that he wasn't the type. Too careful."

"Speaking of Smead," Gil said. "He's sure getting the media coverage and pushing that reward. This sketch is going to bring a bunch of leads. We need to rest up before it hits. I suspect we may be overwhelmed."

Overwhelmed he thought, was probably an understatement. But he didn't intend to have their workload keep them from making love at every opportunity. Maria was an extraordinary woman and he intended to enjoy every moment with her.

"Let's hurry to bed this evening then," Gil said. "We need plenty of bed rest as you suggested."

#

Morgan stared intently at his likeness on the front page of the local paper.

Police ask for tips in Graffiti Shootings

Police are looking for a man that resembles this police artist's sketch. Possibly driving a black SUV. Courtesy photo –LVPD.

Las Vegas police are asking for the public's help in locating the man that may have killed as many as five 'Taggers,' including the son of wealthy homebuilder, Forrest Smead.

Las Vegas police Public Information Officer, Virginia Rodriguez said during a brief news conference Monday morning, "We have no motivation at this time for these crimes, except someone or persons that hates graffiti. According to a profiler's workup, this man also may also be a rapist."

Police are looking for a late-model, black SUV witnesses said was parked near several of the crime scenes.

Rodriguez also said that the police do not believe the shooting was gang-related, or that the shooter knew the victims.

How the hell had those fuckers got this sketch? Think man. Think.

Morgan put down the paper and stared into space, confused and a little frightened. He knew beyond a shadow of a doubt that there had been no witnesses at any of his killings. So somebody had spotted his Jeep, but they hadn't seen him. And rape? Where did they get that bullshit? Running through the list of people he saw on his infrequent trips about town, he had no solid ideas. Landlord? Grocery clerks? Border's Bookstore clerk? Gas station clerks? Neighbors? There was some comfort in reminding himself that he rarely remembered what they looked like so there was no real reason that they should remember him. Still, a drawing of one of the grocery clerks had not yet been splashed all over a front page. But the sketch of him was close enough to make him careful.

But if they wanted to play hardball, he would be ready for them. In the first place, he'd start drawing out money from ATM's to his daily max. One thing he was sure of and that was that he needed to change his appearance. Firing up his laptop he went looking for places to buy wigs and disguises. What he needed now was a plan.

Chapter Fifteen

As Dean Schmidt removed the rifle from its case he told himself that tonight must be the night. Because he was, just as the doctor had predicted, becoming weaker by the day. He hadn't slept well ever since he had spent over half the night watching the road and a utility box already covered with graffiti, crouched behind a pile of dirt that faced a low cinderblock wall.

Dear Gladys, I hope you'll be proud of me. I'll be joining you soon!

He'd picked this spot because he figured taggers would return to this scene, but after four nights of waiting, they had not. He was staring at the area across the street so hard, expecting something, that he was not surprised when a figure appeared there, walking across the street toward the utility box. In the light from a lamppost, he saw that it was a youth in his late teens perhaps, about six feet tall, slender and wearing shorts, tee shirt, and sneakers.

Schmidt felt the hairs on his neck rise as the kid aimed a spray can at the one section of the box not already defaced. A sudden pain shot down his arm as he raised the rifle. Damn arthritis.

Trained as a volunteer cop in Minnesota, Schmidt had been told by his range instructor to always shoot at center mass. Ignoring the pain that was increasing in intensity in his left arm, Schmidt did his best to level the rifle in the center of the young man's back as the paint started to spew forth onto the box. The dim light, the old deer rifle's open sights and Schmidt's' failing eyesight made his task more difficult, but still Schmidt rationalized even if he missed that kid would probably never deface anything again! Gladys would be proud of him. He squeezed the trigger at the instant the excruciating pain that emanated in his left arm exploded into his chest. Teeth clenched, Dean Schmidt grunted, slumped down, turned on his back, and expired.

#

Maria's arm snaked out from under the sheets to silence her blaring cell phone, playing some sort of American Idol ring tone.

"Garcia," she said sleepily.

"Who is ..." Gil began to ask, only to be silenced by Maria putting her hand over his mouth as she sat straight up in bed, her smooth, bare back enticing him to nuzzled her there, at the same time cupping one of her breasts.

"Really?... Where was that again?... Got it... We'll be there in about thirty minutes."

"Now what," Gil asked, as she swung he legs out of bed, showing Gil her cute butt. "Another tagger has been shot over by the beltway at Cheyenne last night," she replied, slipping on her robe. "But they found the shooter and he's dead."

"Maybe this will end all this craziness," Gil said, kicking off the sheet. "Does this mean we're not going for a morning jog?"

"We've got a lot more on our plates than jogging," Maria called back over one deliciously bare shoulder. "And don't pretend you don't know it. Besides, if we did have time, it would be a bike ride."

Late summer was upon the Vegas Valley and the sun was moving farther and farther to the south each morning, but it was still warm at seven when Gil stopped the Crown Vic at the yellow police ribbon. Several officers in uniform were standing around, some looking at the body lying near a low pile of dirt. A CSI tech was taking pictures of the surrounding area. When Maria saw Detective Hewitt standing with the group of officers over the body, she muttered, "Oh shit."

"That's not our shooter," Gil said as he looked down on the elderly man, clutching his chest with one hand and a rifle with the other. The man's face was ashen gray and his lips had already turned a dark purple.

"Ya think?" Hewitt taunted him. "But he is *a shooter*. I'd say he died of a heart attack or something natural. He took a shot at a kid writing on that utility box across the street."

"How badly is the kid injured and where is he now?" Maria asked jumping into the conversation before Gil and Hewitt could exchange any more pleasantries.

"The bullet winged his left shoulder and he's lost a lot of blood. He's been unconscious since he was shot," Hewitt told her, looking at his note pad. "He was taken to UMC about an hour ago and is expected to live. An elderly couple, out for an early morning walk saw the boy lying next to the utility box with blood running down the sidewalk. When we responded to the 911 call, an officer saw the old man lying over here, probably the victim of a coronary, from the looks of it." Hewitt pointed at the old man again.

"So what do we have here?" Maria speculated. "A copy cat or our profiler is so far off base that it's not funny?"

"Any vehicles parked around here?" Gil asked. "How did this guy get here?"

Gil, thinking a mile-a-minute, was determined to outthink Hewitt and get on top of the situation.

Hewitt handed Gil a plastic bag that contained a wallet and a box of rifle shells. "This guy was a Dean Schmidt and he lived over there in Sun City. He probably walked to this site. We've been to the house and there's no answer. We're processing a search warrant as we speak."

Maria bent down to have a closer look at the aged man's face. "He's dressed all in black," she mused. "Which means he *could* be our shooter, but the rifle isn't a 30 caliber so maybe he has two rifles. In addition, it looks like the tagger got to write quite a bit before he plugged him. I wonder what Sam Brown can make of the graffiti. It looks like it says, *"PV and MC are going,"* she added, squinting to look across the street at the utility box.

Maria stared into the man's unblinking eyes and had no idea of why Dean Schmidt would spend the last night of his life crouched behind a pile of dirt trying to kill a tagger.

Staring down at the body of Dean Schmidt, a CSI tech handed the plastic wrapped rifle to Gil, breaking Gil's reverie of trying to put this older gentleman's visage into that of the serial killer they were hunting.

"You can look at this if you want before I take it to the lab," the tech said, matter-of-factly, "but we're sure the caliber doesn't match that of the other killings. Got any ideas?"

Gil looked at Maria, still staring at the body, "Nope, well, yes, I think it's a copycat."

As Gil and Maria were returning to the car, Maria pondered, "Holy Crap! If we have one copycat, are there going to be others? The media is going to have field day!"

Chapter Sixteen

The Showtime Costume and Wig store, tucked into the corner of a mall, was close to the Las Vegas Strip and was doing a brisk business for a late summer day. It was twilight when Morgan came out carrying his bag of disguise materials hoping he hadn't been recognized by the clerk or other shoppers, mostly entertainment types who were absorbed in pawing through capes, hats and other accessories.

Walking the block to where he had parked his Jeep, he placed the package on the front seat next to him and put his non-logoed hat and dark glasses into the bag. He was all set now for the drive to California where he would trade in his Jeep for a Toyota, Honda or other model that had a lower profile than the Jeep, in gray which seemed to be the most popular color here in town. Still fuming over the 'slightly resembles' sketch and SUV description in the newspaper a few days earlier he decided on driving to Bakersfield, a city large enough to have many car dealers. And when he returned he needed to move from his apartment and rent a place where he could use another identity. Another name. It occurred to him that he needed a new driver's license as well. He would have to keep an eye out for men whom he resembled in height, coloring and age. He was going to have to use some of his accumulated cash for all this. An idea began to hatch.

Turning to southbound I-15 toward Los Angeles, Morgan glanced down at the shopping bag on the seat and saw tufts of the brown, streaked blond hair of the wig poking out of the opening. It reminded him of the day of his final exam at the Marine Corp advanced sniping course where he adorned his helmet and uniform with tree leaves, twigs, and native grasses. It was, he recalled, a damned good Ghillie Suite that he had crafted from the tree and shrub branches from the area. He remembered Sergeant Johnson bellowing, "Okay, Corporal Morgan. Let's see if you really earned that corporal stripe. Remember the object of the exercise today. You have six hours to move the three hundred yards to a place you can take a safe shot at the target on the hill over the next rise. Spotters will be looking for any movement and if they see you before you take your shot, you fail! Remember, only one in twenty passes this test the first time."

"Got it, Sergeant." Morgan had smiled confidently as he had slithered into the thicket, his face camouflaged, grass pieces hanging down from his helmet.

Morgan had already known what he was going to do, having spent the night before studying the topo maps and aerial photographs of the test course from which he had practically memorized each gully, tree, thicket, and bush. Figuring that if he moved to the right, that would be reported to the spotters by Sergeant Johnson. Morgan didn't trust anyone. He feinted to the right and then moved instead to the left. The ascent to the target from there was the long way to go around, but it afforded the best cover after he traversed a more open area. It was the first fifty yards in this field that was the riskiest. If Morgan made it past that, he would have an easier time coming in from the left flank. Morgan counted his progress in inches, aware that even the slightest movement of grass would give him away. He needed this course to complete his sniper training. Although he was already the best shot on the team, he needed to pass the stealth part with the same high marks.

Morgan was pretty sure that he had about three and half hours to cover the fifty, relatively open, yards. Inch by inch, his sniper rifle safely concealed in burlap, grass pieces and twigs arranged across his back, Morgan had a sense of invisibility.

Ever so slowly Morgan lifted his watch cover. Elapsed time - two and half hours. The fact that there had been no warning whistles and Marines running in his direction indicated that he had not been spotted. Having passed through the most open area Morgan continued to be covered by a dip in the ground that was high enough to cover him if he stayed in the prone position. Figuring he could move a little faster now, he advanced at several feet rather than inches every fifteen minutes, certain now that his patience was going to pay off.

Rolling onto his back Morgan unslung his rifle and turned onto his stomach again, pulling the rifle underneath him. Not too fast now, he reminded himself as he raised the scope to the metal target perched about ten feet above the observers who, he could see now, were still scrambling to locate him. Their binoculars seemed to linger on the area far to his right. Perfect. Sergeant Johnson had told them he had started his maneuver to the right which meant that he had a full ten minutes left, the target now being centered in his cross hairs. Morgan had cleverly dialed in the distance on his scope before the test and assumed he would be at this spot to fire. Range was perfect.

Bang! Ping!

When the bullet hit the target, the observers all yelled simultaneously, pointing in the direction of the rifle smoke. Barely fifty feet from them, Morgan stood up and raised his arms in victory, ignoring his aching muscles.

#

"Christ Maria, you can't be serious." Gil exclaimed, jumping up from the kitchen table where he'd been drinking his morning coffee.

"I know, I know, Gil" Maria put her arms around him. "I didn't really want to ask you to delay your vacation. I know how much you were looking forward to seeing your daughters, but shit, you've heard the sheriff and mayor and read all the news accounts. Vegas is in an uproar about our sniper. Copy cats, dead rich kids, rewards, a million leads, and blind alleys. The media is being relentless. All we can do is keep the pressure on and figure this out."

"I know you're right, Maria," he admitted. "My daughters will be devastated, but you know the thought that I had first? That shrew of an ex is going to have my hide! I can't even imagine how I'm going to start the conversation."

"Oh Gil, I'm so sorry," she told him. "And if I didn't really believe you're sorely needed, I wouldn't insist. I'm doing the right thing in asking you this. But jeez, can't you just tell your ex where to get off?" Maria took a deep breath as he wrapped his arm around her in return.

Gil could tell from the look in Maria's eyes that she was as upset about this as he was.

Maria stroked Gil's hair, "You said your sister-in-law may come

126

to town and help watch the kids. Is that still a possibility, even if you're working most of the time?"

Gil pondered that for a moment. "No. I wouldn't ask her to come to Vegas and watch Liz and Joni while I worked nearly twenty-four, seven. It wouldn't be fair, and besides what would the point be? It would just add fuel to the fire about a cop's life for that shrew to continue to hammer home. I can just hear her now, something like, 'your dad doesn't care about you girls. He's happy just ignoring you like he did me!'"

Gil remembered how often his wife would nag on him about his lengthy and odd hours and his commitment to the police force over her own interests. No amount of explaining to her the duties of cops and the fact that criminals 'don't keep regular hours' ever seemed to placate her. So often, he remembered, his cell phone would go off at odd hours of the night or on his days off, she would say, 'if that's some police business, tell them you can't make it!' Of course he never ignored the calls and he always ignored her request, or should he say her order. His daughters, even at their young ages, seemed to understand the plight of police officers' call to duty.

"I actually begged Vasquez to just let me handle this while you took some time off," Maria told him, "but he ran the laundry list of events that, well, to be perfectly honest, are a little overwhelming right now. But, as I said before, when he mentioned the mayor, Mr. Smead, the sheriff, the media and all of the citizens' uproar and all those leads coming in for the reward -- I realized I had to ask you to delay your vacation. I just had to. We need you. I need you."

Gil blanched, picking up his phone to call his ex and talk to his daughters. He hoped one of the girls would answer instead of his ex. He wanted Joni and Liz to understand how much he missed and loved them before the shrew could start poisoning them with ideas about his disloyalty to them. Or should he say, *continue* to poison them? His greatest fear was that one day they would nearly forget about their father, and only remember that he abandoned them for a life in Las Vegas. Worse yet, they would think that he had forgotten *them*.

Chapter Seventeen

The Southwest 737 jet pushed Maria and Gil back into their seats as the powerful engines propelled the jet down the runway at Las Vegas' McCarran Airport. The flight heading to San Diego was about sixty-percent full, not surprising for one that left at six in the morning. Gamblers, tourists and other party types hated the thought of returning home so early after a late night in Vegas.

Information was coming at the pair of homicide detectives almost faster than they could process it and last night had been no exception with orders from Captain Vasquez for them to get on the first flight to San Diego in order to question a lady that may have identified the tagger killer. The lead had come in from the San Diego Police Department. An SDPD detective was going to meet Gil and Maria at the airport.

Gil raised his voice above the aircraft's noise in order to read aloud from the preliminary report e-mailed from San Diego.

"A Selene Newson claims that a Ben Morgan, for whom she

worked with several years ago, fits the description of the sketch in the paper. It seems that he nearly raped her on a first date."

The engines' roar subsided somewhat as the plane gained altitude and started to level off. Maria was digesting what Gil said and what Vasquez told her last night.

"Hopefully, when we return tonight," Maria said, "the team will have run down Ben Morgan. At least we'll know if this isn't some wild-goose chase."

"God, we really need a break, Maria," Gil closed the folder after reading more of the sparse data, and placed it in his briefcase. "Let's hope this Selene lady has the right suspect. What with his picture plastered all over the papers, if indeed Morgan is our guy, he's long fled Vegas and gone into deep cover somewhere. We can only hope that the team will have an address where we might find him. Or perhaps his Jeep – if it is his - can be located."

Maria agreed with her usual frankness. "I want that son of a bitch more than you know," she said grimly and Gil thought, not for the first time, that she had an extraordinary way of being as tough as anyone in the force and twice as determined, at the same time maintaining a sultry sexiness that did him in every time.

"Remember that question you asked Sam Brown about whether he used UC's?" he asked her now, as the plane leveled off at 35,000 feet. "If I remember right, it reminded you of something but you couldn't think what it was. Any further thoughts on the subject?"

"Not yet, Gil," she told him, "but when I think of it, I'll let you know. What I've been thinking about most lately is that if our suspect keeps on trying to take out taggers, he may have screwed up killing that Smead kid. I'm just thinking he'd want us to continue to think these crimes are gang related."

Maria paused as if to gather her thoughts.

"Go on," Gil urged. "I think I see where you're headed."

After a moment, Maria shook her head, "I'm just not sure how we could use an undercover cop. Last time I talked to Rodolfo, he hadn't been able to get a line on any gang shootings involving tagging. Somehow, we need to get the word to the gangs that are tagging their territories that our shooter may be a gang member. I'll talk to Rodolfo when we get back. Perhaps he has some ideas. We need to draw out this guy somehow."

Gil wasn't sure if Maria was confiding in him completely and providing him all her thoughts about this case. He couldn't figure why she would be withholding her thoughts and potential strategies from him. But then again, perhaps she, like him, really didn't have a clear strategy and a plan of action. They would have to take this one day at a time and hope for some more luck and timely leads.

"I've got to give it to Rodolfo," Gil said. "Hanging with those bad-ass, gang banging Eastside Maestros types. Dangerous God damn work!" And then, as an afterthought, he said, "Sam Brown may be right too. It could be the work of an ex-gang member, but he could be from anyplace. San Diego, Atlanta, Seattle… Who knows?"

The uncertainty, Gil realized, was getting to him. By now there ought to have been evidence that would allow them to focus on just who this killer was. Because if that didn't happen soon, more people were bound to die.

#

The Asian massage parlor was the same as all of them. Bakersfield had its seedy areas with large rundown apartment complexes, strip malls that had seen better times, and a busy main drag that had plenty of car dealerships. More importantly to Morgan was the presence of a small motel that took cash for his two-night stay without asking for ID, giving him an idea for when he returned to Vegas. Doing a quick calculation of his cash reserves, he figured he could buy a car, move to another location, find a storage facility, and last a couple of months before moving on and getting another job in a city of his choosing.

Morgan settled onto the massage bed ready for the Asian girl to start plying his body with her soft small hands, knowing that eventually she would jerk him off, sending spurts of desire into a towel. Once he was relieved of that, he could concentrate on the deeds at hand.

Having tipped the girl an extra twenty dollars, Morgan was just finishing getting dressed in the empty cubicle when he heard the soft sounds of conversation in the room next to him.

"Sweetheart," a man said, "I've got to go to the restroom. Can you stop for a moment?"

"Okay. Me go too," the girl replied.

Peeking out of the curtain covering the opening to his cubicle, Morgan saw the couple disappear through two doors at the end of the hall at the rear of the building, and saw a man about his height and weight wearing just a towel around his waist. Slipping into the recently vacated cubicle next to him, Morgan saw the man's watch and a tri-fold wallet on the small table, next to the hooks on which he had hung his shirt and pants. Inside the wallet Morgan found a driver's license buried two deep in a credit card compartment. Putting it in his pocket, he left the building without being seen.

Back at the motel, Morgan pushed on his mustache to make sure it was stuck tight and looked at himself in the full length mirror. Rolling up a sleeve of his new Hawaiian shirt, he put a temporary tattoo of a Tiger's head on his upper arm. *Graffiti of the skin!* He pushed some of the strands of his light brown wig under his ball cap. God, he hated guys that looked like he did now but at least now he could proceed on foot to the car dealer confident that his new appearance wouldn't match anything about his normal make-up, except of course his weight and height.

Parking his Jeep backwards into an unmarked parking space, in a large apartment complex a few blocks away, he overcame a momentary pang of remorse at leaving his car gathering dust and looking forgotten in this place. Well, he rationalized, looking back at his black beauty, with the price of gas being what it is, may be it wasn't such a bad move after all. He made his way to the main drag on foot. So far things were going well. The Jeep had no plate on the front so it was unlikely that the police would ID it and now that he was in possession of his new identity, that of Victor Gregory Packard from Visalia, California, he was feeling better about eluding the police. He had to remind himself several times that his main objective was following God's plan to rid the world of as many property defacers as possible. He only wished he could figure out how his Jeep and police sketch made it to the attention of the cops. He never liked questions that had no answers.

An hour later, Morgan left the car dealer's lot driving a two-year-old gray Hyundai Sonata, confident that the young salesman would never connect him to the police sketch thanks, in part, to his moustache and the salesman's eagerness to close the deal when he had realized this would be a cash deal. Morgan was now ready to return to Vegas and execute the balance of his plan, which was to continue to confuse the police and avoid capture. But first, he had to shed his disguise and wash off his disgusting Tattoo.

The Hyundai cruised along very nicely on the trip back to Vegas. Things would continue to go along according to plan, particularly if Packard didn't realize his license was missing for several days and even then, with any luck, he might suspect that one of the girls at the massage parlor had taken it. And he could hope that his Jeep wouldn't be found for a least a week or two, tops. That would give him time to secure another place to live, pick off some scumbag, rotten ass gang members and shoot at least one, perhaps two more taggers in the act. He now thought Mexico would be a good place to run after he finished in Vegas, thanks to his frequent trips to ATM machines he had plenty of cash. He'd always figured that people who kept the bulk of their funds tied up in stocks were nuts.

Morgan had carefully examined the four Budget Suites hotels in Vegas and decided on the one over by Sam's Town Gambling Hall and Casino. It was by far the largest complex, had out-of-the-way parking, and he could quite literally walk the two or three miles to some gang neighborhoods where the action was soon going to be big time.

#

During the drive from the airport with San Diego PD homicide detective Frank Roosevelt, Gil and Maria learned that the San Diego police were going to investigate the whereabouts of Ben Morgan. The man Selene Newson had named as a possible suspect, based on the pictures and descriptions that appeared in the San Diego papers. She had, she'd told them, known Morgan as a coworker at a tech support company where they were cubicle mates working the same shift. She had also told the police, she had reluctantly agreed to a date, a date that had turned into a disaster.

Roosevelt, a very tall black man, maneuvered the Chevy with a deftness that made Gil think this guy had to have been in traffic before landing in homicide.

"Detective Roosevelt," Gil said, as the Chevy raced along a San Diego freeway. "Do you remember the five or six stranglings of taggers here a while back?"

"You bet I do," Roosevelt said. "I was on the homicide team on that and please call me Frank. What made you ask that?"

"We think the guy we're looking for in Vegas may have committed those crimes here in San Diego too," Gil told him. "We've been working on a theory that there's a self appointed vigilante moving about the country and trying to singlehandedly eliminate graffiti artists. Our data indicate that our guy in Vegas who's shooting taggers with a sniper rifle, may have started his spree here in San Diego before moving on to Atlanta, Seattle and now in Vegas. According to our theory and some profiler's descriptions, this guy may be one in the same."

"Holy shit!" Roosevelt exclaimed, looking in the rear view mirror at Maria to see if his swear words had any discomforting affect. "Are you kidding me? We've almost given up trying to find this guy. He was certainly clever. Tell me more."

Gil and Maria filled Roosevelt in on their theory, the timing of Lemke's analysis, some obscure evidence of a black SUV, probably a black Jeep and a hopeful 'the-guy-fits-the profile' match at an Asian massage parlor. This lead in San Diego was their first big break and they hoped beyond hope this lady would give them the opportunity they needed to solve these crimes.

Selene Newson was visibly nervous as the three police detectives sat on her couch in a small house in the San Diego suburb of Miramonte, and questioned her about her relationship with Ben Morgan.

"Okay, Ms Newson, I understand you being nervous," Maria said. "We can't tell you enough how grateful we are that you came forward, no matter how this turns out. We're really here to help and trust me, what you say will remain as private as we can manage. We can get started anytime you're ready. You don't mind if we use this recorder, do you?"

"Oh, you can call me Selene, and I think I'm ready. Go ahead."

Gil could tell from the way Maria had modified her behavior that she was going to temporarily bury her aggressive persona and do her best to win this woman's trust.

The recorded interview lasted about forty-five minutes and it was clear Selene was nervous. She edged about in her chair and twisted a strand of hair as Maria leaned toward her. She recounted Morgan's outraged comments about the initials carved in the tabletop of the restaurant where they had dinner before the rape attempt. By the time she had finished, Gil was sure that Morgan fit the profile that Dr. Samuels had outlined a few weeks earlier.

Maria switched off the recorder, placed it in her purse as they thanked Selene once again with her promises to call them if she thought of something else.

"Interesting that Morgan stopped attempting to rape Selene after she called him weird," Gil said as they walked back the San Diego Police car. "What did you think of that Maria?"

Before she could answer Gil's question the San Diego police detective's cell phone rang.

"Roosevelt." The cop answered. "What's up?"

Roosevelt waved them to be quiet. "Mmm, yes... I know where that is..." He said pulling out a note pad and scribbling something. "No it's not far, we'll head over there right now... Gotcha..."

Closing his cell, he told them that they were going to see a Shirley Cummings. As the trio climbed in the car Roosevelt briefed them on the call. When the SDPD had run Morgan's identity, starting with the telecommunications company where he and Selene worked,

136

they got a social security number and all kinds of work history and an address.

"Great," Gil and Maria said simultaneously. "Is that where we're going now?" Gil asked.

"We're going to his place of employment," Roosevelt explained. "It's a place called WebMaps. This Cummings woman is Morgan's boss. He apparently travels a lot and doesn't have an office at this location."

Gil and Maria traded a 'That-fits' glance.

"Did they say where he was currently working?" Maria asked hopefully.

"Nope. That is why we're going over there in person. Personnel departments don't give out information over the phone, even if we say we are the police. Same old privacy crap we get all the time. But I'm pulling his driver's license picture from the DMV for you to use just in case."

Gil was hopeful that the pieces of this case might be coming together after all. If this Morgan continues to fit the profile, has the ability to move about the country as Lemke's data suggest, and they're nimble enough to respond to his whereabouts and make a quick arrest, then this craziness can came to an end.

Chapter Eighteen

The drive from Bakersfield had been refreshing in terms of allowing Morgan to think out his plan of action, particularly since the Hyundai sedan cruised so nicely at freeway speeds. Since the sedan only had a temporary registration tag Morgan stayed at or below the flow of traffic as to not draw any undue attention from any highway patrol officers.

His first order of business was to cruise the well to do neighborhoods of Vegas' west side and find a gray Hyundai similar to the one he was driving. Make a note of the license plate number and make himself another Nevada plate with that same number. One which, if spotted for any reason by the police, would match that of a car of the same make and model. And because he knew that the police had developed special technology that allowed them to tell immediately if it was a valid plate, he would cover it with plastic to make it more difficult to scan.

As he passed under the Town Center bridge, the site of his last killing, Morgan saw that someone had covered the kids attempt at graffiti with fresh paint. Slowing down, he had noted that the bloodstains on the rocks below the bridge had apparently been freshly washed off too. He smiled as he pushed north on the beltway to Sun City. He wanted to check out the area of the copycat murder and hopefully find another gray Hyundai at the same time cruising around. *Copy Cats! Not a bad thing. Come on people! Get out those guns and keep plugging these vandals. Graffiti is very bad!* But first he had to relocate under his new name.

The Budget Suites, a short walk from Sam's Town Hotel and Casino, was going to be perfect Morgan thought as he entered the registration office to be greeted by a tall, middle aged woman with glasses hanging from her neck.

"Hi, welcome to Budget Suites. May I help you?" The pleasant looking woman said from behind the counter.

"Do you have any rooms?" Morgan said, feeling confident. "I need one for about ten days."

"We sure do," she told him. "Things are a little slow right now. All I need is some ID and a credit card. Where are you from?"

Ignoring her question, Morgan flipped out his Victor Packard drivers' license. "I'll be paying cash," he said.

"Okay," she said, entering his license data into the computer. "But I'll need seven days in advance plus incidentals and to stay another week you'll need to pay in advance four days from now. I see that you are visiting us from Visalia, California?" She entered his license data into the computer as she asked.

"Yep." Morgan decided the less information he provided the better.

"Just fill in this form and add your car's license number," she told him and added, "I have an ex-mother-in-law that lives in Visalia. What part of town is Trails avenue?"

"Oh it's a way out of the main area." Morgan's mind was racing. What if she knows the place very well? Fortunately he remembered the license plate number he had jotted down in Summerlin. *No, I can't do that. She'll ask why I have a Nevada car having just arrived from California.* Morgan decided to go ahead and enter the memorized temporary license number, make and model, just to avoid suspicion.

"She does too," the woman said cheerfully. "In the horse property area, out west of the city."

"I'm close to horse property but not in it," Morgan explained briskly, hoping to shut her up. "There are much bigger houses in there. I only have a small place on the east side."

"Sounds like Trails avenue would be in horse country," she observed, "but then I live on a street here called Valley Of Fire, and I'm not even close to that park."

Morgan counted out the cash and as she handed his license back to him, took a second to study the picture and look at the disguised Morgan. "You've grown a moustache since this picture was taken," she observed. "and your hair is a lot longer. Hopefully, you won't get stopped. You'll have some explaining to do," she added with a laugh.

"Yep," Morgan said. "I've been meaning to get another picture, but the DMV wait is way too long."

"I know what you mean," she agreed. "Here's your key and map of the area. You can park here," she stabbed at the map, "in front of your room, 117."

His room was, he found, in a perfect location, with easy access to the large rear parking lot and two other ways to circle the building in case he needed some alternate routes. Now all he needed to do was make his license plate, find a storage location and then the stalking could begin.

#

The unmarked SDPD Chevy containing Maria, Gil and SPDP detective Roosevelt pulled into a parking space in front of a typical industrial complex, marked with suite doors every fifty feet or so. WebMaps, Inc. was located just to their right.

The receptionist walked the detectives back through a series of cubicles and offices, occupied by computers, atlases, and nerdy looking employees, to the desk of a slightly overweight woman with very short, blond highlighted hair. She introduced herself as Shirley Cummings and offered them seats.

"I understand you want to ask some questions about one of my best employees, Ben Morgan?" she asked, propping her elbows on the desk. "Is that right?"

"Yes Ma'am," Roosevelt replied. "Did personnel tell you the San Diego police called about him earlier?"

"This is a small operation and word travels quickly," she told him. "What's up? I hope nothing has happened to Ben."

Now that's a typical response, thought Gil, who's experience in dealing with homicide suspects had been extensive. It was more commonplace than people believed, that the worst killers seemed so normal and nice to those people that they had day-to-day contact with. Killers, Gil had learned, made it a practice to hide their inner workings from those closest to them. How often he had heard, 'but he was such a nice man, I had no idea he was like that,' from even the closest relatives and neighbors. If this Morgan fellow was their man, Shirley's comments fit.

"We have reason to believe he may be involved in a number of serious crimes," the detective told her. "Can you tell us where he is right now?"

To say that Shirley Cummings was in shock at Roosevelt's statement would be an understatement. The look of disbelief and surprise was unmistakable to the trio of police officers.

"Well, up to a day or so ago I could have told you exactly," she said, trying to compose herself and frowning. "But I received this e-mail from Ben the other day," she said, handing a paper to Roosevelt, "so now I'm not sure."

"Shirley," Roosevelt read the note aloud. "I've had to move out of my apartment as they are converting this place to Condos. I'm going to find some short-term place to stay. Please just hold my mail, including remittance advices and expense checks. Not sure I'm going to have an internet connection, but I'll let you know that soon. In the meantime, I'll figure out how to send my map updates. Perhaps from a coffee shop or something. Ben."

"Holy crap," Maria exclaimed. "Exactly when did you get this and where was he when he wrote this?"

"It apparently had been in my inbox for awhile," Shirley told her. "I didn't see it until this morning. Ben's been in Las Vegas the last couple of months. What's this all about?"

The look on Maria's face told Gil she wasn't going to back off from showing how much she meant business. Gil could imagine Maria pulling out her gun and pressing it to the temple of this lady to get the information she demanded.

"I need the address of Morgan's residence in Vegas right now," Maria said in a voice that Gil knew meant that she was not about to brook any objection. Even Roosevelt looked startled.

"I think you need to tell me what this is all about first," she said, pursing her lips.

"We believe that Ben Morgan may have been involved in some shootings in Las Vegas," Gil said, before Maria could send the fiery order Gil was expecting. "You'd better get that file right now."

For a moment the Cummings woman looked like she was going to dig in her heels, but then, shrugging, she hoisted herself to her feet and hurried out of the room.

Gil was relieved that Maria had evidently accepted his interference with ignominity.

"This has got to be our man," she told him, and he could see the excitement in her eyes. "No doubt in my mind."

"Let's see what that file says first," Gil said. "We have to find out if he was on assignment in the cities where murders of taggers took place. Dates are as important as the locations. Let's not jump to any conclusions."

"Look, the owner is going to have my ass if I let you see this file," Shirley said, holding the file with trembling hands. "Don't you need a warrant to see the contents of this?"

Gil noticed that Roosevelt, cleverly enough, made sure that his badge and gun were visible at all times during this interview. Clearly this man knew what he was doing. "You've got us there, Shirley," Roosevelt told her. "I can get a warrant here in an hour or so. We've got sure fire PC here and I know a judge will grant a warrant post haste, but let me tell you this..."

"PC? What's that?" Shirley interrupted him, her eyes narrowing. It was clear to Gil that her resistance was rapidly giving way to the practical truths of the situation.

"It means that there's probable cause," Roosevelt told her. "Sorry about using police jargon, but let me tell you that if indeed this Ben

Morgan is guilty of the crimes we think he is, he's obviously onto us somehow, and based on the e-mail he sent you, he may be in the process of going underground. So if you want the delay of getting a warrant on your conscious and God forbid, he commits another murder while we sit here twiddling our thumbs, you may not sleep well for the rest of your life."

"Very well detective," she said stiffly. "Let's see if we can compromise. As you can see I have Morgan's file. Why don't you tell me what you want to know and I'll read the info to you. Is that okay?"

"That'll work," Gil said before Maria and Roosevelt could protest. "Now tell me Mrs. Cummings. What cities had Morgan been assigned to before Las Vegas?" Gil asked.

"Well, it looks like Atlanta was his first assignment," she told him, flipping through the file. "Then he was sent to Seattle and then Vegas, I was about to send him to Denver, but Vegas had so many new streets in the northwest side of the city, I told him he had to stay there for another four weeks. Would you like the dates of his assignments?"

When she read them out, Maria and Gil locked eyes. Because this was the proof they needed, something that might make the case against Morgan more than just circumstantial. The Cummings woman proceeded to go on about what a fine employee Morgan was, but Gil didn't listen.

"Do you remember those taggers who were strangled here in San Diego a while back?" he asked her when she paused for breath.

"Yes, I do," she told him, and for the first time, Gil saw her confidence fade. "It was in all the papers and on the news. You're not suggesting Ben Morgan was doing that are you?"

"Where was Morgan working at the time?" Gil went on. "I don't remember you telling us when he started here."

"I don't remember the dates of all those terrible stranglings exactly, but I think he joined us after all that," she said. Her face, he noted, was a pasty white now. "We sent him to Atlanta shortly after he came to work here and he had received his training. I just can't believe this. Ben Morgan was the perfect employee and gentleman. He was always on time with his assignments, turned in accurate expense reports and did superior work."

"I sure as hell remember the dates of those stranglings here," Roosevelt said in his deep baritone.

"Where did he work before you hired him?" Maria asked, and Gil was relieved to see that she had apparently realized that, in this case, it would be just as well not to be heavy handed. Maria the consummate police professional knew how to work witnesses.

"In a PC repair shop," Shirley Cummings said. "However, he'd had great Marine Corps training in map making several years earlier. He fit what we wanted perfectly. Computer literate. Cartographic skills. He was great."

"Military training!" Gil exclaimed, locking eyes with Maria's once again. "Shit that fits too!"

"You mentioned expense reports and paychecks," Maria asked the other woman. "Did Morgan have a bank here in San Diego? Direct deposit? Account numbers?"

"Yes, his expense checks and paychecks were direct deposited into an account at La Jolla Federal," she told them, folding back a page in the folder. "I just know I can't give you that information. Sorry."

"That's okay, we'll get a warrant for that too, but time is of the essence when it comes to locating Mr. Morgan." Gil told her, standing up. "And you've given us the information we need to begin to deal with that. Thank you so much for cooperating. Oh, and one more thing. Do you know what kind of car Morgan drives?"

"Yes, I do," Shirley said, looking through the file. "In fact, part of our employment contract is to pay our field reps car expenses including annual registration. It's cheaper than providing a company car. I see that Ben has a 2008 black Jeep."

Oh my God, Gil thought. That's just gotta be him. All the pieces seemed to be fitting together, all we need to do is grab him and finish this.

After getting the California license plate number and reminding Shirley to call if she heard anything at all from Morgan and warning her not to say anything that might make him suspect that they were on his trail, the trio headed out. Once outside Maria called Captain Vasquez providing Morgan's' address and the complete car description. "And please Captain, Gil and I will be back in town in a few hours, will you please wait until we get back before going over to his residence?"

Gil snapped his cell phone shut after relaying the information to Lemke. "What did the Captain say about waiting for us to return?"

"He said he could wait a little while as the warrant might not be ready for at least an hour. He also said he'd put surveillance on Morgan's place to make sure he doesn't run before we get back." Maria paused. "But there's a little complication on our vigilante theory versus gang related shootings. The press is going to reveal tomorrow that the Smead kid had some white supremacist material in his room and may have had friends in a supremacist gang."

"Damn! How'd they figure that?"

Maria said, "Hewitt was doing a routine search of Tim Smead's room and found the stuff."

"How did the press get it?" Gil demanded, thinking somehow

Hewitt was all about destroying his theory of a single killer, and that the killer had no part in gangs. Gil was beginning to mistrust that Hewitt even more now.

"Apparently the Sheriff wanted it out to help reduce the likelihood of another copy-cat killing. He thinks if it stays gang related, we're less likely to induce a vigilante approach to pure graffiti crimes," Maria told him, surprising Gil that it wasn't Hewitt that had somehow leaked the information to the press. Perhaps the sheriff was right, in this case.

"Well, I'm not sure how that changes anything at this point," Gil took a deep breath. "All I know is, we need to get back and find this son-of-a-bitch before the press and media make this more of a circus than it already is."

"I'll get you to the airport as fast as I can," Roosevelt, said pushing on the accelerator. "After that you're on your own to get a flight. I'll call to get an APB on Morgan's Jeep in case he's back here in California."

"I asked Lemke to do the same, although we call them ATL's, Attempt To Locate in Las Vegas," Gil told him. "About time I learned the Vegas lingo, huh Maria? I also asked Lemke to go back over the data we have on the Jeep with witnesses claiming it had Nevada plates. He said something doesn't add up. Then I reminded him that he thought our suspect was making forged plates. Let's just see."

"Oh, and one more thing," Maria said, handing her digital voice recorder to the detective. "Would you please download and transmit these statements from Newson and Shirley Cummings to Captain Vasquez for immediate transcription. I'll call and tell him to expect them. You can send the recorder back to me when you get a chance."

When Maria thanked Roosevelt effusively, Gil could not but silently agree. But just how much help would this man be to them in the end remains to be seen?

#

Just after sunset, Morgan pulled his plain looking Hyundai Sonata into Travel Town, an RV park off Boulder Highway on Vegas' east side. Having discarded the temporary paper plate from the dealer in Bakersfield and replaced it with his well-crafted forgery of a Nevada plate, Morgan was still feeling confident. The cardboard boxes and luggage he didn't immediately need, including his collection of weapons, were stacked in his back seat, front seat, and trunk. Thanks to his addiction to crime novels, TV police shows, and his own research, Morgan knew very well that, to date, any evidence linking him to the murders he had committed could be nothing but circumstantial. But a discovery of the weapons would be something else. When an internet search had pinpointed this place with its small storage units, primarily used by RV renters, he had known that was where he should store them.

An elderly man greeted him from behind the RV park's registration desk. Despite his wrinkled face, the sharpness of his eyes made Morgan glad that he had worn his moustache and baseball cap.

"How can I help you?" The man said as his smile broadened even more.

"Hi, my name's Vic Packard," Morgan said. "My sister is coming for an extended stay in about two weeks, and I promised I'd place some stuff in one of your storage units for her. I won't be here when she arrives."

"Sure thing, Vic. What's her name and I'll look up her reservation."

"Her name's Valerie Smithson," Morgan told him.

"Mmm, I don't see a reservation," the old man said, consulting his computer. "When did you say she'd be arriving?"

"Two weeks from today, actually. I know she said Travel Town. Is this the only Travel Town in Vegas?"

"Only one. Let me look again."

"Nope. I don't have a reservation for a party by that name," he said after an additional search through a worn ledger. "Could it be in somebody else's name?"

"I'm sure not. Let me call her and see what's going on." Taking out his cell phone, Morgan went outside and parodied an animated conversation. He was reminded, as he did so, that he should ditch this phone as soon as possible in the event the police could use it to track him.

"Okay," Morgan announced coming back into the office. "Here's the deal. Valerie said she went to your website to make the reservations and there was something wrong either with her credit card or your website. Then she spaced it. She'd like me to make the reservations, pay her deposit and she'll pay me back."

After the cash transaction for his sister's feigned arrival and extended stay had been negotiated, the old man gave Morgan a site map and the location of the storage lockers. Even though he had asked Morgan for his ID, the reservations were made in Morgan's non-existent sister's name.

Morgan drove to the rear of the RV park to store his incriminating and lethal belongings. He couldn't believe his good luck at the location of the roomy lockers, which were at the rear of the complex, around the corner from the restrooms and showers. The rear wall looked scalable to him. He'd have to check out what was on the other side, just in case he needed to access this locker without coming through the main entrance. He neatly placed his lethal collection, including his license plate making kit stored fastidiously in a metal box into the locker. Luckily for him he still had had the colors for Nevada. *Done with that for now.*

As he headed over to Sam's Town to park his car Morgan got a good look at the layout of the area. The busy six-lane street that fronted the Budget Suites and Sam's Town was awash with traffic. Running between the Suites and Sam's was another six-lane road with double left turn lanes to help manage the heavy flow of traffic. Morgan was lucky to spot a flood control wash running behind the Suites along one of the streets and crossing under the other busy street towards the back of Sam's Town. During his short walk back to his Budget Suites room, he congratulated himself on how smoothly it was going. Now to locate the gang neighborhoods and also do some research on why it was that the police intervention in the graffiti crimes committed there seemed to be so ineffective.

Morgan turned on his PC for some serious Internet searching.

Chapter Nineteen

The apartment complex west of The Orleans Hotel and Casino had long and short-term residents. Several of the short-term flats were fully furnished, just as Morgan's former apartment had been. Gil and Maria, almost out of breath from their flight from San Diego and the quick drive from Las Vegas McCarran airport found Captain Vasquez draped over the open driver's side door, in front of another group of police cars. The cars were all positioned across several parking spaces to the side of one of the two story buildings. Vasquez, who was wearing body armor loosely on the outside of his shirt and tie was talking into his radio, looking very much like a man in charge. Several other black and whites and the S.W.A.T. team van were on the scene. Leading Gil to wonder why S.W.A.T., always the lead on felony warrant arrests, was here. He also observed with this crowd of police cars around that if Morgan saw them it would certainly scare him off.

"Hi Captain," Maria said. Gil noted that Maria had transformed to her full police professional appearance and demeanor from the casual, intimate talking woman sitting next to him on the short flight. "We're sure glad you waited. Anything new since I called as we landed?"

Vasquez looked at his watch, "You guys made good time," he replied. "We have a watch on Morgan's door. The manager on the premises knows little about Morgan other than he keeps his place neat and pays his rent on time. I didn't tell him anything else yet as I didn't want to stir things up too much after we got the arrest warrant. S.W.A.T. has cleared the adjacent apartments and is ready when we are."

"You got an arrest warrant?" Gil exclaimed. "Based on what?" Gil asked. "I didn't think we had enough evidence for an arrest. Only a search warrant based on PC."

"It took some convincing," Vasquez said, "but we have a DA that's really behind us on this. Detective Lemke was a great help too. He provided us with all the information we needed about the timing of the crimes. Put that together with WebMaps and Newson's statements and I guess the judge thought we had enough. I also heard from Roosevelt in San Diego as soon as you left. He transmitted Morgan's driver's license picture and he got a search warrant for Morgan's bank records. It appears that our man is walking around with a hell of lot of cash. Look. Here's some body armor for you. Better put it on now, I don't want to take any chances."

"Oh? What precisely did Roosevelt find out about his cash?" Maria asked, putting on her Kevlar.

"Seems our man Morgan has been drawing out nearly all of his cash at ATM's all over Vegas the last few weeks," he told her. "Over twenty-thousand dollars."

Gil took the photograph Vasquez handed him and studied it

intently. There was, he saw, a definite resemblance to the artist's sketch, which was a damn good thing because otherwise they would have never have heard from Selene in San Diego.

"Any sign of his Jeep?" he asked.

Vasquez shook his head. "His assigned space is empty," he said, "and a canvass of the neighborhood came up with nothing. I'm glad you guys are here now, because it's time to go in and take him." Vasquez said, drawing his gun and circling his arm in the air to the S.W.A.T. team, "Okay guys, time to go knocking."

The scene that followed was an all too familiar one. After issuing a warning over the bullhorn and receiving no reply, the S.W.A.T. team bashed in the door and entered the room, batons, guns, shields blurring as they rushed through the splintered door only to emerge a few minutes later with an all clear signal.

Minutes later, Gil and Maria were looking around the small efficiency apartment. All of Morgan's belongings were gone. The only sign that he had been there was an envelope and a pair of keys placed dead center on the small kitchen table.

Other residents of the units were lined up behind the yellow crime tape that had been strung around the site. The manager, looking understandably concerned had joined them in the apartment. After a CSI tech examined the envelope and started taking pictures of everything in the apartment, Gil passed the landlord the envelope.

"Morgan addressed this to you," he said.

"I have had a family emergency and had to leave suddenly," the shaken man read aloud. "Here is my rent payment for next month, less my security deposit. If I can get back before the end of next month, I will let you know. It's signed, Ben Morgan."

"Well, you can say one thing for Morgan," Maria said. "He likes things all tidied up. Most people in his position would have just taken off."

"What position?" the manager asked. "What are you doing here? What did Mr. Mor..."

"Perhaps we'd better be the ones to ask the questions," Gil interrupted him. "Did this man pay cash for his rent?"

"No," the manager replied. "He always paid on time and with a check drawn on a bank in San Diego. Why..."

At this point, Vasquez having joined them, Gil left further questioning of the manager to Maria and explained what happened and what they found to the captain. Gil noticed Hewitt standing in the doorway, but did his best to ignore him and not show a concerned expression to Vasquez.

"We need to talk about what steps we'll take next," Gil said when he finished.

"I'll tell you what your next steps are," Hewitt said forcing his way into the conversation. "This Morgan fellow is probably not who you're looking for. What kind of serial killer would leave cash for rent? I'd say you are on a wild-goose chase."

"Look Hewitt," Gil said angrily. "You don't know what we found in San Diego. Morgan was... "

Vasquez cut him off mid sentence, holding up his hand, and looked at the landlord who was obviously enjoying the inside conversation, "Say, ah Mister, ah, you can leave now. Thanks for your help, if we need anything else we'll let you know."

"Who's going to pay for all this?" the manager demanded.

"Go to our website," Vasquez said. "I think there's a form there you fill out. And Hewitt, I want to talk to you for a minute."

Gil couldn't hear what the captain said, but from the look on Hewitt's face, he guessed it was a "butt out" message. Gil was also anxious to tell Hewitt what's-what, but it would have to wait for another time as he watched Vasquez dismiss Hewitt by taking him by the arm and escorting him out of the apartment.

"So what do we have now?" he asked Maria, staring at the full color picture of Morgan. "He told WebMaps that he had to move because this place was going to be turned into Condos and he told this place he had a family emergency. I suspect Morgan is just trying to buy some time with these fabrications. He could be anywhere and I will bet he is not in Vegas anymore. Hopefully a national ATL will snare him soon. That God damn Hewitt. I wonder why he's being so difficult?"

"I have no idea, but it is frustrating." Then showing more exasperation, Maria sighed, "I wonder where that son of a bitch Morgan is?" Then she brightened a bit. "Hey Gil, want to bet another great dinner that Morgan is still in Vegas?"

#

The alleyway behind a row of houses smelled putrid to Morgan as he moved from shadow to shadow, watching, listening, silently making his way through mounds of trash. The neighborhood, about a four-mile walk north from the Budget Suites, was, according to his Internet searches and the crime statistics map on LVPD's website, a hub of criminal activity. Morgan had been surprised and pleased with what he could find on the police website. He could position his cursor on any neighborhood or cross streets, indicate the parameter and voila, the amount and type of crime would be highlighted up to a diameter of up to three miles. The website also highlighted the various crimes, drugs, burglaries, robberies, auto theft, domestic violence. This place, with the cinderblock walls lining the alley, was clearly a graffiti crime Mecca.

This was Morgan's second night of exploratory work. The first night he had cruised around in his Hyundai, memorizing the layout, including alleys, and possible meth houses, frequent gang centers. Now on foot, he was even more aware to the degree to which the neighborhood had decayed with its abandoned cars, trash-strewn streets, and loud, thumping music emanating from open windows and passing cars. *Fucking animals!*

Morgan's silenced 9mm Browning, holstered in the small of his back, helped him feel even more omnipotent than usual. The possession of the gun had given him a rush ever since his first days of training in the Marines. The use of his handgun was a little more removed from the exhilaration that came from stabbing and garroting, and the knocking off scum with his high-powered sniper rifle had nearly removed the adrenalin rush all together. He loved being up close to these bottom dwellers. Loved hearing them die.

In a sliver of light from a distant street light, he folded back the cuff of his black jersey pullover to see his watch. Three-forty-five. Enough time to walk back to the Suites while it was still dark. Tomorrow will be another night. He was sure he'd find some scum walking in this alley soon. He didn't care at this point whether they would be tagging or not. He needed to kill some of these badass men and put the cops back on a wild goose chase, which would leave him free and clear.

Chapter Twenty

Maria flipped through the myriad of leads that had come through the usual tip lines and Crime Stoppers calls, and sighed. This was the third Tag Team meeting and there was still no sign of Morgan with the result the team, especially Hewitt and Hughes, were growing impatient and grousing about the lack of good leads. Hewitt had openly challenged LVPD's "rush to judgment" as he put it, that Morgan must be the suspect. I can't believe you got an arrest warrant on such flimsy data, he would say. Everything, absolutely everything is circumstantial. Even Dr. Samuels, while proud that her profiling had actually helped to finger Morgan, was beginning to profile the sort of ex-tagger that Detective Sam Brown had described. "Well, perhaps you can explain why Morgan fled just as we were getting close," was Gil's usual response, even though he could see that Maria was beginning to have her doubts, as well.

"Maybe he's only a rapist and the newspaper and TV coverage

scared him off," was Hewitt's usual rejoinder. "I'm beginning to think this is really gang related like we and the press had it at first."

And on it would go.

Maria was clearly getting sick of the squabbling and had said as much to Gil over breakfast this morning.

"Let's cool the arguing today Gil and keep the team focused," she'd suggested. "We have Morgan's bank activity being monitored. He'll have to get more money sometime and his Jeep just *has* to show up somewhere. We'll have another few hundred leads to follow-up on today so stop baiting Hewitt, even if he has some less than productive comments to make."

It had seemed to Gil during their breakfast chat, that in spite of a delicious night of sex, Maria was more than just perturbed about Gil's deteriorating relationship with Hewitt. She had implied that his taking a more forceful lead in questioning witnesses and conversations with the captain were not sitting well with her. She was, she reminded him, in a subtle way as he remembered it, that she was his senior. Gil was determined to keep this intriguing, sexy, smart woman in his life, but continue to work hard at solving these crimes, even if it meant he would remain being aggressive. He'd have to strike a good balance at keeping her interested in him without offending her sense of being his senior.

Now they were waiting for the team to arrive, Gil looked at his watch and saw that they were late. It was minutes before Hewitt, Hughes, Dr. Samuels, and Sam Brown made an entrance with Hewitt looking like he had just collared an America's Most Wanted. Gil hated that smirk! Absent were Bob Lemke and Captain Vasquez who, because of his tremendous workload, couldn't make every meeting. Lemke, on the other hand, was a solid ally who always assisted Gil and Maria argue salient points with Hewitt and Hughes. He found himself wishing that Lemke was on hand. He and Maria needed all the help they could get.

"Okay, let's get started," Maria said. "I've got a hunch..."

"I need to say something first," Hewitt said, interrupting her. He alone had not sat down at the conference table.

"What is it?" Maia said, and Gil knew that he was not the only person who heard the scarcely veiled exasperation in her voice.

Hewitt waved a piece of paper. "With the help of Dr. Samuels here and the deputy DA," he said, "I've had the warrant for Morgan's arrest rescinded."

"What?" Gil and Maria exclaimed simultaneously. "You can't do that," Maria added.

"Yes, you dumb son of a bitch," Gil swore getting to his feet. "Why the fuck would you do that?"

"Okay, Detective Hewitt, why don't you explain this," Maria said, and Gil could tell from the determined look in her eye that she intended to make this challenge stick. "I don't know where Captain Vasquez is, but he should know this too."

Gil did not feel good about this. He'd like to smack that smirk off Hewitt's face, but for the first time he felt he was losing his grip on his theory. Gil thought that he'd been a quick thinker and a real team player in all this. And watching Maria too, was a treat, even though she was a little headstrong. Gil just couldn't fathom a strategy like Hewitt's. Undermining fellow officers. It just isn't the way it's played.

"Captain Vasquez has been briefed by Undersheriff Ogden," Hewitt told her insolently. "Captain Vasquez said he would try and drop by later."

The Captain just can't have gone along with this stupidity, Gil hoped. Then thought, there must be something else going on that Maria and he just didn't understand.

"Okay, here's the way it is," Hewitt said. "You know that I've been a little critical that we were moving way too fast on the Morgan guy."

"A little," Gil muttered. "That's the understatement of the year!"

Gil saw the warning glance Maria cast his way and threw himself down in his chair. His thumbs circled each other as he clenched his hands together, knuckles turning white, chaffing at the bit to get this situation resolved.

"I do realize that Morgan has probably been up to something illegal," Hewitt continued, "but the facts don't quite add up to him being our sniper. Anyway, as you know, I've thought for some time that our sniper is probably three or four different guys and the timing of his killings in previous cities was just coincidence, or happenstance at best. I know, I know," He added. "Morgan's WebMaps assignments coincide too, but come on. Do you expect me to believe that he changed his MO just to fool us?"

"Look, Hewitt, I don't know why the fuck you would try to undermine us like this," Gil said impatiently. "I've never heard of an arrest warrant being rescinded before an arrest has even been made."

"Well, there are a couple of precedents," Hewitt replied, swaggering around the room and taking a seat opposite Gil. "The only way to rescind a warrant is if it was learned later that the submitting officer provided false or incorrect evidence, either intentionally or accidentally. In this case, I believe and the DA now agrees, the original arrest warrant was based on some pretty farfetched assumptions. The new judge ruled it accidental. Not pointing any fingers, but you know the pressure on a "tower caper" is tremendous and the original signing judge was feeling the pressure too."

"God damn it, Hewitt," Gil retorted. "Even if that's true why take away our best tool? You know we had some good hits on this guy, Morgan. I mean we had a good profile, some dates, and locations that matched. Morgan has now run for cover. We had a Jeep spotted at several crime scenes. He's worked in cities other graffiti artists have been killed. And it's probably not a coincidence that he's been there during the time the murders were committed. You can call that circumstantial all you want but..."

"But think about the lack of witnesses," Hewitt interrupted. "That and the blurred photographs are a defense attorney's dream. If you guys had arrested Morgan the DA wouldn't have anything to give a jury, not enough to find a guilty verdict, never mind enough to bind him over for an arraignment. We need weapons, DNA, prints, bullet matches, something. Not some PowerPoint charts. And now we know that the Smead kid was probably involved with a white supremacist gang, so there's serious reason to believe all of these are gang related killings."

"Well, now we can't use any resources to even find Morgan," Maria said ignoring the gang related comment. "With an arrest warrant and find weapons and other evidence, you numbskull."

"I thought of that," Hewitt said. "That's why I made sure Sam Brown and Dr. Samuels were here today. I think Dr. Samuels has something to say. Jayne."

As was her habit before she spoke, Dr. Samuels rubbed the bridge of her nose and replaced her glasses. "I am profoundly sorry about all this, but I do have some thoughts on another profile that doesn't include some of my previous assertions. It's more in line with Detective Brown's experience with ex-vandals or vigilantes. I also found some frightening data on the web sites Detective Brown gave me, data that's in line with our previous assumptions."

"Wait a minute!" Gil said. "What about the hit we got at the massage parlor. That was right on, Dr. Samuels. What about Selene in San Diego, the woman Morgan almost raped? Remember what she said about him hating graffiti? We also know for sure he was driving a black Jeep. It all fit. God damn it, you know we had the right guy."

"I understand your frustration, Detective," Jayne said, using her best clinical psychologist's voice. "But think about what Detective Hewitt has suggested. You don't know for certain that Morgan hates graffiti so much that he would kill because of it. After all, he only made some comments about markings on a table in a restaurant. And as for your match at the Asian massage parlor. I think that was brilliant detective work and running those articles in the press was clever too. But we don't know anything for sure."

"Sure enough to make the arrest warrant stick," Gil said. "And since when do we use profiler information as a sure thing?"

Dr. Samuels winced. It was obvious to Gil that she was a brilliant profiler and LVPD had dozens of cases where her profiles were so accurate the police had obtained arrests in the majority of them. True, he had to admit, that when the suspects were found that fit her work-ups, hard evidence was also discovered. If he thought about it, he'd apologize to her later. In private. Perhaps, he could determine where Dr. Samuels was getting pressure to change her original profile, other than from Hewitt.

"Well, you got lucky with that one," Hewitt interjected. "All hell would have broke lose if you'd nabbed that guy on the warrant you had then weren't able to locate any weapons for example. Like I said, no judge would have bound him over for trial and the DA agrees with me. Go ahead Doctor Samuels, let's hear more about your modified profile."

"Well, I think our suspect has many of the same qualities that I previously outlined for you," she said. "Whoever it is, is more of a get-even and an 'I'll-show-you-who's boss' personality than the sort of man who thinks he's both judge and jury. There's more of a chance that he's more of an ex-tagger. I was intrigued by Detective Brown's volumes of data and his own experience in dealing with tagging crews and the hostility they show towards each other."

Jayne looked at her laptop and hit the scroll button. "Remember, except for one instance - and I'm excluding all the crimes from San Diego, Atlanta, and Seattle - our shooter took out gang members. Gang members in this sense mean a criminal gang or tagging crew gang."

Gil slouched in his seat. This was, he thought absurd. Why was she so willing and able to change her whole outlook concerning her former profile? He couldn't wait to discuss this with Maria, in private. *And where was Lemke?*

Jayne was going on and on but Gil was no longer paying full attention. Her new profile consisted of similar traits but with minor differences. Now she was saying he may, or may not have been ex-military and his demeanor may not be motivated by 'God's will.'

Shit, thought Gil. There were way too many maybe's, could be's, may have's for him.

Maria tried to reposition her leadership of the team, but wasn't successful until Captain Vasquez made his late appearance and worked his 'I'm the boss' routine in an attempt to quell the very acrimonious feelings in the room.

"Look, I'm disappointed too, that our warrant has been rescinded," he heard Vasquez say. "But Maria has been guiding the team brilliantly and she'll continue to lead, of course. And she may still decide to make Morgan her main suspect. But I'll tell you this, Hewitt," he added contemptuously, "you'd better well start looking in other directions, as well. Now get to work!"

After the team filed out, muttering amongst themselves, Gil and Maia sat there in silence, dazed by what had happened. Maria was the first to move. Taking out her cell phone, she pressed the speed dial button so hard that her knuckle went white.

"Who are you calling?" he said. Gil was thinking a mile a minute about which one of several things he wanted to do first. Calm down, he told himself. We can sort this out. The good news, he reminded himself, was Vasquez's order to Hewitt to start looking in the other direction and allow Maria and him to keep Morgan in their sights so to speak.

"I want Lemke's side of this," Maria told him and when Lemke answered, "He's just now pulling into the parking lot. He'll be here in a few minutes, and explain everything."

"I'm sorry I couldn't be here," Lemke said when he joined Maria and Gil ten minutes after the others left. "Let me explain about the warrant fiasco. I was helping process a search warrant for Morgan's place. I confess that I didn't even think about an arrest warrant. Vasquez gave me more details about what that woman named Selene told you, and also the info from WebMaps about his having a black Jeep and being stationed in Atlanta and all. When I cornered Tom in the DA's office and told him what we had on our suspect he said something to the effect that we had all we need for an arrest. At least that's the way I remember it."

"You must've said something else, or Hewitt wouldn't have been successful at getting it rescinded," Maria said, getting up to pour herself another cup of coffee. It was Gil noted, her third. "Did he look at the photos from the Mall and the Oregon Highway Department?"

"He kinda' leafed through the file. I remember now that I did tell him we had photos of Morgan's Jeep at crime scenes, but he didn't look at them."

"What about Judge Walters?" Gil asked. "Did he look through the file?"

"No. He was swamped, as usual, and Tom just said that we had a lock on this guy. Photos, witness statements, the whole nine yards. That's when Judge Walters signed it."

"Crap." Gil swore. "That's gotta be it. Those blurred photos aren't in any way conclusive and there are no statements by witnesses that actually saw a crime. I think Tom pulled a fast one on the judge. Well intentioned, I'm sure, but still a fast one."

"Hopefully," Maria said. "The DA won't be too harsh with him. He's a really good ally. But why would Hewitt step into this and screw us up. There has to be more than Hewitt's assertion that if you guys had arrested Morgan the DA wouldn't have anything to get a jury to find a guilty verdict. Because *I think* if we had arrested Morgan we could have found out where he's keeping his weapons."

"They're probably in the back of his Jeep," Lemke said hopefully. "You know, that's another mystery. The Jeep, with whatever plate it might have, has never shown up or been spotted anywhere. If in fact he forged the plates most patrol officers would spot them in a minute."

Twenty minutes followed, during which time their conversation ebbed and flowed, mostly Hewitt bashing and motive questioning. First one conclusion and then another until Maria said, "Okay what's done is done. Let's figure out what we do from here."

"Vasquez said we could continue to look for Morgan," Gil said, thinking that the three of them could focus on Morgan, and continue to mine data from Morgan's bank, cell phone and laptop I.P address, while leaving Hewitt and the others to proceed to fish for a new suspect.

Maria and Bob Lemke nodded. "I'm sure we agree that we'll provide some investigation on the leads that have been piling up," Maria said, "but that Morgan will be our main effort."

"Based on what we know and what we believe," Gil said, beaming for the first time this morning and reiterated, "Morgan is *our* suspect. Roosevelt in San Diego is still watching his bank account activity and the ATL on Morgan's Jeep is still out there, since San Diego PD based the warrant on evidence we discovered in California and not on the warrant we used to have here."

Gil was glad he had confronted Hewitt and that Vasquez pointed at Hewitt with a tone that said he was upset at Hewitt's meddling. But at the same time, he had upped the ante. Maria and he were now putting their eggs in one basket. What if they were wrong?

#

Turning out the lights, Morgan carefully peeled back the drapes of his suite. Pressing open the mini-blind with two fingers he studied the random lights spraying across the parked cars near his building. Finally, confident that no one was around, he slipped out of his suite, retrieved his car at Sam's Town and drove to within a few blocks of Travel Town where he jumped the back wall and retrieved his 9mm Browning from the storage locker. After that it was off to roam the gang neighborhoods once again.

The stolen driver's license of Victor Packard continued to nag at him. He wished he knew what the California DMV did when a driver reported a stolen license. Did they put out the word nationally? Did Packard think a Chinese girl lifted it when he was getting a massage? Or had he just gone to the DMV and got a new one?

But none of that really mattered now. Not tonight. Tonight was the night he was going to confuse the cops by plugging a member of a gang. He could hardly wait!

Chapter Twenty-One

The black and white car of patrol officer Brad Lara pulled into Budget Suites and a space marked for Registration Only. Brad worked the swing shift for LVPD and hoped, particularly when his children reached middle-school age, to get on to the day shift. With the profile of an athlete, straight white teeth and an infectious smile, he looked the model of a clean-cut patrol officer, although he could look menacing enough when confronting a criminal. A handsome, strapping Hispanic man, Brad made the ladies swoon. It was, he had often thought, a good thing he was married to a beautiful woman, or he might have got himself into a lot of women trouble.

Officer Lara's routine had been the same for the last year of his five years on patrol. On his last day of his workweek, he'd pull into the Budget Suites and ask office manager Marge Thomas for a list of the registered guests, take the list back to his patrol car and run it against open felony arrest warrants. It was a simple but boring data entry job, involving as it did, typing in the names, and then waiting for the search engine to display results. Some nights he had better connection speeds than others. Or was it the database taking longer? Brad couldn't remember, nor did he care why it was sometimes slow, but over time he had got into the habit of tapping on the screen to hurry things along. Budget Suites was one of only a dozen places that cooperated with the police this way. They had helped Brad score more than his share of felony warrants in this manner because Vegas was considered the fugitive capital of the United States. Once Brad had a hit on an open warrant he could legally enter the room to perform an Identify, Detect, and Locate action. Because of Brad and officers like him the Las Vegas Police Department could boast having captured more of America's Most Wanted than about any other city!

More often than not, he'd score at least one hit per night, after giving Marge the name and wait for her to call the suspect's suite with some suitable ruse to get him to come to the office where Brad could make a safer bust. If the guest didn't answer, Marge would give Brad a key and he'd knock on the door of the individual registered. If the warrant was for some really bad dude, Brad would call for back up first. If there was no answer to Marge's phone call, and the warrant seemed innocuous enough, Officer Lara would enter the room and have a look around. Several times, he would find Meth producing apparatus, stolen guns, cocaine, or marijuana in open sight. The beauty of this process was that it wasn't illegal or against police procedures in any way. The list of registered guests at the Budget Suites was information available to the public and apparatus and drugs lying around in the open precluded the DA from have a fainting attack and some defense attorney salivating over an illegal search.

Tonight Marge had been very friendly as usual providing flirtatious chatter as she printed the guest list. "Missed you last week, Brad," she said. "What happened to you?"

"Oh I had a big convenient store robbery over on Nellis. Had to stand around like an idiot waiting for the big shot detectives to sort things out. We never did catch the guy."

"Well, you certainly lead an exciting life," Marge said. Then, trying to keep the chatter going, "So Brad, any plans for the weekend? Going to the lake as usual? I love the thought of you in a swim suit."

"Not this weekend, Marge," he told her, blushing a bit and scanning the freshly printed guest list. "The wife has us shopping for back-to-school stuff for the kids. Not really looking forward to that, but I have to do what I have to do. Anything or anybody on here that you don't have a good feeling about, Marge?"

"You know me better than that, Brad," she replied. "I don't think like you guys. I've never been very good at spotting the criminal types. I'm a trusting soul, I guess, but I try to make some intuitive guesses. I'm more interested in whether their credit card will allow the charges. Once I get the approval back from the processor that the charges will be paid to us, for the most part, I forget the faces and names."

"I understand," Brad said. "When I was in the academy we spent a lot of time on observation skills and it included suspicious behavior and appearances. I did very well on all the tests, but some people, like yourself, never seemed to get it right."

"Maybe you should send me to that academy, Brad," Marge teased him. "After all, I feel like I'm an agent of you guys providing these lists."

"Good idea Marge, I'll talk to the sheriff about it," Brad said, laughing. "I'm just going to take this list out to the car to check it. Be right back."

Brad punched the names into the database in his car and smoked a cigarette as he waited for each result. One-hundred forty five names tonight, which meant business was down a bit for the Suites, with its well over three-hundred rooms. After about a half hour of queries, Brad struck out except for a misdemeanor bench warrant, probably for an unpaid traffic fine.

"Jeez, Marge, what's going on?" he said, having returned to the office. "Do you have a new policy about renting out to only respectable citizens? You're certainly not living up to your name today."

"What name is that?" she asked, grinning.

"Felony Suites." Brad told her. "You know that the word is anyone can come here and do whatever the hell they want, thus the silly slogan *"What happens in Vegas stays in Vegas"*... ugh, I can't stand it. This city is appealing to criminals and those wanting to blend in and always has been. Thus, the reason I do these IDL checks with you."

"So not one hit at our lovely Felony Suites?" Marge said. "Too bad, Brad."

"Not one felony, Marge. I only received one bench warrant for a misdemeanor. Talk about coming up empty handed. There's this guy named Victor Packard from Visalia, California, and that's it."

"I *remember* him," Marge said. "He had a moustache and long hair that didn't seem quite right to me and what looked like a fresh tattoo on his arm. He did act a bit strange now that I think more about it. However, he paid cash and he did have a driver's license. He checked in nearly a week ago."

"Paid cash, huh? I'd say your observations skills were working fine. What do you mean when you say he acted strange?"

"I just thought he didn't look like his picture," Marge said, "and told him so. Some lame excuse, I thought, about letting his hair grow and when talked about Visalia – I know somebody that lives there, he didn't really seem to know much about it."

"I hate to strike out tonight, Marge," Brad said, frowning. "Call his room and we'll see if he's in. If he answers just tell him he needs to come down to the office and deposit a bit more cash. I'll watch him from over there by this potted palm. Let's see what impression he makes on me."

After a few seconds on the phone, Marge hung up. "No answer, Brad," she said.

"I know I shouldn't do this one when it's only for a misdemeanor, but let me have a key, I'll go check him out."

Brad decided that it was too risky to cross any lines, particularly as there was no evidence that anything incriminating was going to turn up. But that didn't mean he couldn't check it out. And when no one answered his loud knock, some sense of what he ought to do kicked in. A woman in the next suite cracked the blinds enough to see him waiting at the door. He ignored her and unlocked the door, his gun drawn and called out, "Anyone here?" Turning on the lights, he took a look in the three small rooms that constituted the suite. No one was there.

Holstering his gun, Brad considered the fact that it looked as no one lived there. Poking around in the desk, however, he found some maps of Las Vegas neatly stacked in one corner of a drawer and a laptop computer, with the mouse cord coiled in neat circles positioned dead center. The clean kitchen revealed nothing, except Brad thought it odd that under the sink were bottles, cleaning cloths and spray cans of cleaning fluids of assorted kinds. Inspecting the bedroom, he found nothing but neatly piled underwear and socks in the chest of drawers and nothing in the nightstand, save the ubiquitous Gideon Bible. The closet revealed neatly hung slacks and jackets, three pair of shoes that were aligned perfectly on the closet floor. One pair was a flat black expensive pair of cross-trainers. A small soft-sided overnight case was placed tidily on one side of the closet floor. We really have a neatness freak here, Brad thought.

Still sensing that something was not exactly right, he carefully unzipped the case, knowing he was really pushing the rules with this "invasion" without any probable cause. Except for Marge's very vague and inadmissible comments, a misdemeanor warrant, and his own gut feeling he went ahead. If this search came out, no doubt a judge would come down not only on him but the entire LVPD with a heavy hand. The case contained underwear, neatly folded over several books.

Taking them out, Brad shuffled through the titles. As a result of his ambition to become a member of the homicide squad, Brad was very familiar with the "tower caper" involving the shootings of taggers including the killing of a prominent citizen's son, a case he had followed with eagerness. These books sparked a connection. Certainly it was an odd collection of reading material for a guy visiting from Visalia. The book titled *Crimes Of Style: Urban Graffiti and the Politics of Criminality* by Jeff Ferrell caught his attention the most. Curious reading at best. Carefully placing the books back into the case, Brad went through the medicine cabinet and made another interesting find. A small bottle of costumers spirit gum, used to stick on facial hair and wigs, was hidden in an empty plastic soap container.

Officer Brad Lara knew he couldn't act on the information that he came across so illegitimately, but perhaps, he thought, a private call to Homicide Detective Maria Garcia was in order.

#

"Oh no, no!" Maria cried into the phone. "I can't believe it...

Oh shit, oh dear… I'll be there soon… No, I won't say anything to anybody… No. I'll call Radcliff."

Hearing her voice falter, Gil sat up and asked her what was wrong, only to see tears glistening in her eyes.

"Jesus. What happened?"

"Oh damn, Gil," Maria buried her face into Gil's bare chest and started to sob. "Rodolfo has been shot along with a couple of Eastside Maestros gang members in an alley a few miles from here. They're all dead. Right now we're not to let it be known that Rodolfo was a UC for us," she added, wiping her eyes with the back of her hand. "They're calling in everyone on this. It will be a zoo when we get there. Nothing's worse than a cop killing. Let's go!"

On their way to the crime scene, Maria told Gil of the many cases she had worked with Rodolfo and what an exceptional officer he had been. UC work was so draining on cops, that home and social lives were non-existent and Maria was one of just a few homicide detectives with whom Rodolfo had a good relationship. And now he'd been killed in the line of duty as an undercover cop, which meant the department might not even reveal his real identity to the public. Gil knew that usually when an officer is killed in the line of duty police departments almost shut down to honor their fallen brethren. Speeches, parades, memorial services, newspaper accolades, interviews with the bereaving family members and/or widows and on it might go for days and weeks, sometimes years. In his opinion, a fallen officer deserved all of this. It would, he thought, be interesting, and perhaps revealing as to just how LVPD would handle the loss of this officer, particularly since Rodolfo had been an undercover cop. One working with a dangerous gang could be tricky.

When her cell phone rang again, Maria listened for a few moments before grabbing a note pad out of her purse. "Look Brad," she said,

"I'm just pulling up to a crime scene and I'll have to call you back. Give me that number again please."

"Who was that?"

Putting the note pad and phone back into her purse, "That was a patrol officer named Brad Lara," she told Gil as he parked the car next to one of nearly a dozen black and whites. The cop cars nearly filled the small alley and adjacent side streets along with all four of the media remote reporting vans with their antennas protruding nearly twenty-feet into the early morning sky. There were yards and yards of yellow crime scene tape. "He said he'd run across something that might be directly related to the case we're working on. When we get through here, I'll give him a call."

"Did he mention what kind of interesting thing?" Gil asked.

"No, he said he'd rather not talk about it on the phone."

They ducked under the yellow tape, ignoring the reporters clustered about calling for statements or information. Patrol officers, CSI techs and several plainclothes cops already on the scene were standing around the chalked outlines of the deceased, who had apparently, already been taken to the morgue.

"Hi, Maria," Captain Saldeña, head honcho of the Gang Bureau said, giving her a hug. "This is so sad."

"What happened?" Gil demanded.

"Here's all we know right now," he said. "Rodolfo had penetrated some local members of Eastside Maestros, and in our last communication with him he told us that there was a drug deal about to go down. Rodolfo also told us he was going to hang very close to the members that were going to buy the drugs. Do everything they did. Go everywhere they went. We had detectives ready to move the moment he gave us the signal. Although he wasn't wired yet, he was wearing a "Bird Dog," you see, so we could track his movement.

He didn't signal us so we're not sure what happened at this point. It appears Rodolfo and these two people you can see outlined here may have been ambushed. A preliminary look-see by CSI indicates thirty-two caliber or nine millimeter bullets. Each victim was shot once close to the heart and this one took a shot in the head after he was on the ground."

Maria's eyes welled up again, "Was that Rodolfo?"

Gil could see that this was taking a toll on Maria and Gil damned himself for skipping out on the lunch with Rodolfo sometime back. He'd liked to have known Rodolfo a bit better too. Her tears exaggerated her large brown eyes. She seemed more lovely and vulnerable than ever, in spite of the pain she was feeling.

"No, Rodolfo was over there to the left," Saldeña said quietly. "CSI thinks the deaths were almost instantaneous. At least we know Rodolfo didn't suffer very long."

"That was going to be my next question," Maria said, amazing Gil once again by her ability to pull herself together. "Thanks for telling me that. Any sign of cartridges, bullet fragments, anything?"

"No, we've scoured the area pretty well. Looks like our suspect picked up his brass too, but we have a bullet fragment from the asphalt where the Eastside Maestros' guy took it in the head. We hope to get at least one bullet from a victim, because there wasn't an exit wound on the other Eastside Maestros member. We'll continue to look for fragments over there in the alley. You guys are homicide and I'm sure you'll have a look too."

"Did the Eastside Maestros members have any marker tools, pens, spray cans in their possession?" Maria asked as she watched Gil working the scene away from the body and peering at walls, fences and telephone poles.

"You'll have to ask the CSI tech over there. I do know that one of the gang members was armed but didn't even have a chance to draw his weapon. The contents of all their pockets are in those little plastic bags."

"What about Rodolfo's stuff?" Gil asked rejoining them. "You retrieve his Bird Dog and cell phone? Was he armed too? What are you going to tell the press?"

"Yes, his items are with us. They're safe. We took them from CSI so they don't somehow get into the regular evidence handling system. Strangely, Rodolfo wasn't armed this time. This is such a shame Maria. Rodolfo and I agreed that if this drug bust went down like we thought it would, we already had his cover story concocted for when we would arrest him. I'd let him have some office time, give him a chance to stay out of the field for a while. Perhaps he was unarmed because he didn't want to arouse any suspicions on the drug deal about to go down. I just don't know why he wouldn't be armed. The Sheriff's order right now is we don't reveal we had a UC shot with these gang members."

"You probably already know this, Captain," Gil said, "but I would say the suspect shot at them from somewhere over there, perhaps hiding in the telephone pole alcove cut into the wall. Rodolfo and the gang members came along from that direction and our suspect jumped out and plugged all three in very quick order. One vic was close to the wall and the other in the middle of the alley. Given the fact that Rodolfo had been hanging back a bit, this must have been almost a military maneuver as far as the shooting was concerned."

Was this, Gil wondered, Morgan's doing? While Gil returned to scouring the wall closest to the outline of the body of the boy, Maria went to the CSI van and asked the tech that was taking off latex gloves, "May I see the possession bags from the vics please?"

"Captain Saldeña has the other one for some reason," the tech told her, handing over two bags."

"That's okay; I just want to see these two anyway," Maria said, looking at each bag both marked with cross-correlated photo numbers and some sort of CSI index. She held one up. "I want to know which vic had this big dark green felt tip marker."

"This bag presumably came from this body," the tech said leading her to one of the outlines, the one closest to the wall. "After we fingerprint the bodies and the contents we will know for sure."

"I'm pretty sure it came from the victim closest to the wall," Gil said, coming to stand by Maria. "There's the start of some fresh graffiti or gang tagging on the wall right in front of him. Hard to see, but the green letters look pretty fresh to me. What color was the marker in the bag?"

"Green," the tech and Maria said at the same time. "And the cap was off," Maria added.

"We should get Sam Brown over here to take a look," Gil told Saldeña when he rejoined them. "From what little I know about graffiti, the Eastside Maestros use green markers. He was about to write over the red color of their rival gang."

"I noticed that, too," the captain said. "Incidentally, Sam Brown is already on his way here now."

With Captain Vasquez's permission, Gil and Maria, after taking copious notes, left the crime scene and went for coffee at a diner on Boulder Highway. Neither of them felt like eating anything, and from time to time Gil saw that Maria was close to tears. But, just as he would have expected, her professionalism won out and it did not surprise him when she called Brad Lara on her cell phone and arranged for them to meet later at a place on Craig Road. He could tell from the tone of her voice that she was even more determined than she had been before to nab Morgan.

#

Meanwhile, Morgan, looking forward to getting some sleep after his adrenalin rush of shooting three bottom-dwelling gang members a few hours ago, was returning from Sam Town's coffee shop with the local paper. It had been gratifying to have come upon three scumbags just as one of them was actually starting to write on the wall. *Fucking filth!*

He had moved his car over at Sam's Town from one parking level to another so that hotel security would think it belonged to just another local gambler that spends too much time playing the slot machines. Feeling confident, he had picked up all of his brass and escaped the neighborhood without being seen or heard. He was just going into his suite when a woman emerged from the room next door.

"Hi there. I see you're a long term resident here like me," she said before he could unlock his door. "You in town for business?"

Oh shit, thought Morgan. That's all he needed. A conversation with a neighbor, busy-body. She had caught him off guard enough that he couldn't help but say hi back, almost automatically. He now hoped to end the exchange quickly.

"Yes. I'm working on a housing project deal," he told her. "I should be finished up any day now."

"I hope everything's all right," she said as he opened his door, ready to make his escape. "I noticed a policeman knocking on your door last night."

Morgan backed out of the entry to face her directly. She was a woman in her early forties, nicely dressed in a black skirt and blue blouse, her graying brown hair, pulled back into a French twist.

"Police? Here?" he said. "I can't imagine why. When was this? I've been busy with the project so I haven't been here much. And," he added trying to be as nonchalant as possible, "I'm spending way too much time in the casino. What do you suppose they wanted. I've paid all my traffic tickets."

"I'm sure I don't know, but the officer did go into your room for a few minutes. I hope everything's all right. My name's Jackie by the way."

"Thanks for the information, Jackie," Morgan said, his mind rushing through all the possibilities of why the police had been in his room. Victor Packard was wanted? Did they have the wrong room? They can't possibly know I'm Ben Morgan. Can they? This lady was attractive and he needed to avoid acting too suspiciously. "I'm Victor. I've got to go right now, but perhaps we can have drinks or dinner or something?"

She was agreeable to the suggestion, just as Morgan had known she would be. It was easy to sort out the ones who were hungry for any sort of attention. He pretended to be paying close attention while she rambled on about being in Vegas to open a new design center, noting that she mentioned having been divorced several times and one just recently. Morgan concentrated on her breasts, which weren't bad. Besides, he wasn't fussy at this stage of the game. He put an end to the encounter by thanking her for telling him about the visit by the police. She was an unlikely ally, granted, but for right now he needed all the help he could get.

Morgan studied his room as if he was a cop trying to spot something suspicious. Everything was neat and orderly, just the way he liked it, although he always had to clean his mini-kitchen and bathroom after the maids were finished, because they didn't do it right.

He had to reassure himself that he had nothing to worry about. Any incriminating evidence was securely locked away in the RV park storage locker. His car wasn't here on the property, and there was nothing out of the way here in his suite, certainly nothing that would ID him as Morgan.

And then he thought of the fucking books! Shit. They were the only things here that would indicate his interest in graffiti and gangs. After a thorough examination Morgan couldn't be sure his books and clothing hadn't been disturbed. But it didn't look like they had.

He knew he'd have to move to another location soon, and he'd better store the books in his RV locker.

And he would do it.

Soon.

Chapter Twenty-Two

"That's gotta be Brad," Maria said as the clean-cut man wearing street clothes got out of a Toyota in front of Denny's where they were waiting for him. "He said he looked like a cop. That's gotta be him."

The cop-looking man walked toward the door of the not so busy Denny's. "Brad?" Maria hailed.

"Detective Garcia, so nice of you to meet me," Brad said when Maria called his name.

"This is my partner, Detective Radcliff, let's go inside and take a booth at the back where we can talk."

"Are you guys still looking for that sniper that's been taking out graffiti vandals?" Brad asked as soon as they had ordered coffee. "I heard some scuttlebutt that your investigation turned south a bit when an arrest warrant was deemed illegal. Some sort of typo. Is that right?"

"God, it's incredible how word gets around the department," Gil said. "And generally gets screwed up. But in this case you're about right on. Do you have something for us?"

Although Brad took pains to tell them exactly what he had done at Budget Suites in the past, he did not divulge the fact that he had searched the room of someone who was not on the felony wanted list. The room someone whose only claim to criminal fame was being listed for a misdemeanor bench warrant in California.

"Listen Brad," Gil said. "Please tell us you found Ben Morgan before the warrant was rescinded."

"Jeez, I wish that was it, but here's what I found and you'll know why when I tell you that I really can't take this up my chain of command without getting a serious reprimand for sure. Maybe even some time off without pay and that would kill my budget right now. But this is what happened."

When he had finished, Gil looked at him speculatively.

"Just when was it that you searched his room?" He asked.

"It was after eleven," Brad told him. "Probably between eleven-thirty and midnight. Why is that important?"

"Those three gang members were knocked off sometime early this morning," Gil told him. "Could be a coincidence that Packard, or whoever he is, wasn't in his room, but he *could have been* wandering the streets."

It was, Gil thought, one of those lucky breaks that had been waiting for, and when Brad handed them a slip of paper with Victor Packard's name and address in Visalia, California, he knew that they might have hit the jackpot.

"I know a Sergeant in the Sheriff's department in Tulare County," Maria said. "I'll call him and ask what, if anything, he knows about our man Packard."

Leaving Maria on her cell, calling her friend in Tulare County,

Gil went to the car and retrieved his briefcase, returning to slide into the booth next to Maria just as she was saying good-bye. "Yes, nice talking to you too Jim, hopefully we can meet at another seminar sometime soon."

Noting her ability to manipulate men, making Gil wonder if she would ever try to manipulate him. Somehow he did not think so. There was something in their relationship that created a balance of sorts. He hoped it could be maintained. "So Maria, what's next there?" Gil asked.

"I gave my friend Jim all of the Packard information," she told them. "There is nothing in their database but an unpaid ticket for parking in a handicapped parking space, but he's going to do some more checking and will call me back, hopefully today."

Gil pulled the license photo of Ben Morgan out of his briefcase, sliding it across the table to Brad, asked him when he was due at work.

"Oh, I'm off for three days," he said. "I'm supposed to go school clothes shopping with my wife and kids later this afternoon, but I can do whatever you want me to do with this photograph."

Gil envied him. Brad could take his girls shopping any time he liked. The last time he saw his girls, he had taken them school clothes shopping but ended up with iPods, ear buds, video games, and DVD's. His ex wife had not, he presumed, been pleased, but there was little enough time for him to spoil them.

"What I'd like you to do is go see Marge at the Budget Suites with this picture ask her to make it look as much like Packard as possible by drawing on the moustache and longer hair. I'm playing a hunch here."

As Maria beamed at Gil's suggestion, he couldn't but feel she was impressed with his thinking.

"I'll do that after five tonight, when Marge comes on duty," Brad said, "but I need to run right now. I'll call as soon as Marge gives me some feedback on this," Brad folded the picture into his shirt pocket and got up to leave. He shook their hands, thanked them for lunch and left.

Gil agreed when Maria said that they would have to protect him. It was not every officer who would risk his career in order to do what he knew was the right thing.

"I wish that phone would ring," Maria grumbled. "I'm owed a lot of calls. Captain Saldeña needs to let me know about what Sam Brown thinks of the graffiti. Captain Vasquez owes me some info about the autopsy and forensic findings and Jim needs to tell us about Victor Packard."

"Needless to say we also need to hear whether the department is going to announce Rodolfo being a UC or not." Gil added, "And by the way just how well do you know this Jim from Visalia?"

Gil thought they had been, up to now at least, brutally honest with each other about their feelings for each other, past lives and loves, likes and dislikes. He was confident in their feelings towards each other and no matter how she answered, he trusted and respected her.

"We attended a seminar together in San Diego a few months back," Maria said. "We hit it off pretty well, and had a few drinks together..."

"Don't tell me anything more," Gil told her, interrupting and grinning. "I'll just let my imagination run wild."

"I'm pretty sure we are thinking along the same lines," Maria went on, all business now. "If they get a nine-millimeter bullet out of those gang bangers and we can get a match on a Seattle shooting, we have our man. At least we'll be sure it is the same man. It's my bet Morgan is the guy! Right now we need to go by the office and pick up some data and file some reports. I also want to cancel tomorrow's Tag Team meeting."

"How come?" Gil asked her, sliding out of the booth, thinking that they ought to tell the team something.

"Even if the powers-that-be decide to keep quiet about Rodolfo's being shot, it's still a cop killing and I'm sure as hell not ready to announce that the man we're after is responsible for these shootings." Maria said, plopping into the passenger seat. "I'm still mulling over what to do about Brad Lara's find at the Budget Suites. The last thing I want to do is put him into any kind of jeopardy. I wish I could read Vasquez better."

"That's a reason to cancel the meeting?"

"No. the real reason is I'm sick and tired of looking at Hewitt and his smart ass grins and comments."

That was Maria all right, Gil thought. Impetuous. Sure of herself. He only hoped she was not going too far.

#

The Tulare County Sheriff's patrol car turned onto Trails Ave where the homes were small and about forty years old, but decently kept up. While he had been on this street several times before he was sure he had never had occasion to call on the Packard residence. Jim counted down the house numbers and pulled into the driveway of the house he wanted.

"Hello Ma'am," he said to the elder woman who came to the screen door. "Sorry to bother you, but I'm looking for Victor Packard. I'm Sergeant Jim Warren," he added holding up his ID and badge. "Is he home?"

"No I'm afraid Victor's off camping in the Sierras," the woman said. "What is the problem? What's he done?"

"Nothing Ma'am," Jim assured her. "I just want to ask him a few questions. Apparently he has an unpaid parking ticket. Nothing serious, really. Do you mind me asking who you are?"

"I'm his mother, Edna Douglas," she said stiffly. "And I certainly don't know anything about any tickets. It doesn't sound like Victor, but he doesn't tell me everything. He goes camping for two weeks in the Sierras with some friends this time every year."

"That's nice, Ma'am. Does Victor carry a cell phone?"

"Oh yes he does, but he called just before he went out of range, saying he'd get in touch with me again in about ten or eleven days."

"How long has he been gone now?"

"I'd say about a week now. I lose track of time these days."

"Is Mister Douglas home?"

"Oh no, Jimmy passed on a few years ago too," Edna bowed her head slightly. "Rest his soul."

"Sorry Ma'am. What about his friends he went camping with? Do you know their names?" Jim wasn't going to ask to come in; it may upset her even more.

"I'm afraid I don't know for sure. Victor is in sales at Visalia Crane and Tractor and I think he goes with some customers or something."

"No names?"

"No. I don't know his friends very well. What's he done Sheriff?"

"I assure you it's nothing; I'm just doing someone a favor. Do you have his cell phone number, just in case?"

When Edna returned with the number, Jim asked one final question. "Do you know where he camps or what trailhead?"

"I sure don't. Somewhere over Yosemite way, I think. Victor's a grown man and I don't keep an eye on him like I used to."

"Do you know if Victor traveled out of town anywhere before he left to go camping?"

"I'm sure not anywhere special. He travels up and down highway ninety-nine from Bakersfield to Modesto as part of his job."

Further questioning of Packard's mother was less revealing. Warren determined that, in fact, Packard, at least in previous years, went camping, returned home dirty, unshaven and "stinky." His mother couldn't rule out that Victor didn't slip off to Vegas or some other place, but she was sure he didn't because he loved camping in the backcountry so much.

Warren returned to his car and dialed Victor's cell phone, only for it to go right to voice mail, which verified the fact that he was, indeed out of the service area or his cell phone was off. Next, he called Visalia Crane and Tractor only to find they were on a two-week summer shut down. Lucky bastards, he thought to himself. Next he called Maria. As he punched in the numbers, he remembered the time they had together at the CSI Investigative Conference for Homicide Detectives with a considerable degree of fondness. Maria was one attractive woman. Bright, smart, competitive and ambitious, and boy, could she throw back the tequilas. He also remembered how jealous she was of the many hats he wore in Tulare County. Deputy Sheriff, homicide investigator, robberies, burglaries, traffic accidents. "Good life there in Tulare, Jim," she would say. Too bad they hadn't had sex, he thought as he waited for her to answer. Perhaps another time.

Chapter Twenty-Three

Bob Lemke, Maria, and Gil sat in the Tag conference room, surrounded by empty pizza boxes and empty Coke cans. The odor of stale coffee permeated the barely moving air. Piles of papers and notes were scattered about.

"So what we have so far is that it will take the Seattle PD at least several more days to lift the nine-millimeter bullets from their tagger-killings' evidence lockers and another several days for us to try and match them," Lemke said, rubbing his shaved head.

"Right and I don't think we have that much time," Gil said. "Marge at Budget Suites doctored up the picture of Morgan and agrees that he might be masquerading as Packard. Of course, this is inconclusive and we'd never get a warrant on that alone. Packard may legitimately be camping or it could be him here in Vegas. Morgan may have found or stolen Packard's license and Packard doesn't realize it's missing. Happens all the time."

"I like the stolen license theory," Maria said, "but Jim told me

Packard hadn't left the Visalia area at any time before he went, allegedly, camping."

"I like your use of allegedly Maria," Gil said. "Keeps us on our toes. All options open. Damn!"

Gil pondered. Was that Maria backing off what appeared to be a great lead? Was she softening in her beliefs that we had Packard pegged as Morgan? Did she still believe that the original profile of Dr. Samuels, that lead us to Morgan, was the single sniper?

"We're also certain, that the Eastside Maestros gang banger was in fact starting to write on the wall when he was shot," Lemke added.

Thanks Bob, thought Gil, for bringing a certainty back into this.

"I wonder what those a-holes Hewitt and Hughes think of that," Gil said disgustedly.

Maria stood up and stretched her arms above her head, reminding Gil what a great creature she was, and also reminding him that they had been at this questioning, concluding, discarding, and postulating far too long. He needed to stretch out himself. "Oh, they probably feel that these shootings prove he was right about the shootings all along being gang related. Damn, I wish we could hurry the forensics on those bullets, and where is that damn Jeep?"

After some further conjecture and 'next steps' conversation, Maria suggested that Lemke go on home and get some rest. "Gil and I are going over to Budget Suites with Packard's license picture and talk to Marge," she told him. "We may just check around the area too. If Brad told us Budget Suites has a record of the make and model of Packard's car, it's slipped my mind."

Gil was placing cups and pizza boxes in the small trash can, "I don't recall Brad telling us the Suites had Packard in a car."

"Hello. Are you Marge?" Maria asked the tall, middle-aged attendant at the registration desk at Budget Suites.

"Sure am. You need a room?"

Although Gil would like to have told her they were up for a half an hour stay, he followed the usual identification routine.

"Brad Lara has been working with us on a case that may involve one of your guests."

"Oh yes. Victor Packard. It's pretty exciting. All that disguise stuff and all."

Marge squinted at the real Packard's picture and then declared that she simply couldn't say if it was the same man or not, but reiterated that the doctored picture of Morgan looked more like the guy who checked in. When Gil asked her about his car, there was a positive response.

"Let me check. I do recall something strange about that," Marge told them going to her computer terminal and typing in some keys. "Yes, here it is. Packard recorded his car as a 2006 Hyundai. He filled in a license number with a temporary California license number. I thought it odd that somebody could remember the long number. Let me print all this for you."

"Why do you think that's strange?" he asked her. "Don't you require license plate numbers from registered guests?"

"Not really, there's a space on the form they fill out," Marge replied, "but we generally don't check or insist that they write in their license numbers, so when a guest goes to the effort to put in a temporary number, it's strange, that's all."

This sure sounds a lot like Morgan's MO, Gil thought. Leaving cash and a note for his landlord and letting WebMaps know he was moving is certainly strange behavior for a serial killer, and now he had gone to the trouble to give Budget Suites a temporary number. If in fact this Packard is Morgan, Gil pondered, we're facing a strange bird indeed.

"So Suite 117 is at the back," Maria said scanning the map.

"What about calls made from his room," Gil asked.

"Nada," She told him, looking at into the computer terminal again. "No calls at all."

Five minutes later Gil and Maria, with lights of their unmarked Crown Vic turned off, circled the grounds and in between several buildings looking for a Hyundai with temporary registration before they parked one building over from the building housing suite 117. As Gil backed into a parking space, so they could keep the front door of 117 in sight, Maria called in to run a check on the Hyundai. They sat in silence waiting for the results.

"Well shit," was all Maria could muster after dispatch finished telling them that the Hyundai Sonata had been purchased in Bakersfield, California a little over a week ago by a Victor Packard in Visalia. It was gray.

"I know," Gil agreed. "I expected to find it was non-existent or something. But, something is just not right."

"I can call Jim again and ask…" Maria began.

"Is this Jim guy married?" Gil asked grinning. "Because it looks like you'd use any excuse to get him on the line."

"He told me he was divorced," Maria said and chuckled. "But isn't that what all guys say when they're off at a convention?"

"Yes, I suppose we do." Gil laughed and said, "How do you know I'm really divorced for that matter?"

"Look you blond piece of crap," Maria said, rapping his knuckles with her pen. "We've got serious matters here."

Serious indeed, thought Gil. Over a dozen killings in four cities was damn serious. The national media had picked up the story and because of late night comedians like Jay Leno, the nation was abuzz about graffiti. Several more copycats had surfaced in Houston, Philadelphia and Miami. Thankfully, thought Gil, the local police had pinpointed those as copycats and it didn't cloud their Las Vegas investigation. Dr. Samuels' profile had led them to Morgan via damn good police work, and thanks to the strategy of placing his picture in newspapers, it provided the impetus for Selene in San Diego to come forward with testimony that fit exactly who they were looking for. Morgan inexplicably abandoned his apartment just as they were going to make an arrest. Gil was sure this Morgan guy wasn't getting tipped off, and had, fortuitously for him, fled just in time. Perhaps Morgan saw the artist's sketch in the paper and a description of his black SUV. That's all it would take to drive him undercover. Now, thanks to the work of a caring and smart patrol officer, they may be on to Morgan disguised as Victor Packard. Gil could only go with his gut on this, but his gut, often more right than not, told him Packard was Morgan.

"I think," Gil said, "we should watch this Victor Packard twenty-four-seven and see what he's up to."

"I'm not sure we'll able to spend the time doing that," Maria said "Vasquez will never let us because we've got no basis other than some books about graffiti, which were, I'll remind you, discovered quite illegally by one of us, and a Budget Suites clerk who thinks that Packard looks like Morgan in disguise."

"Don't you think that if you talked to Vasquez off the record, he might let us establish a formal stakeout on this guy?"

"How could he do that?" Maria demanded. "We've still got the media and the Sheriff to deal with and Smead pleading for justice. And there's the little matter of gang members being shot, and poor

Rodolfo dead. We can't even deal with that properly and give him the decent burial and eulogy he deserves, not to mention…"

She broke off and wiped her eyes. Gil was about to put his arm around her when he saw a man coming out of Room 117.

"Look," he said. "That must be Packard. Duck! Don't let him see us. Okay. He's gone around the corner of the building. Let's go. Somehow I have a feeling that he's just not going out for a nighttime stroll."

When they reached the corner around which the man had disappeared they moved to a position in the opening between the next two buildings. Turning the next corner they found themselves staring at a busy street, cars whizzing by.

"There he is," Gil said. "He's just going into the Sam's Town's garage.

They crossed the street with difficulty, holding up hands to the oncoming cars as they walked and then ascended the parking garage's three levels, keeping eyes peeled. Although cars were coming out, not one of them was a Hyundai.

"Shit Gil," Maria sad breathlessly, "I've got to get back to working out instead of just going to bed."

"I think we're getting good workouts," he told her. "Very aerobic. You see anything?"

"I looked down from over there and saw a gray Hyundai pull on to Boulder Highway. But I was too far away to do anything."

"Was it a Sonata? See a plate?"

"Couldn't be sure. All those cars look the same to me. Particularly from above. I'm pretty sure it did have a plate and not one of those temporary paper ones."

Gil's gut was still telling him this Packard fellow needed constant surveillance. Even if his gut was wrong that Packard was Morgan, this Packard man is far from clean. He'd have to rely on Maria's ability to convince the higher ups that they needed to continue to pursue this man.

They walked slowly back to the Suites discussing their next options, including the pros and cons of talking to the Captain, performing surveillance on their own time, and asking Lemke to pitch in. All of it.

"Look," Gil said. "I'd think we should risk getting the key from Marge and look inside this guy's room. Let's hurry, before he comes back."

When he returned, key in hand, they started putting on their latex gloves and Gil suggested Maria stand watch outside. She didn't argue long, and agreed he may be the better evidence finder of the two of them.

"Well, take off those gloves if you're not coming in with me," he told her. "If Packard comes back, he'll wonder what the hell you're doing with them on, standing outside his room. You'll have to signal me and delay him until I have a chance to get out."

Slipping the magnetic card key in the lock and hearing the familiar whirr of the lock opening, Gil stepped inside quickly, closed the door behind him, and switching on his flashlight, looked around in the dim light. His first impression was that the place was in extraordinarily neat condition. Occasional pillows lined up perfectly on the couch and easy chair. The coffee table was all squared with the couch and end tables. The small kitchen table, counter tops, and the small microwave oven seemed to shine in Gil's beam of light.

He looked under the bed, in drawers, under the sink, behind and in the toilet tank, everywhere, including the soap container – where he found the spirit gum Brad had mentioned. He shone the light around the sink and on the floor, looking for one tell tale strand of hair. Nothing.

Opening the closet, Gil saw the neatly hanging clothes, perfectly arranged shoes and the overnight case, which reminded him of the books. Unzipping the case, he felt through the neatly folded underwear, stacked tee shirts, handkerchiefs, and two leather belts. His first thought was to verify what Brad had found and take the patrol officer's fingerprints off them, but there were no books in the case. Morgan must have removed them. But why? And where were they now?

Gil went back to the desk where the laptop was closed and in place, the mouse cord neatly placed in a circle. The Power cord, on the floor near the outlet was all wrapped and tied neatly, as well. If this *was* Morgan, Dr. Samuels had this guy right on. A man from Visalia, who lives with his mother and goes backpacking every year can't be this neat and tidy. But where are those fucking books? Without them they didn't have a thing.

Gil was about to call it quits, when a speck on the kitchen table got his attention as the beam of the flashlight danced across the table's surface. There was a tiny blue speck of paint or something near the edge. The fake wood grain of the laminate top made it very hard to see without the proper angle and light. Even a fastidious guy like Morgan could have missed it. Removing the small penknife from his pocket, Gil scraped the small speck into his clean white handkerchief. It was probably nothing important, but you could never tell.

They were on their way back to the car when a woman called to them. They both jerked around and saw a woman standing in the doorway next to Packard's suite, waving at them. "Are you the police?" she called out.

"Shit, that's all we need to be out here talking to her when

Packard arrives. And how the hell did she know we're the police." Gil said quietly as the woman approached them. He held up his badge to the pleasant looking woman, who was wearing a dark skirt and a light colored blouse. Gil couldn't help but notice the woman's breasts, uncontained by a bra, jiggling as she walked.

"Yes Ma'am," Maria said. How did you guess that? We're just out doing some routine work. How are you tonight?"

"I'm fine thank you, but I couldn't help notice, you being next door and all," the woman replied. "Seems my neighbor has been drawing the police here frequently."

"What do you mean frequently," Maria asked.

"Well, there was a uniformed officer here last night and he went into the suite, as well."

"It's just routine Ma'am, nothing to worry about," Gil said with all the sincerity he could muster. "Have you seen your neighbor lately?"

"Yes, I saw him this morning. We chatted for a bit. We introduced ourselves. He seemed very nice."

"What name did he give you," Maria asked.

"Victor. I'm pretty sure he didn't mention his last name."

"What did you talk about, er ah Miss…?" Gil asked, hoping she would fill in the blank.

"Well actually, I told him an officer had come by and gone into his room. Oh dear. I hope I didn't do anything wrong. My name is Jackie Fitzgerald, by the way."

"Look, Miss Fitzgerald," Maria said, "this is just a routine matter as my partner said. However, we'd appreciate it if you didn't mention this to the resident. Here's my card. If you see or hear anything unusual, please give me a call, anytime, day or night. But it's important that you don't mention our being here."

"You're in homicide!" the woman exclaimed, staring at the card. "Am I in any sort of danger living next door to this man?"

"Oh good lord, no, Miss Fitzgerald," Gil said, doing his best to put her at ease. "If there was any danger at all, we wouldn't even be talking out here. Your neighbor's no threat at all to you. This is just routine, honest, but please don't mention this to Victor. The case is complicated and we just don't want to mess it up. Everything's okay. Really."

"Okay then," was all that a clearly dubious Jackie could muster.

"God damn busy bodies," Maria grumbled as they returned to the car. "I hope she didn't fuck things up. Now, what did you find in there?"

Gil told her about the spirit gum, the speck of something or other that he had scraped off the table and the fact that, contrary to what Brad had reported, there were no books in the case.

"If that woman told Packard or Morgan or whoever he is about Brad going into his room last night, he may have moved them," Maria said.

"I'd think it more likely that, if this is really Morgan, he would have left town," Gil speculated.

"I just wish we could have spotted him getting into that car so that we'd know for certain that was him driving off," Maria said. "I think we're stuck for now, but I am going to talk to Vasquez in the morning."

Jim called again, this time to say that he'd called Packard's mother about the car, and she told him there's no way her son would buy a foreign make.

"That's interesting," Gil said hearing Maria's report. "The pieces of the puzzle may be coming together. Packard's mom must be getting concerned with all of Jim's questions."

"According to Jim, Packard's mom said he's a died-in-the-wool Ford truck guy," Maria said. "He'd rather be dead than buy some foreign car."

"Well, there's another piece of circumstantial evidence we have to deal with," Gil said, thinking that his gut feelings about Morgan versus Packard are flip-flopping back and forth. "Are you going to tell Vasquez that, too?"

"I'll think about it. All we know for sure, well make that a maybe, is that this Packard guy is probably not really Packard but we're less sure it's Morgan because the books are the only thing that tied us to him, and now they're gone."

"True," Gil said, "But right now, I trust our intuition. And I trust yours very much."

"I don't know about you," Maria said, "but all this use of my intuition and running around a parking garage has made me tired."

"How tired is that?" Gil asked her.

Maria grinned at him. "Is 'My place or yours?' enough of an answer for you," she said as he took her in his arms.

#

In the process of placing his Browning 9mm gun in the storage locker, Morgan spotted his sniper rifle case and decided that he'd just have to risk being seen with the scope. If the cops had not made a mistake checking out his room, but actually had Packard under some sort of surveillance, he needed the night vision capabilities to spot any kind of stake-out. Making sure he was still alone at the row of lockers, Morgan removed the night vision scope from the rifle, closed the case and the locker, walked the few feet to the rear wall, and boosted himself over to his car.

This time, Morgan slid into a parking space on the third level of Sam's Town's parking garage for a change. After checking around for any signs of surveillance, he decided to walk through the casino instead of going directly back to his room. Carrying the scope under his armpit, he, for all the world, looked like a gambler entering the casino to try his luck again. He couldn't wait to get out of his wig and moustache and take a long hot shower. The day had been busy, although he had managed to get a few winks, in the afternoon. Right now he was pleased that, during his drive around the city this evening, he had found two promising spots to lie and wait for graffiti criminals, one of which he had used before.

When he went to buy a candy bar at the casino gift shop, he happened to see a rack of calling cards for sale, and bought one. He thought that his cell phone maybe being monitored and hadn't risked using it. The idea of calling the detective heading the team investigating graffiti crimes had been percolating in his mind for some time and tomorrow he would call and give him a piece of his mind.

Investigating graffiti crimes indeed. The police needed to be more like him and just get rid of the foul taggers. Catching them in the act was the way to go.

Chapter Twenty-Four

"**P**ermission to talk, Captain," Maria said hesitating at the door to Vasquez's office. It was very early at the homicide office and Gil was already off to the lab to have that small piece of whatever it was he had removed from that table the night before examined.

"Sure, Maria, Vasquez said. "Come on in. Tough times huh? I know you and Rodolfo were pretty close. Go ahead, close the door and come sit here. It's high time we had ourselves a private chat."

The first topic of conversation was, of course, Rodolfo. Maria was not sure how she felt when she learned that the department was not going to reveal they had lost a darned good cop at this time. As Vasquez explained it, there were one or two other UC's working the Eastside Maestros and other gangs and it would put them in danger if the gangs were to find out they had been penetrated by a UC. The story that three gang members had been shot would stand. They agreed that the press and TV were covering the situation to death and was becoming tiresome.

The next topic was Ben Morgan. Maria made as convincing a case as she could for her and Gil's theory that he was presently impersonating a Victor Packard. Presenting the evidence in a truly professional manner, Maria included Packard's suspicious behavior of the night before and their somewhat illegal entry into Packard's room. She revealed her calls to her sergeant friend in Visalia and the fact that, according to Packard's mother, he would never have bought a foreign car. And then there were the books and the spirit gum and the Budget Suites clerk's identification of Morgan's picture in disguise. She left out nothing except specifically naming Brad and the fact that Gil was examining evidence in the CSI lab that had been gathered in his unlawful entry.

Maria took a deep breath, moved ever so slightly closer to Vasquez and ended with a plea. "Captain Vasquez. I know this stuff is all circumstantial at best and we probably couldn't get a search warrant, but I would like you to approve detective Radcliff and I being pulled off the Tag Team temporarily so we can perform twenty-four-seven surveillance of Packard until we get a break. We just know that this Packard man is probably off in the mountains somewhere and somehow Morgan has his identity. The only way Morgan could have disappeared off the face of the earth is to have pulled off something like this."

Vasquez leaned back in his chair and locked the fingers of both hands together behind his head, his eyes expressionless. After a few moments, he unlocked his hands and placed his elbows on his desk and leaned closer to Maria.

"Maria, Maria," he said. "Damn you're a good detective, but jeez you've put me in a tough spot. You know I can find out what patrol officer violated the rules and searched that suite. It'd be easy to find out who was working that night, and what officer normally performed these felony warrant matches and made frequent arrests."

He raised a hand, "But I don't want to do that, *yet!* Nor am I going to reprimand you and Radcliff for performing the same kind of search, *yet!* Here's what I know about allowing you guys to do this."

Maria's face relaxed, sensing that Vasquez would acquiesce to her request, in the end. But first she had to listen to him, and listen hard.

"As homicide detectives, your work is hard and requires great attention to detail," he began. "It takes an instinct to sense when things aren't right. But we must follow these instincts according to the rules. You and I both know that overzealous cops have made investigative mistakes that have resulted in criminals walking free because the DA couldn't get a conviction. And this may be one of those cases. You've presented me with some convincing circumstantial evidence. But even if you find weapons and can positively link them to Morgan and the murders, there are elements of the investigation that would send the DA to the loony bin and the defense attorney laughing all the way to kingdom come."

"Captain, I promise that..." Maria began, but Vasquez cut her off.

"Don't make me any promises that you can't keep," he warned her. "It's too late to correct what you, Radcliff, and that patrol officer have done."

"Captain I... "

"Stop and let me finish," Vasquez scooted his chair further under his desk, clenched his hands together so hard, his dark knuckles turned white. "There are times when we must act against our inclinations. You and Radcliff are good detectives with great instincts and right now I'm going to trust them," he said as his hands relaxed their forceful grip on one another. "I may regret this, but I'll let you two stakeout Packard. You'll have to figure out how to do split shifts or whatever, but go ahead. I'm getting sick and tired of standing in front of those news cameras everyday without anything to say. So turn up something. Anything!"

"God bless you, Captain," Maria exclaimed. "I know we're right about this, just like Radcliff was right about this being a single suspect. We're going to catch this son of a bitch. But, what are you going to tell the Tag Team, especially Hewitt?"

"Oh, I'll think of something," Vasquez told her. "Now get out of here."

She had just reached the door, when Gil appeared. "Sorry to interrupt," he told the captain, "but I have the lab test results on that spec of paint I picked up last night."

"Close the door, Gil." Vasquez growled. "What spec?" Vasquez's face turned dark.

"Sorry, I assumed Detective Garcia told you."

"No, she didn't." Vasquez glared at Maria. "What spec?"

"When I was in Packard's suite last night I found a small spec of something on his kitchen table. I scrapped it off and took it to the lab this morning."

"Oh Christ another piece of evidence you illegally picked up?" Vasquez scowled. "You're gonna get us all in very serious trouble."

"Right Captain, but this spec is hobby paint that has light reflective characteristics."

"I don't follow," Vasquez said, still obviously pissed.

"The fact that Morgan's Jeep, spotted with different license plates had us in a quandary." Gil said. "Were the witnesses and fuzzy photos wrong, or was Morgan making false plates? I think the answer is he was making false plates. Nevada plates, to be precise. According to the lab tech, this blue is almost a dead match to the color used by the state. And with reflective properties, it will look like a Nevada plate except to a trained eye and those optical plate readers that many police patrol and NHP cars have."

"Well, shit, that may be another piece of very illegally obtained piece of circumstantial evidence, but it sure fits," Vasquez said. "However, we never had this conversation. Is that clear? And I expect some results here or the department is going to look damn bad and you're both gonna be in serious trouble. However, if there's anything I can do or provide let me know."

"Well, now that you mention it Captain there is something," Maria said. "I'm going to requisition some Bird Dog devices, some night vision apparatus, a surveillance van, and a car other than a Crown Vic, and maybe some other equipment."

"You don't need my permission to get that stuff. Why are you telling me this?"

"Because I'd like to borrow Bob Lemke to go along with the equipment. He's got some expertise on this stuff." Maria feigned a duck from an imaginary blow from Vasquez. "We're going to be really short-handed and it would be great to have a third pair of eyes and ears."

Gil was not surprised when Vasquez announced that he was sorry that he had offered Maria anything. "I'll see if I can free the guy up," he said grudgingly. "Now, both of you get out of here before I change my mind."

"You don't mind that I asked for Lemke, do you?" Maria said when the door was safely closed behind them.

Gil assured her that he didn't, that in fact, it was a brilliant idea. And he found he meant it. Because something told him that they were going to need all the help they could get to keep this maniac, whoever he was, from killing again.

#

Graffiti Crimes Detective Sam Brown turned on the power to his PC, placed his little cold case holding three cans of 7Up, under his desk, and waited for the computer to boot up. His cubicle, one of the many that constituted the cubicle 'farm' at the Gang Bureau's semi-secret location, was decorated with photos of graffiti, along with shots of wanted taggers and the Governor of Nevada's current proclamation that this month was Graffiti Awareness Month. "I'll say," he muttered to himself. "With all these shootings, the community had never been so aware!" He was, however, pleased that there were less new graffiti now than had been the case in the last year. In fact with the sniper shootings and copycat crimes going on recently, the only graffiti still appearing in a meaningful way was in neighborhoods that already had tons of it. But there was still work to do to provide more analysis for the Tag Team, work that involved searching his records for vigilantism cases and cross checking the whereabouts of the vigilantes.

Brown pulled a sample shot of graffiti in the form of initials from his printer and thumb tacked it next to the Governor's proclamation. Most ordinary citizens couldn't read the graffiti of gangs and 'Tagging Krews,' but Sam had been doing this so long he could not only read the scrolling letters all bunched together, but could even determine the moniker of the vandal involved. This particular picture had come from the power box up in Sun City where that old man had been found dead. It was the typical 'Bubble Gum-Graffiti,' which is to say it was less significant, much like carving initials into a tree or writing your name in wet cement. To Sam, it looked like the kid had been beginning to scroll his initials and those of his girl friend. One thing was certain. This was not the work of a Tagging Krew. There was absolutely no sign of a moniker.

Monikers were the way the vandals established their personal fame. Every moniker could be identified by Detective Brown who knew immediately whose work it was and had in fact a secret database of them. Some of the more prolific taggers came to mind. Some of the best known were "Just ask Lil" "Capone, Lil" "Ump, Lil'" "Shiester, Lil" "Sweat, Lil" "Nutty, Lil" "Wee Wee, Lil" "C Rag, "Lil' Spit, Lil" "Mookie, Lil" 'A", "Lil' B" and "Lil's C through Z." He had thousands of nicknames in his LVPD Gang Crimes Bureau computer database of aka's and street pseudonyms, a collection that was closely guarded because it's so valuable, and valuable particularly since he had to deal with gangsters who didn't know their peers' real names.

That didn't mean he could just go out and arrest them, but it allowed him to start building a case. The moniker, or tag name of a vandal, was usually unique to them, often a treasured possession that they will fight for and go to great lengths to defend. When more than a single graffiti artist makes use of a specific tag moniker, a fight, or "tag battle," often ensues to decide ownership of the moniker. A tag battle occurred when more than one vandal competed for ownership of the tag name. Sam still thought these shootings recently in Vegas were a result of this kind of activity that had gotten out of hand, an opinion that he'd already been able to sell to Hewitt and that profiler, Dr. Samuels.

When the phone rang, Brown heard an unfamiliar voice on the line.

"Detective Brown," a man said. "I hope you appreciate all the help I have been giving you in regard to the recent so-called graffiti crimes!"

The hair on the back of Sam's neck stood up. "Why's that? Who is this?"

"I think you know who this is, Detective Brown. Haven't you seen a reduction in graffiti crimes lately?"

"Come on," Sam said grimly. "Who is this?"

"You'll figure it out, detective. I'd like to know what you are doing to combat these defacers."

Putting the phone under his chin, Sam rushed to find his tape recorder, which was somewhere. God knows where. "Well, I do my best, Mr. er..." he said in an attempt to buy time.

"I'm certainly not going to tell you who this is, and I really want to know what a detective does when it comes to graffiti crimes. Tell me, detective, why is there so much of it around the country?"

"Look, whoever you are, I do my best, and actually, even if I do say so myself, I do a pretty good job based on the resources I have." Sam clamped the recording device on the phone and hit 'record.' He needed to keep this guy talking.

"Well, I don't think you are pretty good at your job," the caller mocked him. "If you were, you wouldn't need me. I think you should detect more, detective."

"What do you mean need you? What do you do to help me?"

"Oh, I think you know, detective. You may arrest a few of this scum, but I bet dollars to doughnuts they're on the street again in a few hours. My solution is permanent removal." The voice chuckled.

"So you're the guy going around and blowing away taggers, including a fifteen year old kid?" Sam said.

"Yep. That would be me. Too bad about that kid, but he shouldn't have been trying to deface public property. He won't grow up to deface property any longer. Is it true he may have been into white supremacy like I read in the paper?"

Man this guy is a sicko all right thought Brown. "Look if you have a minute let me tell you about some graffiti crimes that you may not know." He needed to get a lot of this voice recorded. It might help in the prosecution.

"Sure, go ahead, Detective Brown. I'm always interested in hearing about incompetence. And I know you can't trace this call because your department is too cheap to upgrade their phone system. So take your time and tell me something I don't already know about graffiti scum."

Damn, thought Brown. This guy does his homework. We can't trace calls and don't even have caller ID.

Brown was furiously trying to think of something that would make this man give him some facts homicide could use in finding this son of a bitch. "Okay," he said, "let me tell you a few things. As you know, creating graffiti is a crime. It is only going to be managed though investigative means used by law enforcement. Not vigilantes like you. These means include traditional investigative methods and other methods that are geared toward the investigations of graffiti..."

"That's a matter of opinion, detective," the caller interrupted him. "Traditional investigative methods are bullshit. You can stop with that touchy-feely crap."

"Hey you wanted to know what I do and I'm telling you," Sam said. "Should I continue or not?"

"Yeah, go ahead and fill my head with your investigative nonsense. I'm listening."

"Okay," Brown continued, thinking if he could really piss off this guy he might reveal something useful. "I am an expert in the area of gang investigations, but I also possess skills in all areas of criminal investigation. This is important due to graffiti vandals being involved in a variety of criminal enterprises."

"No shit, detective. Go ahead."

"Many investigations involving graffiti do, in fact, result in arrests and criminal prosecutions for other crimes, including crimes of violence."

"Yes, but it's not good enough," the man said. "Arresting and letting them out is not the solution."

"Look, whoever you are, this is a long, uphill battle. Graffiti vandals usually begin their illegal activities in their junior high or middle school years. This is a tough time for youths…"

"Well good for you, detective," he said, butting in again. "I told you, enough with the touchy-feely crap. Your process takes too long and I know it doesn't work."

"Hey," Sam told him. "I didn't say this was an overnight success story, but I have data that show it does work for a longer term."

"Not good enough, detective. These guys need to be stopped in their tracks. And they need to be stopped now! You need to lock up this filth and start patrolling high graffiti areas."

"You share the opinion of most citizens that are frustrated just like you, but they don't go around committing murder," Sam told him.

"Well maybe they should and it would stop. God bless that old guy up in Sun City. That's what needs to be done. Kill the fuckers."

"Thank God most other people aren't as crazy as you. Look, it's important for a community to come together in this fight. Even if we made graffiti a capital offense and encouraged vigilantes like you to kill the perpetrators at random, it wouldn't disappear completely. Someone would always be out there, taking out their hostility by defacing property. You're not going to solve this you know."

"So you think I'm crazy, do you? Sounds like you're a bit nuts too. I like your idea of allowing the public to shoot these low life vandals. Graffiti would disappear immediately. Trust me on this, detective."

"Listen you crazy fuck." Brown said hoping to elicit some specific information the police could use. "I was talking theoretically, you moron."

"Well, detective, get ready to watch your theory in action over the next couple of nights."

Sam was desperately trying to remember some facts from that arrest warrant Hewitt had rescinded. What was the name of the suspect that Radcliff and Garcia had their eyes on? Oh, yes, Morgan. "Say, Mr. Morgan," Sam said slyly, "you know we'll catch you."

There was a pause, not a long one, but notable. He might have struck a nerve.

"Morgan, huh?" the man said. "Well, you don't know shit, detective."

"I don't huh? Well let me ask you a question, Ben Morgan. Do you like strangling your victims as you did in San Diego or stabbing them like in Atlanta?"

There was a moment of silence. "Nice talking to you Graffiti Detective Brown. Keep up the poor fucking work."

And with that, the call came to an end.

Sam Brown turned off the recorder and stared at the phone, confident that he had been talking to Ben Morgan, that Ben Morgan was the sniper. Dr. Samuels and Detectives Garcia and Radcliff had been right. Who, he wondered should he call first?

#

Lying on his bed, Morgan stared at the ceiling, scowling. It was certainly not good news that he'd been fingered by the police, but perhaps he had learned a lesson from Brown about how to deal with these scumbags.

Tonight I'll plug one or two for sure and then I'll be outta here.

Chapter Twenty-Five

The newly formed surveillance trio of Garcia, Radcliff, and Lemke sat in the back of the van and plotted out their next few days of scrutiny of Morgan, aka Packard. They had decided to refer to the object of their efforts as 'Optik." As Gil put it when he came up with the acronym, it was shorthand for Obsessive Compulsive Tagging Killer. They laughed, but agreed it would work, particularly when they were communicating over radios and cell phones.

"Okay my Mini - Tag Team partners," Maria said. "Let's get a move on. We're sure Optik is in his room, thanks to Marge having just called his room to ask if housekeeping could come in. Bob, why don't you stay here and move the van to get a better angle on Optik's door. Gil and I will take the Audi through Sam's Town parking lots and see if we can spot a Hyundai."

"Oh sure," Lemke said. "You guys go gallivanting around in a comfortable police plain-clothes car and leave me here in this crummy van."

"Let me have one of those Bird Dog units out of the case," Gil said holding out his hand. "If we run into the Hyundai, I want to get one planted, if possible. What's all this other stuff, Bob?"

"Oh that," Lemke said. "I managed to snag a van that has all this experimental equipment we're testing. Sonic Sound technology gives you the ability to direct sound where you want it and nowhere else."

"No shit," Gil said.

"I went to a demonstration of this stuff a few weeks ago," Lemke explained. "We're not sure how we may use it yet, but it's pretty cool."

"Cool isn't good enough," Gil told him, his curiosity really peaked. "So how does it work?"

Lemke beamed. He loved technology. "This stuff's mostly proprietary and works with the combination of an ultrasonic powered emitter and a proprietary signal processor and amplifier. It can focus sound into a tight beam for sound directionality."

"You can do that with sound?" Gil asked.

"Hey you guys," Maria said. "I know men love their toys and all, but, come on."

Lemke and Gil ignored her. "To answer your question," Lemke said, "it's similar to a beam of light. You can actually use ultrasonic energy to shine your sound on a very specific area. This type of sound forms a column in front of the emitter, which remains as focused as a laser beam of light as it encounters a listener located in the narrow column of sound. I saw this work up on the test range and it works fantastically. We tested it towards another officer over two-hundred yards away. I got my turn to be on the listening end and it was really weird. The beam was focused on a wall in front of me and I perceived the bounced sound, so to speak, as if it was coming from a spot on the wall. The angle has to be just right."

"Was it very loud?" Gil asked.

"Oh, it could be," Lemke said. "In the case of the test, it sounded like someone talking right next to me in a normal voice, however, the volume controls are a bit tricky. If it's set too high and a person is too close, it could have devastating effects on one's eardrums!"

"That's great," Gil said. "I think there may be a use for this in the department. Take for example crowd control, when we're trying to disburse a rowdy crowd. Just aim and shoot!"

"Or better yet," Lemke said, "we could talk to a jumper on the top of a high rise and convince him not to jump."

"Come on you kids. We've got work to do," Maria told them.

"Hey, I just had another idea," Gil said. "This talk about sound toys and Bird Dogs. Not only should we plant a Bird Dog on Morgan's car, we should consider planting one on a piece of his clothing, shoes, or something."

"I agree," Maria chimed in. "Something we know he'd take with him, particularly if he decides to hoof it and not take his car to wherever he goes."

"Do you think we could afford to have one of us risk that when he leaves his room?" Lemke asked. "I mean when he finally does, it will take all three of us to keep tabs on him."

"Maybe we'll get a chance later," Maria said hopefully. "Now, let's get to work."

Maria handled the blue Audi deftly as they cruised up and down all of Sam's parking lots and garages, keeping their eyes peeled for a gray Hyundai. "Optik is really smart," Gil observed. "He's been one-step ahead of us all the time. No wonder San Diego, Atlanta and Seattle had a tough time trying to identify and nail him. For example, he's pretty damn clever to park here. I bet he moves the car often enough as to not arouse suspicions from the Casino Security boys and

I doubt LVPD cruises through these lots looking for stolen cars. I suppose the only time a stolen car gets found at a place like this is if it wasn't moved for several days. Security might call on it then."

"Might explain why we haven't found the Jeep yet too," Maria said maneuvering the car up the ramp to the third deck. "It's probably sitting in a place that wouldn't draw suspicion for days, may be even weeks, perhaps in Visalia or Bakersfield."

"There," Gil said. "Drive over there."

"What did you see?" Maria turned the car toward the far corner of the garage. "Oh, I see."

Maria parked a few spaces away from the Hyundai and Gil got out to examine the car. Nothing was visible on any of the seats. After jotting down the VIN on his note pad, Gil squatted down and got the number of the rear license plate. The plastic covering, was, he knew, unlawful in Nevada. The police and Highway Patrol, could pull you over if your plate was covered in this manner, but some people still did it, thinking that it protected the renewal tags from being stolen.

"License plate is definitely a fake," Gil said, jumping back into the Audi. "I'll call in the VIN and this plate number to make sure. I'll bet smart old Optik got a license number from another Hyundai."

"That way if some patrol officer was just doing a routine scan, the data would come back with a match to make and model and not stolen," Maria agreed.

As Gil called in the Hyundai data, Maria's cell phone rang. Two things going on in the car at one time made it difficult to hear so Gil stepped out of the car and while waiting for the information he had requested, watched Maria carry on an animated conversation. By the time he got back into the Audi, she was concluding with a "That's great, Sam, please call Captain Vasquez with this. I suspect from now on we'll be having more than just the three of us working on this."

"What did you find out about the Hyundai?" Maria asked.

"Tell me about that phone call first," Gil demanded. "Sam who?"

"You'll never believe this. That was Sam Brown, our resident graffiti expert and guess what?"

God damn it, Maria, Gil thought, this isn't the time for guessing games. We've got serious problems here, don't beat around the bush for Christ's sake.

"I'm not going to guess Maria, what did Sam want?"

"Well he can't be absolutely positive, but he's pretty sure that Ben Morgan just called him."

"No shit! What did he say?"

Maria told Gil about Sam's conversation with the man he was quite sure was Morgan. The caller had admitted to killing taggers. He hates them and wished people did more like he was doing to rid the planet of graffiti.

"Holy crap!" Gil exclaimed. "Did Sam record the conversation?"

"Yes he did and I'm trying to think what's the best way to handle this now."

Gil scratched his head, "Well, we could get the voice to Shirley at WebMaps and Selene. They're the only two people who we know about who might recognize his voice. All the background data on Morgan was pretty well blank except for his Marine Corps duty and he has no family left."

"That would work," Maria agreed, "but I'm not sure we have the time. I'm also not sure it would tell us anything we don't already know. Sam said the guy told him that he was going out to take down some taggers again real soon."

Gil felt his insides churn at this news. He was excited, and now so sure they had this Morgan fellow in their sights. He prayed that this Packard character was going to turn out to be Morgan. No. He didn't need to pray for that. He already knew in his gut that Packard was Morgan and they'd better get on with proving it.

"What's Sam going to do now?" he asked her.

"He said he was calling Vasquez next. I think that'll bring in the cavalry."

"Well, we'd better be ready," Gil replied. "I'm going to place that Bird Dog on the Hyundai. The VIN is registered to Victor Packard and plate is registered to a woman who lives on the west side, in Summerlin. Dispatch called the owner and she said her car is parked safely in her garage."

"Hot damn," was Lemke's first response after Maria and Gil briefed him on the phone call from Brown and the Hyundai registration. "Well, tickle me pink with a feather. I was right about all the data pointing to one suspect. We're gonna get the bastard now."

"First things first," Maria said. "I'd be willing to bet that Hyundai doesn't have a trunk full of incriminating weapons. He's gotta be stashing his stuff somewhere before he goes out on his nightly raids. That Bird Dog had better work. Until Vasquez calls, let's make sure we're covering his room and his car. Any volunteers for who does what?"

"Well, the van is positioned well right here, so we shouldn't move it," Gil said. "I'll take the car and the Bird Dog receiver over to Sam's Town garage. You and Bob can have the first shift here in the van. We've got about two hours until dark. Then we can switch around again. Meanwhile I'll grab some sandwiches and some coffee. Sound okay?"

"Yes, but you'd better hurry before Optik goes out and the Bird Dog lights up," Maria said. "And don't forget my three sugars."

Reminding Maria to let him know if she had any more news from the captain, Gil grabbed sandwiches and coffees before parking as close to the Hyundai as he dared, not close enough to see the Hyundai, granted, but close enough to go in hot pursuit of it if necessary. Having plugged the Bird Dog receiver into the lighter, he didn't have long to wait before Maria was on the cell, briefing him about Vasquez's call made after Sam had talked to him. Much to Maria's disappointment, the captain had discounted what he called the "alleged" call, saying that it could've been any nut posing as a sniper. He had cited the fact that the caller had never really admitted to being Morgan, and he also said his hands were tied when it came to getting more resources. He'd also issued a reminder that, faced with a cop killer, as they were now, the department's resources were being strained to the limit. And more disturbing still, he had added that he'd been talking to Hewitt, although what about was not clear.

What the fuck was wrong with Hewitt now? Gil asked himself. Whatever it was, it probably meant even more trouble.

Thankful that it was finally dark out, Morgan turned off his lights and cracked open the curtains and opened the horizontal blinds with two fingers, only to see nothing suspicious, at least not with his naked eyes. Retrieving his night vision scope, he powered it on. This scope was the latest in military technology and he loved it. Every time he saw the scope, he imagined centering the crosshairs on one of the vandals. Then through the same opening in the blinds, he pointed his scope and scanned each vehicle one at a time looking and looking.

There! In the white van parked about a dozen cars down and just past a mesquite tree, Morgan could see two people sitting in the front seat. Turning the focus and increasing the lux reading to the maximum setting of luminance and luminous emittance, he made out that one was a black man and a white woman. A stakeout! *What do I do now?*

Morgan paced around his darkened room thinking of all the possibilities. Had Victor Packard reported his license missing? Had his Jeep been found at the apartment complex in Bakersfield? That fucking Sam Brown had known his name. How in hell had they tied him to San Diego and Atlanta? *God Damn it! WebMaps!* Somehow that picture in the paper and on TV. Why did it show up in San Diego? Who had seen him? The cops weren't *that* good. Or were they? He needed to show that Sam Brown how to eliminate graffiti. All that education bullshit. He needed to get out of the room without being spotted. Think man, think.

It took ten minutes for him to come up with a plan. Picking up the phone he called the room next door.

"Oh hi, Victor," she said after a brief pause. "I - I was hoping you'd call."

"I'm beat tonight," he said, "but I thought that we might go out for a meal tomorrow evening, say about six o'clock."

"Why yes, Victor, that sounds good," she said after a pause.

He asked her if any more cops had come around, trying to sound as though it didn't matter.

Again that pause. She cleared her throat, "Why no," she said a little too brightly. "Why do you ask? Is everything all right?"

She was falling into his trap, thought Morgan, and knew now that he had to skillfully play out the next steps with lonely Jackie.

"Well, I wasn't completely honest with you," he told her, "because it's really complicated. It has to do with a partner here with the builder that I'm working with. There's been some serious embezzling going on. Partners not trusting each other, that sort of thing. And I think I'm in the middle of it."

"Are you in any danger?"

"No, no, not at all. These guys are paper pushers and not violent at all. So I have both sides of the deal trying to find what I know. It has made my job here really difficult."

"I can imagine," Jackie said sympathetically. "Anything I can do?"

"No, well, maybe," he told her, relieved that she had given him the perfect response. "I'm a little concerned about these partners hiring private investigators to follow me. I wonder if you could do me a favor."

"Are you sure you're not in danger or putting me in danger?"

"No. Like I said these guys use paper as a crime. Nothing violent at all. But I spotted a white van parked about eight or nine cars down on the left. There's a man and woman sitting in it and I wonder if you'd just go down and ask them if they're there because of me. If it is about me, I'd like to know. If they're sitting there minding their own business, that's fine too, but I have to know what they're doing there. I have absolutely nothing to hide but if it's that money grubbing partner's private investigators it will tell me something about what's going on. They think that I may know something about the checks they've written."

"Are you sure it will be safe?"

"Absolutely. I'll keep an eye out, as well. I promise you'll be fine. I just need to know if the partner's going to want me to testify or something."

"Why don't you do it then, Victor?"

"Like I said, it's really complicated, but I don't think they know

I'm in my room right now." And confessing again, "I didn't go to work today and they are probably wanting to ask me where I was."

"Where were you?"

Morgan felt confident she was falling into his little ruse. "I was at the forgery and fraud unit of the police department making statements. If the partners knew that before the police are ready to use the evidence, their case doesn't go well, so these guys are trying to find out where I was today. I'm not a very good liar and don't want to face them myself. Will you do it for me?"

"Okay, Victor. I'll do it, but I need to throw on some clothes first."

The thought of him talking to a near naked woman right next door gave him a fleeting sexual thought, but he had to discard it quickly and stay focused. "Thanks Jackie, you won't regret it. We'll have a very special night out tomorrow."

But tonight, Morgan thought, will be a hell of a lot more special, once I evade those fucking cops!

Chapter Twenty-Six

With radio checks with Gil who was parked at Sam's Town providing the only breaks in the silence, Bob Lemke, sitting behind the wheel of the van, suggested that Maria crawl in the back and get some rest. He had argued that there had been no sign of activity in or around room 117 for some time.

"No I'm fine Bob," Maria said, "it's still early and I'm way too wired, but if you want to, go ahead."

Lemke refused the offer but took the opportunity to try and engage Maria in some personal chatter asking about her real relationship with Gil, both of them keeping their eyes on Optik's door, but she wasn't biting. "LVPD is worse than Peyton Place," was her curt reply. "Right now we need to concentrate on the job at hand. Wait! Look! That woman who lives next to him – Jackie something or other – is coming out. Oh, shit! She's walking right towards us. I can't see Morgan's door."

"Good evening," Jackie Fitzgerald said to the pair. "I couldn't help but notice you guys out here." Spotting Maria sitting on the passenger's side, her expression changed to one of relief. "Oh, you're that policewoman."

"Can we help you Ma'am?" Lemke asked.

"Actually, I'm a little confused now," Jackie said, pointing back towards the building. "My neighbor - well he wants me to come out here and ask you what you were doing. He - he said you were private investigators – but you're not are you?"

Lemke reached out of the car and pushed her to one side, to regain his view of the door. "Damn," Lemke said, "I think Optik's already made his escape!"

"Shit," was all Maria could mutter before she hit the microphone button. "Gil. Head's up! Optik may have eluded us."

"Got it," came Gil's reply over the radio, "I'll be ready."

"Oh dear," Jackie said. "I think I've done something wrong, it's just that…"

"Bob, you take off to Sam's," Maria said, cutting off Jackie. "I'll stay here in case he's still here or comes back."

Maria was barely out of the van when Bob sped off with a squeal of tires and exhaust smoke.

Maria took Jackie to a spot where she could not be seen from Optik's room, just in case he was still there. Gil heard on the radio Maria demand an explanation from the frightened woman.

God damn it, Gil thought as he let go of the talk button on the radio, Morgan's on the loose again. And yet when he looked at the receiving screen of the Bird Dog placed under the front bumper of the Hyundai, the flashing light said the device was not moving.

#

Having been nearly hit by a speeding car while jay walking across the busy highway, Morgan ran to the rear corner of the parking garage, aware that he had only a few minutes before those cops talking to Jackie would realize he'd sent her out as a decoy. The barely used staircase at the rear of the parking structure, leading to the third level, was covered in dust and bird droppings. Keeping his head low, he looked through the complex of hand and guardrails and spotted his Hyundai. He could, he realized make it to his car by a series of low moves in front of a row of cars and then passing to the back of another. Aware that there might be another team of cops keeping an eye on his car, he crept along slowly and watched, just as he had been taught to do in his Marine Corps training in urban warfare, using inanimate objects as shields and protection.

Peering through the rear and front windows of an aging Cadillac, Morgan saw a man in the front seat of an Audi. Morgan wasn't sure if what this fellow was doing had anything to do with him, but he sure as hell wasn't going to take any chances.

Morgan made it to the front of the Hyundai, confident that he hadn't been seen. Still crouching, he tried to the see the Audi from this particular stall, only to realize that even if he stood up straight he wouldn't be able to make out the Audi. If it was a cop in that car, then why wasn't he parked in a position to see the Hyundai? There was only one answer to that. They must have put a transmitter on it.

The ambient light in the parking garage was adequate to discourage muggings and the like, but was not bright enough for him to search for a small transmitter. *How small are they these days?* He searched the front bumper, and under the rocker panels. When he returned to the back bumper, he found it, a small button like device. Carefully easing it from its adhesive lair, Morgan slowly carried it to the car in the next space, hoping the movement of a few feet wouldn't transmit the movement to the receiver. The adhesive was still tacky and it stuck nicely under the front bumper of a nice new Lexus.

Morgan slipped his car into gear and idled out of the parking space before speeding up, and taking a route that wouldn't put him past his suspected surveyor in the Audi. Emerging from the ramp, he turned left into a one-way alley behind the casino and exited onto the busy street.

The RV park was actually a short distance away, but Morgan took a circuitous route, just in case. Parking down the street and over one block from the rear wall of the RV park, he walked the hundred yards or so and climbed over the wall. After making sure that no one was observing him, he opened the locker to retrieve his sniper rifle only to realize that he had left the scope in his room.

Morgan swore at himself for making such a stupid mistake. It only took a few moments for him to get his mind around the problem and congratulate himself for eluding the cops once. Now, he'd have to do it again. Thanks to his reconnoitering skills, he knew the layout of the streets and flood channels in the area so well, that he could safely return to the Suites on foot.

#

With Jackie out of the way, back in her own apartment, advised to let them know if Victor contacted her, Maria monitored the radio conversation between Bob and Gil.

"I'm just arriving on the third level," Lemke said. "Any movement yet?"

"No," Gil told him. "Bird Dog's quiet. Drive down row three 'F.' The Hyundai is near the end. I'm over on three 'E', I wonder where that son of a bitch is?"

"He could still be in his room," Lemke replied. "We only *think* he left when we were distracted and he could be walking somewhere. Any sign there, Maria?" Lemke let the key on his mike go.

"Nope," she said, and it was clear to Gil that she was still steaming about having allowed Jackie to obscure their view. Horney, lonely woman, Gil thought, ready to do any man a favor.

"Gil, I'm at the end of the row," Lemke said. "Where'd you say the car was?"

"Right there. I can just see the top of the van. You're right there."

"There's an empty space here, but no Hyundai. Are you sure I'm in the right spot?"

Gil rechecked the Bird Dog receiver and it was dead still, right where he put it. "I'm coming over," he told Lemke.

"What do you mean coming over, Gil?" Maria said impatiently into her microphone. "Where's the car? Is Morgan there? What's going on?"

A moment passed before Gil came on the radio, "He's given us the slip, God damn it," He said. "Car's gone and the Bird Dog's on the car next to him. Shit!"

There was nothing left to do but regroup in the van. "Look, it's okay," Maria said holding up her hand. "Nobody's fault really…"

"Yes it is. It's my fault," Gil said interrupting. "I should have had a visual, as well."

I'm going to have to step up my game, Gil thought. This Morgan is a far better opponent than he had given him credit for being, even after all of Morgan's successes to date. But this must stop tonight! We just must find him!

"Man, that's hard to do in that parking garage Gil," Lemke

assured him. "That bastard is really smart. How could he figure we had his car planted?"

"It doesn't matter now," Maria said. "What's done is done. Anybody got any ideas?"

"Do we have any smaller Bird Dog devices in the van?" Gil asked, fingering the campaign-sized button he had removed from the Lexus. "Because I have an idea."

"We've got several smaller Bird Dogs," Lemke told him, "but their range isn't nearly as good as the one we planted and they don't work as well with a GPS system, but if we're within about half a mile they work fine." He fumbled in the back. "Here's one of them."

"Boy, this is small," Gil said taking the matt-black, watch battery sized device from him.

"Yes it is," Lemke said, "And if we want to track this, we'll have to use the van receiver and not the portable one in the Audi."

"I'm going in his room." Gil said, holding the Budget Suites key. "Cover me."

"No," Mara demanded. "I'll do it. *You* cover me!"

"No point in you breaking the law too," Gil said, getting out of the van, holding up the small device. "I'm already on the hook for an illegal search, no point in both of us getting reprimanded, or worse."

Confident that Maria and Lemke could not been seen from Morgan's front door, and just as certain that Morgan could not be in his room, Gil slipped in to the dark room. Standing with his back to the closed door, he clicked on his flashlight. Gil saw that Morgan's room was still as neat and tidy as before as the beam flashed around the space. He parted the shades and blinds just as he imagined Morgan had done and peered out the window, and found that he could just make out where the van had been parked. How the devil could he have seen Bob and Maria sitting there, he wondered. As he turned away from the window, he stumbled over something, and flashing the light on it, saw that it was the night vision telescopic sight. Putting on his latex gloves, Gil picked up the scope. The matt black finish and the brand markings indicated it was a Dakota Magnum's telescopic riflescope. So that's how he saw us, he thought, with the latest night vision stuff.

His instincts kicked in then. He knew that the scope would be an important piece of evidence, but that by itself, it would be just another piece of the circumstantial incriminating stuff that continued to pile up. A clever defense attorney would get any and all evidence taken from this room without a warrant suppressed.

Taking the small Bird Dog out of his pocket, he unscrewed the battery compartment, nicely machined into the scopes' body, and placed the transmitter under the coiled spring that held the battery in place, where it fit perfectly. Screwing the cap back into place, he turned on the scope to make sure it worked, and found that, yes indeed it did. After putting it back where he had found it, he quickly scanned the rest of the small suite and seeing nothing else was worth noting, left as hurriedly as he had come in, confident that he had set a trap, which, with any luck, would do Morgan in.

#

Meanwhile, the man in question was emerging from the flood control channel that ran behind Budget Suites and under the road separating the Suites from Sam's. It was still hot in Vegas, in spite of the late summer weather when, usually the evenings cooled a bit and the concrete wall, slanted at about forty degrees, was still warm to his hands as he scrambled up the side.

Standing on the side of the channel, he paused to get his bearings, and then easily scaled the eight-foot block wall topped with chain link fencing that served as the perimeter to the rear of the Suites, silently dropping to the ground between the wall and the covered parking structure, near the cars parked three buildings away from his own. He must, he knew, make sure he could spot any surveillance activity before he approached his suite.

Actually, he was hoping that the police were scratching their heads right now, puzzled over the tracking device, not knowing that he had placed it on another car and that they would assume he was out for the evening. It had been a stupid mistake leaving his scope behind, he scolded himself repeatedly. No doubt Sam Brown has reported their conversation and they would be on alert for him somewhere. But they couldn't possibly believe Packard was Morgan. He needed that scope, even at great risk. He knew where he was going to go with his sniper rifle. He'd plug some graffiti vandal, and hightail it out of town. Although he despised most other forms of crime unless it fit his purpose, he knew he was going to have to steal a car and perhaps steal somebody's identity again. Some of his thoughts hadn't yet worked their way into a plausible plan. First things first, he thought. *Gotta get that scope.* Everything else in his suite could be abandoned.

Morgan stealthily moved through the parking lots and buildings. Watching. Standing absolutely still in the shadows. Watching some more. He saw several skateboarders, dressed in cargo shorts, but otherwise no one. If he was lucky, the owner of the Lexus would be leading them a merry chase right now.

Fitting his card key in the lock, he opened the door, and sighed with relief. He'd tricked them.

Snatching the scope off the floor, he was out and over the wall in less than a minute, off to make his last kill in this lousy town.

#

"He's moving," exclaimed Lemke from the back of the van. "He's going across the back of the Suites."

Gil dropped the van in gear and came out from behind the gas station across the street, bumping over the curb. Tires smoking, the van sped to the street behind the Suites.

"Careful Gil," Maria said. "We don't want to get too close. Remember, he's seen the van."

"That Dakota Magnum's telescopic sights goes with one powerful weapon," Lemke chimed in. "No wonder he could knock off targets over two-hundred yards away."

"That scope does nothing for us," Maria said. "We need the rifle to tie him in to all of this, and we need to find it on him before he gets a chance to use it on another tagger."

"Or us." Gil said. "Where is he now, Bob?"

"He's still on foot, is my guess," Lemke replied, looking at the blinking light. "Looks like he's walking along the flood control channel. You can move up about a hundred yards and then slow again."

Gil pulled over to the curb, letting the van move along at idle speed. "What's he doing now?" he said.

Gil pondered all the possibilities that the situation presented. They could bust Morgan right now for possession of the scope and hope that they could locate his weapon through interrogation or some other evidence they might find on his person, or continue this cat and mouse chase, hoping he leads us to the rifle stashed somewhere close by. He was on foot, and they knew he'd taken the Hyundai, so he had to be going to where he left it. Or did he? Might he had already picked up the rifle, stashed somewhere along these streets? Maria had been strangely silent since he had out fumbled her for the 'privilege' of invading Morgan's room again. Gil noticed that she was just staring ahead.

"He's still on foot," Lemke replied. "Move up again."

As Gil pulled away from the curb, strong high beam lights and red and blue flashing lights came on behind them lighting up the entire neighborhood.

"Shit!" Gil swore, and jumping out of the van, held out his badge with one hand and made a slicing motion across his throat with the other. The strong light from the patrol car's post-mounted spotlight lit up his badge, the contents of the van, the surrounding area and gave competition to the Las Vegas strip lights several miles away.

"Look," he said to the patrol officer who was getting out of his car. "We're on a tricky surveillance operation and we'd appreciate it you'd turn around and go the other way. We don't want to spook our subject."

"Sure, Detective," the officer told him. "I cruise this neighborhood all the time and slow moving vans always get my attention. I'll turn around immediately."

"Is he still walking?" Gil asked as he slid the gearshift into gear. It now seemed like a very dark van.

"Well, if Morgan was driving, that little stop may have cost us." Gil said, watching the patrol car u-turn and go in the opposite direction. "Where the hell is Optik going?"

"Dead ahead, Captain," Lemke said. "Rudder dead center. Slow and easy. He's still walking, but at a pretty good pace as far as I can tell."

"If we're to believe that it was Morgan that called Sam Brown, I'd say he's out to get another tagger or two," Gil told the pair in back.

"But why go back for the scope?" Lemke asked. "If it was Morgan and it was really him that killed Rodolfo and those other two gang bangers, he has a nine millimeter gun as well."

"Maybe wherever he's going this time, he needs to keep a distance between him and his intended victims," Gil conjectured, slipping the van back into gear. "I agree with you, that the scope would fit an awesome weapon. Probably explain how he made those incredible shots."

"He's stopped," Lemke said.

"Looks like he's in the neighborhood behind that RV park." Maria observed squinting at the screen.

Gil was happy that Maria was still engaged in their chase.

"Hold it, there, Gil," Lemke said. "He's about three blocks up and over one. "He's moving again. He's moving faster. He must be in his car now. Go straight two blocks and turn right. We'll try and run parallel with him."

Gil deftly turned the surveillance van this way and that, following the directions Lemke was shouting from the back

"Right at the next block. Go straight until you reach Amber Lane, and then hang a left for a block."

And so it went, playing chase and stop with what the trio assumed to be, the gray Hyundai Sonata making a circuitous route towards the downtown area.

"He's stopped," came Lemke's voice from the back. "Pull up to the next corner and let's wait a bit."

"He's walking again. Looks like he's headed toward the general loft construction area near Fourth Avenue. I still have him and he's turned up a block. Let's cruise by where he apparently stopped and then started walking again. We should be able to see his car."

"There it is, Gil. Up there. Slow down." Maria said, pointing to her right as the van inched down the street. "Stop! Yep, that's the Hyundai. Look how he parked, with his back bumper back against the car in back so his plate can't be seen as easily. You still have him, Bob?"

"Sure do, but it looks like he's walking in circles. I think he's climbing up in a building."

Parking the van about twenty-five yards down the street from a loft project gone bad, the trio moved along the street keeping in the shadows for the last dozen or so yards until they came into a small clearing and looked up at the unfinished condo tower, part of the City of Lights Condo project that had either temporarily shut down or filed for bankruptcy because of the very soft real estate market in the Vegas Valley. These downtown projects had been hit hardest. There was a similar unfinished project across the street. The first two floors had plywood sheathing covering the outside of the building and the eight floors above that was still mostly open steel structure with various pieces of structure inside that. In the dim light they couldn't make out too many details.

"There's something very familiar about this place," Lemke observed. "Yes, I remember now. This was near the site of the first sniper rifle shootings. I had this case before you guys took over."

"It's fitting that he came here to the site of his first killing," Maria said. "Probably knows it's his last."

"Let's hope your wrong about this being his last," Gil said. "You should have said 'last attempt.' We have to stop him. I'm sure he's armed with at least his rifle and maybe he's carrying his gun too."

"Let's find a way in," Gil said.

"No. Not yet," Maria told him. "I'm going to call Vasquez and ask for backup."

"No, we can't wait for that," Gil told her. "He may already be in a position to shoot and he will certainly see any police cars arriving even blocks away. We need to get up there and let him know we've got him cornered. Let's peek inside and see what we've got."

They pulled back a plywood panel, which was, interestingly enough, covered in graffiti, that when eased back and entered through allowed access to the building. This was, Gil assumed, how Morgan had entered. After positioning Lemke at the far corner and Maria below the staircase, he climbed the stairs, carefully moved onto the third floor platform, and looked up through the maze of steel beams and open stairways. All he could make out in the dim light was that the top floor was partially completed and the roof above that was mostly open to the sky. He realized that Morgan was most likely on the top floor that was obscuring observation from below, but would allow him clear shots of streets, walls, billboards and other walls surrounding construction projects on three sides.

Explaining the setup to Bob and Maria in hushed tones, Gil elaborated on what he thought was a brilliant idea.

"Bob, do you know how to use that sound gadget in the van?" he asked.

"I could probably use it, but its batteries may need to be charged." Lemke replied, voice in a soft whisper.

"How long would that take to charge them in the van?"

"The van won't do it. It needs one-ten," Lemke looked around the construction debris. "I doubt that there are any live circuits here. Let me go check on the battery."

"Okay and if it has a charge, bring it here along with the night vision binoculars, and the rifle."

"What do you have in mind?" Maria asked when they were alone.

"If I can get that machine in a position to send Morgan a message that we have him surrounded and that he should give up peacefully, we have a chance to end this without any more killings," Gil told her. "But we need to flush him out somehow. From what I remember of Bob's description of how that sound beam works, we're going to have to know precisely where he is."

"Let's hope the battery is charged," Maria said.

"If it is, I think I should take up a position in the building across the street and get high enough to be able to see him on the top floor of this building with the night vision binoculars," Gil said. "I'll take the rifle too, and I'll radio you if I spot him, so the device can be pointed correctly."

"Listen, Gil," Maria said, "you've been doing a masterful job, but it's time I flexed what little authority I have here. As the team leader, I should be the one calling the shots and I think I should position myself in that building across the street, so I can observe what's going on and position you guys accordingly."

"Maria," Gil replied, "I..."

"My mind's made up," Maria said cutting him off. "I'm a decent shot and I want to take full responsibility for the safety of both of you. We know that Morgan is one dangerous man."

"I'm not happy about it," Gil said, trying to sound disappointed. "But if you insist."

"I insist."

"Do you really think that if you get a shot, you can take him out?" Gil probed.

"Yes, I think I can." Maria said, "Once I get a clear shot, I'll shoot him, if he doesn't respond to the sound warnings and give up peacefully."

Exactly what he wanted her to do, Gil thought, as the rest of the pieces of the plan was coming together in his mind. Maria had bitten on the first part, which was to get her safely across the street and nearly out of harm's way. If he could be sure of how to operate that sound equipment, he'd take that on and leave Lemke here, in case Morgan was able to descend to the ground floor after they flushed him.

Maria and Gil were still talking about the logistics of the operation when Lemke arrived, carrying the big metal case of equipment, the rifle and binoculars swaying on straps around his neck. "I think it's got about ten minutes of battery life left," Lemke said handing the rifle and binoculars to Maria's outstretched hands. "So what do you have in mind, Gil?" he added placing the case on the floor and flipping open the latches.

"Is that easy to operate?" asked Gil.

"Not really," Lemke said. "The volume and directional controls are rather tricky. I only saw it operate once, but I think I can handle it."

After discussing the specifics and pros and cons of the plan, they went to take their positions. After discussing what Lemke was to say through the device, Maria headed out on a circuitous route, crossing the street, working her way through several backyards, and coming out on a street one block away and out of sight of the high-rise building. After crossing another street, she entered the building, making sure she would not be spotted from the top floor of Morgan's building. As for Gil, he helped Lemke get the sound laser device set up on the sixth floor. Gil had assumed that the sound beam would bounce off the top floor's partial ceiling, but to get the right angle

Morgan would have to be at the perimeter in a shooting position, which meant that Gil would need to climb to the floor just beneath Morgan.

After the trio was in position, Gil, who was the closest to the target, would use his radio ear bud, although he'd only be able to speak very softly for fear of giving away his presence. Pressing the ear bud into his ear he heard Maria say, "I think I see a figure at the northwest corner. Yes, he's sitting cross-legged, and he has the rifle and scope across his lap. He's scanning the area below me."

"Be careful," Gil whispered into the radio. "He's using the same night vision technology you are."

"Maria. Can you give me how many feet from that wall he is?" Lemke asked.

"He's right in the northwest corner looking due west."

"Shit!" Lemke exclaimed. "I'll have to climb another floor with this stuff to get the right angle. I'll let you know when I'm in position again."

Gil stretched his arms and legs waiting, his Glock grasped tightly in his grip and his trigger finger on the barrel. He press checked the gun several times, making sure that there was a round in the chamber. Once he was sure he and the gun were ready, he waited and listened.

Lemke took his time climbing the metal stairs, doing his best to keep the heavy metal case from bumping the guardrails and stairs beneath his feet. Once on the floor, two below their target and just one beneath Gil, Lemke crept along the skinny temporary flooring, which creaked as he walked along the plywood with his heavy load. There he silently opened the case and pulled out the pieces of the equipment one at a time. The tripod holding the speakers pointed through the opening in the two floors above him and at the partial roof over where, according to Maria, Morgan was perched. Once he turned on the device, the lights, after blinking orange and red, finally turned green.

"I think I'm in the right place," Gil heard Lemke tell Maria. "Has he moved?"

"No, he's still sitting in that corner. He's like a fucking statue sitting there," Maria said, twisting the focus knob on her night vision binoculars.

Gil crept up another set of stairs and thought that he was ready to pop up on Morgan's floor and get off a shot if that son of a bitch made one false move. Everything was working to his plan that he'd be the one to either cuff or shoot him.

"I'm ready then. I hope this works," Lemke brought the microphone of the Laser Sound System to his mouth and took a deep breath. "Ben Morgan. This is the police. We have you surrounded. Throw down your weapon and put your hands in the air."

"There's no reaction, Bob," Maria said. "He's still just sitting there."

Risking exposing his head, Gil raised up just enough to be level with Morgan's floor, he pressed the ear bud closer to his ear, not wanting any sound to escape. "Well, shit!" he heard Lemke tell Maria. "I'll have to move back a few feet and change the angle. "I'm ready again. Is he still there?"

"Christ, hurry Lemke, he's looking right at me!" Maria sounded panicked. "He's starting to point the rifle in my direction!"

"God damn it, Bob, try again. I think we're looking at each other. Shit, he's aiming at me!" Maria threw herself to the floor as Gil popped his head and tried to acquire Morgan in the corner.

There! Gil saw the dark outline of a man standing in the corner, aiming his rifle across the street. We don't need any fucking sound devices, Gil thought. If I can just get a bead on him.

"Oh jeez, Gil," Maria called for help. "Do something for Christ's sake - Gil!"

#

Morgan's patience was growing unusually thin. He could sit and scan for hours at a time waiting for movement and tonight the traffic was light, but so far he had not seen any pedestrians. It was still relatively early for the graffiti scum he was waiting for to appear and probably because of the surveillance activity and all his efforts to avoid being spotted and caught, he was unusually nervous.

And then he saw someone level with him in the building across the street. *What's that? Somebody with binoculars was looking in my direction.* Morgan pulled the night vision scope and rifle to his eye and saw whoever it was throw themselves to the floor as his finger started to squeeze the trigger.

"Ben Morgan," a voice boomed. "This is the police. We have you surrounded. Throw down your weapon and put your hands in the air."

Morgan jerked around, pointing his rifle toward the ceiling, ignoring the figure across the street. *How the fuck had they got on the roof? There's no way!*

"Throw down your weapon and put your hands in the air." The voice was coming from somewhere above the ceiling. Morgan took a few steps toward the stairway, weapon pointing upwards.

"Stand still, Morgan!"

What the fuck? Morgan moving with catlike speed finished the distance to the stairs in a second. *How had they got up there?*

239

He had just placed one foot on the stairs to ascend to the roof, his rifle pointing up, when a voice directly behind him said, "Drop your weapon, and put both hands in the air!"

No fucking way. Morgan told himself as he whirled around and jumped to the side. As he did a shot rang out from across the street and the bullet hit the stair case inches from his foot. Morgan whirled to his right, toward the source of the shot, just as the voice behind him shouted, "Drop it!"

Morgan turned and saw the man in a shooting stance, pointing a gun at him. He aimed his rifle and was about to fire when, suddenly, he saw a flash and pain exploded in his chest. A small dot of light in the middle of Morgan's brain, as in an old television set being turned off, diminished ever so slowly until it went out.

Epilogue

It was all that Gil could do to keep his girls from rushing past the ticket booth in their eagerness to get to the amusement rides that filled the Adventure Dome inside the Circus Circus Hotel and Casino. Maria waited while he bought the tickets for the roller coaster, and then took his hand as they went to sit on a nearby bench. Since the girls' arrival, she hadn't seen much of Gil while he did all the other touristy things in Vegas, including a lot of shopping. Gil unrolled the proper amount of tickets from the large roll he had just purchased and gave the girls tickets to ride on the roller coaster, before sitting down next to Maria on the bench.

"It's so nice to see you with Liz and Joni. They're having such a good time," Maria observed. "The icing on the cake is that they know deep in their hearts you love them and that you've become a national hero."

"*We* are national heroes, Maria," he told her. "We couldn't have brought down Morgan if it hadn't been for all three of us," Gil added.

"Bob Lemke's data. Your intuition and leadership. All of it, earned us all a department Medal of Honor."

"But you're the guy who shot him."

"Only because you missed!" Gil said, grinning.

"Well, it was dark and my arm hurt like crazy from landing on it getting out of the way!" Maria said, taking his hand. "But I'm so relieved that all the pieces finally came together. We were lucky, weren't we?"

"Think about it, Maria," Gil told her. "Within a few days of Morgan being killed, all our missing elements came together. The 9mm ballistics match in Seattle was a godsend, not to mention the saturation press coverage that alerted the guy over at Travel Town to the fact that Morgan, in disguise, had stored something there. Suddenly we have all the weapons, as a result. Then there was Packard arriving safely back from the Sierras, and finally our finding the Jeep in Bakersfield. Just think if we had waited for all of that to come together, Morgan might have killed one or more taggers before blowing town."

"We were lucky," Maria agreed. "Thank God for Captain Vasquez and his understanding ways."

That was a motherly look in Maria's eyes as she looked at Joni and Liz standing in line. It was, Gil thought, a very good sign.

"Yes, Joe was stellar in letting us do our thing," he said, "but there's still one thing that bothers, me?"

"What's that?"

"A couple of things actually. Hewitt is one." Gil told her. "I found out in a private chat with Sam Brown that it was Hewitt that screwed up the Miranda on that Navy Chief. I still don't understand why he seemed to be such a road block to us."

"Well I had some private chats of my own about our Detective

Hewitt," Maria told him. "It turns out that Hewitt had a history, not enough to cost him his job mind you, but a history of being on the vigilantes side in many cases. He was also documented for not doing thorough investigations when one criminal was involved in murdering another. I don't know for sure, but I think he liked having Morgan out there taking care of graffiti scum. I do know that he has severe reprimands in his file. What was the other thing that bothered you?"

"Our favorite patrol officer, Brad Lara," Gil said. "You know he didn't have to come forward to his superior and admit that he'd gone over the line on that search. He's such a good officer but he felt he had to. He was lucky to have only received a stern reprimand. It was tough on him."

"Why does that bother you, Gil?

"Because I didn't come forward as to how I got that paint chip and planted the Bird Dog almost in the same manner as Brad. I was lucky. But I still feel bad about breaking the rules. I still think I should say something."

"You're a good cop, Gil," Maria told him. "The whole department knows that now. I'd just drop it. We agreed that we'd do our best to try and get Brad into homicide. He'd be a good one!"

"Yes, and I suppose that would ease my conscious a little but, I still nee…"

"You know what the best part of all this is don't you?" Maria interrupted him, squeezing his hand. "It's that the Smead reward of one-hundred thousand dollars is being donated to the Fallen Police Officer's Fund."

For a moment both of them were silent and Gil knew that Maria was probably thinking that even this triumph had had a high cost.

But then she smiled at him through her tears, and he knew that it was a really nice way to honor Rodolfo in their own quiet way.

"Come on," he said. "Let's go watch Liz and Joni scream their heads off."

END

Acknowledgement notes:

While this work of fiction, with large doses of figments of my imagination it may paint a negative picture of gang violence and graffiti crimes in Las Vegas, The facts are that, as of this writing, gang related murders are way down from previous levels as reported by the police as are crimes involving graffiti, burglary and car thefts.

I certainly took great liberties with individual officer's behavior for the sake of the plot and story line. What I wrote, should not in any way reflect negatively on any police officer or department's performance and their strict adherence to the rules of police work.

Attending the Citizen's Police Academy provided by the Las Vegas Police Department was a wonderful learning experience. The curricula, over a thirteen-week period, demonstrated, without a doubt, that "LVPD" is one of the finest law enforcement agencies in the country.

As Detective Scott Black wrote in the forward, we did indeed become friends and I'm so grateful for his support, critical suggestions, corrections, and positive feedback. Detective Black epitomizes LVPD's high work ethic, attention to detail, dedication, and tireless efforts to fight crime. He arrests many "taggers."

Yes, the Sonic Sound Technology described in *Tag You're Hit!* is a technology that is alive and well and in use today, albeit I'm not sure it is used by the LVPD, but it could be since it works much like I've described.

Also a huge thank you to my many friends and members of my

family; Diane Vanover, Vicki Niggemeyer, Marilyn Reeves, Shirley Anne Jenkins, Garry Jenkins, Jennifer Angelucci, Lorian Jenkins for their continued encouragement, positive feedback, eagle eyes, great suggestions and well deserved criticism of my early drafts. And a very special thanks to A-1 Editing Service's Mary Linn Roby, whose sage advice and critique were spot on. Mary has written over fifty published books. And of course, my wife Lynda, who graduated from the Citizen's Police Academy with me, for her support and encouragement.

About the Author

Howard Jenkins has had a varied career, in corporate America performing senior executive management of procurement, contract administration, manufacturing, and information technology in industries as varied as Aerospace and Defense, commercial aircraft manufacturing, software and the restaurant business. Career changes moved him from California, to Puerto Rico, to Minnesota, to Arizona, to Kansas, to Colorado and finally to Las Vegas. A willing and capable public speaker, Jenkins has written several columns for Hospitality Technology Magazine as well as several corporate position papers and major project management "how-to" manuals. Jenkins retired from corporate life in early 2004, moved to Las Vegas with his wife Lynda. Since his first book, The Big Deal, Howard has worked hard on the craft of writing

Howard has two sons, and a daughter, arriving when he was very young, and two grandchildren all in California. His new grown stepson lives in New Mexico. Lynda and Howard love Las Vegas.

He was amazed at the often violent outbursts from non-violent citizens at the sight of graffiti. What if one of these graffiti haters was a sociopath? This novel represents that notion.

Jenkins, in addition to writing, listening to jazz, and enjoying great neighbors and friends, volunteers his time with the Las Vegas Metropolitan Police Department helping in the Crime Prevention area.

CPSIA information can be obtained at www.ICGtesting.com

230937LV00001B/8/P